Also by David Leddick

FICTION
My Worst Date
Never Eat In

NONFICTION
Naked Men
The Male Nude
Intimate Companions
Men in the Sun
The Homoerotic Art of Pavel Tchelitchev

The Sex Squad

David Leddick

ST. MARTIN'S PRESS ❧ NEW YORK

Design by Nancy Resnick

Library of Congress Cataloging-in-Publication Data

Leddick, David.
    The sex squad / David Leddick.
        p.   cm.
    ISBN 0-312-18174-4 (hc)
    ISBN 0-312-24326-X (pbk)
    I. Title.
 PS3562.E28444S4   1998
 813'.54—dc21   98-35891
                                                           CIP

First Stonewall Inn Edition: March 2000

10 9 8 7 6 5 4 3 2 1

For
Frank Andrea

I would like to thank:

Keith Kahla, my editor who is precise and practical and good-looking, too. This is my second book for him, and each one is a learning experience for me.

Mikel Wadewitz, his second in command, who is quick and smart and lots of fun.

Patrick Dillon, my copy editor. If I seem grammatical and correct in my facts, it is only because of impressive him.

Kathie Nengel, who puts my manuscript on disk for me, catching many errors and making a lot of sense. And who is so diligent and dependable.

And, of course, all those myriads of people from my dancing past, some real and some now quite unreal to me. Without their glamour and guts, and richness and rashness of character, there would have been nothing to write.

I would like to add that, although there are many real characters in this book, it is entirely fiction.

St. Vincent's Hospital

There was a very black nurse's aide in a very pink dress seated near the foot of his bed. She said, "We have to keep someone with him all the time. He tried to kill himself, that's why they brought him in."

I read the chart at the foot of his bed. Advanced lung cancer. One lung already removed. Seropositive for AIDS. "Shouldn't he be in an oxygen tent?" I asked.

"They're bringing one right now," she said.

Siegfried turned his head and opened his eyes. "Hi, Harry," he said. "Come to watch me die?"

"He knows you, Doctor," the nurse said.

"And I know him," I told her.

"I didn't plan to come visit you, Illy," I said. "I just sort of stumbled upon you while making my rounds."

"You work here?" he sort of mumbled. "I didn't even know you were a doctor."

"Can't we hurry up that oxygen tent?" I said to the nurse.

"I'll go get it myself," she said, and left.

I went to stand by the bed and took Siegfried's hand. Siegfried Ilquist. He had been very handsome when we were dancers together at the opera. The Metropolitan Opera. Thirty years ago

1

almost exactly. I left the opera in 1958. Now it's almost 1990. Siegfried Ilquist was considered the handsomest man in New York. He thought his eyes were too small and wore dark glasses whenever he could. Then he was really handsome. He had a great nose—a perfect nose. And beautifully sculpted lips. It was all still pretty much there but covered in fine wrinkles. Like a beautiful statue worn by the sun and the wind. He smiled and squeezed my hand with his eyes shut, his face towards the ceiling. He knew I was looking at him. "Surveying the wreckage," he would have said.

He was wearing a hospital gown with little figures on it, tied at the back of the neck. With his eyes still shut, he said, "I disconnected my oxygen tank so I could end all this. But Anne found me and called the hospital. So here I am. Still on this earth."

"How is Anne?" I said. I tightened my grip on his hand. He was struggling to breathe. "She's an advertising writer now," he said. "And you're a doctor. It's a long way from *Aida*."

It *was* a long way. Illy and I had been sort-of lovers when we were at the opera. I don't think we were really in love. I, at least, was really in love with Rex Ames. That was before I stopped dancing. Before I went to college. Before I became a doctor. Before a lot of things happened. It was before I was twenty years old, even. Homosexuality? It's just something you get used to.

The nurse came back with the interns and set up the tent, put the oxygen tanks in place, turned them on.

The tanks hissed and Siegfried began to breathe more easily. The nurse put her arm under his shoulders and arranged his pillows; then she pulled him up into a more comfortable position. When she straightened the sheets, I saw how thin his legs were. Those once powerful thighs had dwindled to little more than skin over the femurs. Remembering when they were bronzed and powerful, I thought, Loving people is like loving clouds. His cock dangled down, darkened and small. I remembered that very

2

well, too. Much bigger and wonderfully shaped. It fit the mouth as though the two were designed to fit together.

When I look at people's eyes sideways, they look like glass doll's eyes, and I realize that we are just some kind of machine. How ridiculous it is to fall in love with someone's penis.

I straightened his blanket. "I'll be back, Illy," I said, "Take it easy. You're all right now." He smiled, his lids hooding his eyes. The way he'd always smiled. Something Asiatic about it. Keeping his thoughts to himself. His background was Norwegian. The distant Tartar blood showed a little in his tilted-up eyes with their sheltering lids, or would it be the Lapps from far-off Lapland?

I walked home to Greenwich Street. Interesting theory, the dual universes. That somewhere there is another planet Earth with another New York and another Greenwich Street. I've already lived in that alternate New York. When I was a dancer, my mother and I lived on Sixteenth Street, just a few minutes' walk from here. My lover Rex Ames once lived just down Bank Street, only a few doors from the corner where I now live in half of an almost Revolutionary-period house. When I used to go to Rex's apartment, I passed my house but never saw it. We went to the movies together at the old Loew's Sheridan, which was right across the street from St. Vincent's. Held hands in the balcony while we watched *I Want to Live*. (This was pretty unusual and sentimental for Rex.) There was no clue that someday I would be stalking the halls of that same hospital. Now I walk through the same physical places, but different lives were lived there when I was under twenty. It's almost as though they had been swept away. It's unimaginable that one can be living in a completely different world yet in the very same place. At least they swept away Loew's Sheridan. Replaced it with a place where they store garbage cans, I think. That *is* infinitely more modern.

The other day, I passed the old building on Sixteenth Street where Mother and I lived, and it has been redone. A new brick facade. No more high iron-railed stoops. Nobody drops their

3

garbage out of the third-floor window into the garbage cans in the street anymore, leaving bits of eggshell and orange rind on the windowsills all the way down. But I'm sure the same narrow little apartments are still inside. Squeezing other people's hearts into something like a reasonable shape so they can survive on this planet.

How I Became a Dancer

We came to New York, my mother and I, when I was seventeen. Just seventeen. To pursue our careers in dance. My mother was the one who wanted to be a dancer. I was just along for the ride.

My mother's name was—is—Elizabeth. Everyone back in Michigan called her Betty. Once we left Michigan, she decided she wanted to be called Belle-Mère. She pronounced it Belle-Meer. To rhyme with "peer" and "sheer" and "leer." And "queer." Only when I was studying French in college later did I learn it meant "mother-in-law." When I told her she said, "Who knows? Who cares? That's the least of the things we did wrong." We? I still don't know how much she knows. I'm not going to ask her, that's for sure.

My mother was a *Red Shoes* victim. She did have long legs and red hair, I'll give her that, but Moira Shearer she wasn't. Unfortunately, she was thirty-six years old when she saw *The Red Shoes*, so she couldn't even do a Zelda Fitzgerald. But, by God, she tried.

We were from Whitehall, Michigan. The Potters arrived in Whitehall on the Lake Michigan shore at the time of the Civil War. That was my father's family. My mother was a Glover. I guess the Glovers arrived about the same time, when it was just woods and Indians. When Elizabeth Glover married Harry Potter, it was just what the folks in Whitehall had expected.

They evidently *didn't* expect Harry to run off with Miss Whitehall when I was ten. She was one of the DeBeers girls. As my grandmother Glover used to say, not unkindly but factually, "She was one of those girls from down by the lake." We lived on a bluff called Christian Hill. I think you get the idea.

I didn't see much of my father after he left town. I didn't see much of him before. Like most fathers, he found having a family crushingly dull. My memories of him, when he was home, consist largely of him lying on the couch listening to baseball games and smoking. *That* he found interesting. I played baseball quite well in high school—I'm well coordinated—but I never found it interesting. I'm just not a spectator kind of guy. Even when I was a dancer, I enjoyed doing it but I never particularly liked to watch other people do it.

I'm certain no one in Whitehall expected my mother to become a ballet fanatic. But she did. She dragged me to Detroit to see Roland Petit and Zizi Jeanmaire dance *Carmen*. I must have been twelve by then. It was pretty hot stuff for a preteen. I'd never seen anyone slide up and down someone else's thighs in their underwear before. I haven't often since. Well, that's not true. Anyway, my mother didn't seem to think it was too shocking for her child to see. She loved it.

We followed that up by going to Chicago to see the New York City Ballet. Melissa Hayden in *The Cage*. More sliding up and down other people's thighs. I think Belle-Mère might have started to get discouraged at this point except that Maria Tallchief danced a one-act *Swan Lake* the same evening. And that got Mother all worked up again.

After that, we went back to Whitehall and she began reading. I remember an avalanche of books pouring across the dining room table. While I was studying *Algebra for Beginners,* she was reading *Beaumont's Book of Ballets*. While my eyes were popping open over the big news about the Jukes and the Kallikaks in Biology 1, she was having to force her lids down a little, too, as she discovered what really went on between Nijinsky and Diaghilev. At least as Romola Nijinsky told it.

Ballet bibliography must have been hard to find in the backwoods of Michigan in the early 1950s, but Belle-Mère managed it. I distinctly remember she was infatuated with Mathilde Kchessinska, an imperial ballerina. I asked her what it meant to be "the bauble of the Czar," but she wasn't answering. I knew damn well what it meant, I just wanted to bug her. Secretly, I'm sure she was crushed that there weren't any more czars and that there was no hope of her becoming a bauble.

During that winter, she began to transform her plans for a dancing career for herself to include me. I guess it became increasingly clear to her that to become a classical ballet dancer, one had to start young.

I knew something was in the wind when I came home after a freshman basketball game with Rothbury (we lost twenty-seven to eight). She had been to the game and seen me in my baggy shorts. She said, "You've got nice legs, Harry." I'm Harry Junior. "You've got my side of the family's legs. We all have nice legs. Your grandmother still has nice legs, and she's in her sixties."

I had never thought about having nice legs before. Not many boys in Whitehall High had, I would guess. I ventured, "Yeah, but I've got big feet."

"You're still young," she said. "You'll grow up to your feet and out of your pimples."

Her next step was the purchase of a "Do It Yourself" book on ballet. It was by Zachary Solov, whom we were to know much better later. Then we couldn't have dreamed that someday we would know him. Zachary's book involved complicated photographs of a slightly overweight young woman in zebra-striped all-over tights. They were kind of stream-of-movement pictures so you could see exactly what she was doing in plié, rond de jambe, frappé, développé, the works. And there was a record that went with it. If you were willing to apply yourself, you could figure out

7

precisely what movements went with what music and you could do a barre. Which we did.

I was a strange kid. I was playing football, basketball, and baseball. Football not well—I was too slender and couldn't really run fast—but the other sports not badly. I had promise. I also loved to dance and went to the high-school dances and danced with every girl there. Plain ones, fat ones, pretty ones, popular ones. I was really too young to be dating, but all the girls liked to dance with me because I could dance well. We did something called the Finale then. A kind of jitterbugging. And the two-step. I could waltz and polka, too. Where I learned those, I can't imagine. I must have seen them done somewhere. Not on television, of course; this was pre-television for most of the families in White-hall. Some people had them, but not necessarily the wealthiest. Most people regarded television as they did Coca-Cola, Hershey bars, and Cadillacs. They existed but were unnecessary luxuries.

Belle-Mère was a chaperone at one of the high-school dances, and once she saw that I liked to dance, the jig was up. I had to join her once a day clinging to the back of a chair going through the Zachary Solov exercises. I studied the book, too. I guess I must have thought of it as another kind of sport. Certainly the fat girl in the striped bodysuit didn't lead to any thoughts of airy-fairy carryings-on.

And I loved my mother. We rather dismissed my father's departure, but Belle-Mère now had to work down at the florist shop. I worked after school and on weekends as a stock boy and checkout clerk at the Kroger. We didn't have any money, which didn't really matter, because Whitehall was one of those provincial towns where your family meant more than anything else. But even so. Balletomania was my mother's emotional support, and I wasn't going to be disloyal to her. So I studied our sappy little exercises with her, so she could transform me into another Robert Helpmann. Can you imagine any mother wanting to help her son become like the dainty and overly made-up Robert Helpmann? But she did. What did we know? I think even then I knew more than she did.

It isn't that those days seem so long ago to me now. The past doesn't seem all that distant, really. It's more as though it all happened in that alternate universe. Now, thirty-some years later, a big-deal doctor at St. Vincent's, there's very little opportunity to hang around chatting about your days as a ballet dancer and what a great pair of legs you had.

Make that *have*.

The only person I talk about those days with is Belle-Mère herself. She comes around a couple times a year to look at my daughters' legs. Margot's are all right, but what little girl doesn't have long legs at twelve? And Yvette seems to be more interested in horses and boys. At fourteen, it's too late for a girl anyway.

As it turned out, fifteen wasn't too late for me. That's what Edna McRae said when Belle-Mère hauled me off to Chicago for an interview and an audition.

It was in the spring after I was fifteen that Belle-Mère and I both realized that we'd pretty well done it with the one ballet book and the pudgy girl in the zebra tights. Belle-Mère had met some people from Chicago at the florist shop over Easter weekend. They had come in for some lilies. Which someone had said looked like the lilies Giselle tosses over her head to Albrecht in the second act of the ballet *Giselle*. They had just seen it in Chicago. My mother then asked them if they were dancers. They laughed and told her they weren't, but one woman had studied dance at one time, with a teacher named Edna McRae, who she said was quite famous as a teacher.

So my mother called the operator in Chicago and got Edna McRae's number. Called the McRae studio and inquired about studying there. And was told that students had to come in for an audition if they were no longer children.

Belle-Mère chickened out and told them about her wonderful, talented son, not mentioning herself. And they gave her an appointment. On a Saturday.

We got up very early on that Saturday morning and took the bus to Chicago, about four hours away. Belle-Mère had been to Chicago enough to find her way around. I was completely overwhelmed: the Loop with trains traveling above our heads, the streets jammed with people. I tried not to show it, but I was terrified of being separated from Belle-Mère. I was sure I would be lost forever once swept off in that mob of shoppers.

We found Edna McRae's studio in an office building. Just a little office with some dressing rooms at one end and a doorway into a large studio at the other. I looked in the door and saw Edna McRae.

I may have been afraid of Chicago, but I was even more frightened of Edna McRae. Five feet two, weighing in at 150, 160 pounds, wearing bright red hair. In the opposite corner, each weighing in at about forty pounds and wearing pink tutus, was a covey of little girls. They all had their guard up.

We had been told by the receptionist to take a seat on a bench just inside the door. That way we could watch the class and Miss McRae would talk to us after class. I had never seen a ballet classroom before. Big, rectangular mirrors covering one wall and long wooden railings running around the other three walls on two levels. One about waist height, the other lower.

As we tried to silently walk to the bench, without turning to look at us, Edna said, from the corner of her mouth, "What do you want?"

Belle-Mère pushed me in front of her. She said, "We want to dance. I mean, *he* wants to dance."

Edna, who had somehow wedged her refrigerator-shaped body into a black slipcover, turned and advanced towards us. The refrigerator was supported on two beautifully arched feet in immaculate pink kid slippers. She looked at me. Then at my feet. Then gestured towards the bench and turned back to the children.

10

"Let's get this straight, girls," she said, "this is no Dolly Dinkle school. We are here to work." The little girls fluttered to the lower rank of the wooden railing and took their places, one behind the other, one hand grasping the rail, their heels neatly together, their feet turned out, looking straight ahead.

She gestured to the pianist, an elderly lady, and chords struck. "Squatty-vous, girls." she said, and they were off. We proceeded to see our first ballet class. I was interested but Belle-Mère was in a trance. *The Red Shoes* was happening to her. As each of the exercises unfurled, one following another, I remembered the chubby girl in the striped tights that we had copied out of our instruction book back in Whitehall. Miraculously, each exercise we had clumsily done now was passing before my eyes, in exactly the same order, only now it was rows of slender little pink legs that were doing them.

I suppose then what attracted me most was the feeling that everyone knew exactly what they were doing, when to do it, and had faith that it was for some reason.

The little girls squatted down in their pliés, feet together, then feet apart, then feet in front of each other, just as the book had shown. They pointed their little feet: in front of them, beside them, behind themselves. In the flesh, it didn't look so hard, and I was sure I could do it. Beside me, my mother was jerking a little spasmodically this way and that, doing those ronds de jambe and grands battements right along with the class. Pretty obviously, she was going to have to go to class, too. But, I decided, not with me.

When their barre work was done, the class, like a flock of little pink pigeons, whirled out onto the floor and fell into rows behind each other. Evidently the pecking order had already been established.

Miss McRae turned towards me and gestured towards the wooden barre. "Do you think you can do that?" she said. Belle-Mère said eagerly, "Of course, of course." In a voice that could have etched glass Miss McRae said, "Oh, I *know you* can: I was thinking more of *him*."

11

I nodded several times to show my enthusiasm. She turned back to her little pink flock and put them through their paces of pirouettes and jetés. They weren't half bad for a bunch of little kids from Chicago. Finally, she let them go, all perspiring faintly. Each in turn had to come up and shake Miss McRae's hand and curtsey before they could leave. Eager mothers' eyes peered around the doorjamb, and each snatched up her little pink pearl as she rolled out into the reception room.

Poor Belle-Mère. I'm sure she thought there would be endless enchanting days of watching ballet class. She didn't know it was to be her last for some time. Miss McRae had a strict rule that no one was to watch class—with rare exceptions. Particularly mothers.

After the class Miss McRae rather kindly explained to me that if I wished, I could go to the Capezio store down the block and buy black tights, a black dance belt, and either black or white ballet slippers. She preferred white because of the "finished" look it gave the foot.

I didn't know what a dance belt was and had no idea what a "finished" foot looked like, but I said nothing. I was game to try.

With these purchases, I could wear a white T-shirt, white socks, and a belt to roll the waist of the tights over. Obviously the dance belt was something other than this. This was her regulation classroom uniform for boys, and I never wore anything different in the years of classes that were to follow.

Later, in New York, dancers would come to class in assorted dilapidated sweaters, floppy knit leg warmers, ankle warmers, and even sometimes wool scarves. Some boys even affected low-cut leotards to show off their chests. But anyone who had started at the McRae school scorned this look as being "French." In our opinion, the French could do everything well that had to do with ballet—except dance it.

But I get ahead of myself.

Late in the afternoon, I had a private class with Edna to see what she thought of my possibilities. Belle-Mère stayed in the reception room, carefully rolling her head scarf from one corner to the opposite into a long tube, then unrolling it, and after several repetitions changing corners to roll it in the opposite direction. So it wouldn't get too wrinkled, I guess.

I was in the studio standing near the piano wearing my new outfit. I had discovered what a dance belt was: a wide belt of elastic, with a strap between the legs, wider on one side than the other. It was pinching my little privates very uncomfortably. Miss McRae explained to me the importance of the first position: heels together, legs straight, toes turned out as far as possible while holding the arches up.

She took the time to explain why she wanted me to do these things. She told me later that she had spotted me immediately as being a "mental" dancer; and she made the effort because I had such nice legs. "A shame to not get them on the stage," she said.

"We're training your legs to turn out at right angles from your hips," she said. Then she laughed. "In fact we're deforming you. Like the Chinese used to bind feet, but not so bad." I'm sure she knew that anyone of my age would love that. "If your feet turn out and your legs don't, we have accomplished nothing.

"Ballet requires that dancers move in flat planes across the stage, framed by the proscenium arch. The audience has to see your torso, arms, and head from the front, while they see your legs in profile. Once you are deformed, you can make beautiful images for the audience."

Of course I loved it. Maybe I wouldn't bend and weave like a lotus blossom on tiny deformed feet, but I was sure I would have some kind of exotic allure. I'm sure I didn't think I was doing this to drive men mad with desire, but it must have been under there somewhere. And I'm positive that's why Belle-Mère wanted to dance in the first place.

All the while, the pianist was tinkling away, playing the classroom melodies I was to come to know so well: Chopin for the petits battements, *Faust* for the grands battements, the second act of *La Bohème* for the ronds de jambe, Tchaikovsky for the adagios,

Strauss sometimes for the allegro part where you jump and hurl yourself about. After an hour and a half, Miss McRae decided it was not too late for me to hope to dance. But, she demanded, *did* I hope to dance? She was a perceptive old bird. The hovering mother told her something. She was used to hovering mothers, of course, but not so accustomed to fifteen-year-old boys.

Now I can't imagine what I hoped for. I guess I hoped for something wonderful to happen to me. I was bored in Michigan, and I suppose I was enthusiastic as much for Miss McRae's sake as for my own. Like every interviewee, I wanted to give the right answers.

Chicago, Chicago

Thus it came to pass that Belle-Mère and I moved to Chicago. Moved to an apartment of which I only remember the smell of gas heaters and drying damp dance clothes. Belle-Mère was taking the adult beginner evening class at Miss McRae's school, which began when my last class ended. We passed like ships in the night. Exhausted, thin, pale, and happy.

I had to finish school, so I was enrolled at an academy for theatrical children where one attended classes in the morning only. God knows that most of the student body was theatrical if not destined for the theater. At other schools, they said that our school had to call off the Virgins' Parade; one was sick and the other one didn't want to march alone. Since I was always in good health, I guess I qualified as the one who wouldn't march alone.

At ballet school I took two classes every day. In the afternoon I was the lumbering oaf among the little girls in pink. Edna told me this would be my trial by fire. If I could stand being made a fool of by a bunch of little girls, I stood a chance of building a true technique.

In fact, it hardly bothered me at all. Like two kinds of wild animals grazing side-by-side in the Serengeti, the little pink ones never paid any attention to me. They were too young to feel any

15

kind of boy/girl thing, and I wasn't old enough to be a parent. So they ignored me. And I ignored them.

In a few days, I was concentrating so hard on feeling my body and trying to get it to do the things that Miss McRae was showing us, I could have been training with a troupe of trained orangutans. I was so busy getting those drooping elbows up, those knees straight, those toes pointed that I wouldn't have noticed if anyone was laughing at me. Which they weren't. The children just flung themselves about and repetition did the trick for them. All they needed was instinct and the right proportions. Time they had. But I had to concentrate, and I found I liked to.

The five o'clock class, my second class of the day, was another matter. This advanced class was entirely made up of adult students and late teenagers. There were occasionally dancers from the Chicago Ballet (which *did* have some good dancers—a few). The Broadway shows on tour also contributed dancers to the class when they were in town. (Often they had good techniques, but they tended to be bouncier.) Our local contributions, on the other hand, were largely pleasant girls with their hair pulled tightly back into a bun and large thighs and buttocks. Now they probably tell people, "I would have had a wonderful career as a dancer if I hadn't met Fred/Frank/Bill."

For the most part, the boys were a cross-section of Chicago's best-looking young homosexuals. Do most homosexuals decide at some point in their lives that they must dance? This group changed frequently. Not in style but in identity.

Going to ballet class as an adult male, in those days, was really putting it on the line. This was pre–Edward Villella, and ballet boys were never butch. To enter the ranks of admitted homosexuals required a certain level of physical beauty and noticeable personality. As with everything else, standards have slipped, and everyone including your uncle Fred is out of the closet. Men used to walk the streets looking for someone to love. Now they look like they're walking the streets looking for someone to kill.

16

In the company of these passing beauties of the day, I changed into my dance clothes every evening in the dilapidated little boys' dressing room. For my first class, I was all alone, but for the grown-ups' class I was in a twittering birdcage full of "Oh, my dears" and "Well, I said, Mary . . ." They were all friendly in their babbling, cheerful way. And it was from them I learned all the minutiae of dressing for ballet. Getting the exact size of shoe, so tight that your toes can't move; putting your full weight on the ball of one foot as you went onto demi-pointe would soon stretch it a lot. My first pair, which fit like bedroom slippers, were soon so loose they were dangerous. And they didn't stick tight to the foot so as to look good when you pointed your toes. Talk about "Oh, my dear!"

The boys showed me how to bend the back of the shoe to find the exact spots to sew on elastic. And they pointed out that I, or someone, had to sew the elastic carefully inside the shoe, so it looked good, but neatly under the binding of the drawstring, so it wouldn't give you blisters. Years later, I read that Oscar Levant had said that ballet was homosexual baseball. It was all of that and more. Tough, tough, tough on the feet, the ankles, the knees, the back. It may look like you're drifting about like a dandelion, but you're actually whanging and banging away like a trench digger.

They taught me how to correctly wear my dance belt, too. I supposed the wide side was to cover the crack in my buttocks and always wore it that way. Billy Somebody noticed this one day and said, "You've got your dance belt on backwards." I muttered that I thought if I wore it the other way around, it wouldn't cover my rear end. "But that's the whole point," said Billy, somehow tossing his blond crew cut and his perfect fanny at the same time as he exited the dressing room. I didn't quite understand what point he meant, but I turned it around anyway.

Every day I looked forward to watching the professional class, which immediately preceded ours. Student dancers were allowed to watch from the door, and I was always early for my class in order to watch the "real dancers." And the fact that we couldn't dance anywhere near as well as professionals didn't keep us from being critical.

The students in this class were largely from the Chicago Opera. I came to realize that touring companies flocked to Miss McRae's classes also, because she was famous in the ballet world for her ability to improve technique. When you wanted to turn more pirouettes, jump higher, improve your feet, beat those feet back and forth faster and more times, you went to Edna McRae.

When I saw luscious, curvy Mary Ellen Moylan of Ballet Theatre, I realized that a girl dancer didn't necessarily have to be straight up and down and sinewy. And when I saw Melissa Hayden with her cocky, bantam-rooster demeanor, I realized that a girl didn't have to be curvy to be sexy.

Belle-Mère took me to see all the visiting companies. The New York City Ballet, Ballet Theatre, and Colonel de Basil's Ballet Russe de Monte Carlo, with the inexplicable Nina Novak as the leading ballerina, were some of them. I began to be able to contrast some dancers on stage and in the classroom. Elegant André Eglevsky wasn't very different in the classroom from the aloof, impeccable prince in *Swan Lake*. He did pirouettes in a kind of funny loopedy-loop manner, like a shot putter getting ready to throw the shot. Miss McRae used to scream, "Up, André, up! Push down with your foot more." But he never changed. John Kriza was so butchy, ballsy sexy you didn't much care how well he danced—which wasn't fantastic. Watching them, I learned the secret of the stars: "Don't ever try to do anything on stage you don't do well." On stage you never saw their faults; they always seemed perfect.

I saw Claude Bessy, guest-starring with Ballet Theatre from the Paris Opéra. From her, I learned to feel the thrill of watching a dancer accomplish difficult steps she *might* not be able to do. The American style was to suggest that nothing was difficult. The French way was to suggest that these steps were very difficult but somehow you would conquer them. She was a star who used the excitement of a tightrope walker to get her audience out of their seats.

When the legendary Alicia Markova, born Alice Marks, appeared in *Giselle* for Ballet Theatre, not a ballet student missed a performance, standing crushed together at the back of the theater in standing room. We all had heard that she had never taken class with other students. All her life she had had private classes. This made her into a kind of deity for us. She was also famous for her "spotting." When we did a series of turns, we were taught to pick a "spot" to look at, hold it with our eyes as long as possible as we turned and then whip the head around to pick it up again immediately. In this way, you didn't get dizzy. But Madame Markova didn't do this. She had four little spots, perhaps the corners of the stage. And when she turned, her little head went bing, bing, bing, bing like a hen plucking at grain. This was exotica. We loved it. We tried it. Impossible.

Ballet students are true students: for them, learning is everything. And like baseball fans, they are infatuated with the players. Markova had been trained by Enrico Cecchetti, teacher of Pavlova and Nijinsky. Cecchetti had left Russia with the famous Diaghilev company, which Markova had joined as a young girl in the 1920s. We were intrigued and wondered if her birdlike "spotting" was in the tradition of the Russian greats, or was it her own little London-born thing?

Both Belle-Mère and I fell under the spell of ballet tradition. We read about the great Romantic ballerinas. Marie Taglioni, first to get up on pointe and drift about in the early *La Sylphide*. First to be respectable and marry a count. Fanny Elssler, the sexy and less respectable ballerina specializing in Spanish dances. A peppy Austrian, she. Adorable little Carlotta Grisi, the Italian dancer who created *Giselle*. Choreographed for her by her lover, the dancer Jules Perrot, who sported a nifty pair of thighs if the old prints have it correctly. And the elegant Lucile Grahn. Danish. The most truly beautiful of the bunch.

Mom and I just loved imagining all these ladies and their

carryings-on in the 1830s and 1840s. One of our new dancer friends told us about *Taglioni's Jewel Case,* an artwork created by Joseph Cornell and on view at the Museum of Modern Art in New York: glass ice cubes fitted neatly into blue velvet cubicles in a small mahogany case. It was Cornell's homage to the story that Taglioni was en route through the snow to dance for the Czar in St. Petersburg when stopped by bandits. They demanded her jewels and her maid remonstrated with them: "Don't you know who this is? This is the great Taglioni." The bandits agreed if she would dance for them they would return the jewels. Her maid readied her in her huge white tutu, her wreath of artificial flowers, her pearl bracelets, her tiny pink satin slippers with only a little crocheting across the ends of the toes to help her stay on pointe. The bandits built a huge fire and laid blankets on the ground. And she descended into the polar night. Under the stars, like diamonds in the navy-blue sky, she danced to get her own diamonds back.

This was the world Belle-Mère longed to enter and the world she was dragging me into, willy-nilly. To be honest, I wasn't hanging back very much.

When we saw Alicia Markova, the last of the delicate, birdlike Romantic ballerinas, dance floating in a cloud of tulle skirt in the second act of *Giselle,* we could imagine we were at the Maryinsky Theater in St. Petersburg seated not far from the imperial box. Her tutu seemed larger than others I'd seen and seemed to be always moving. I caught her catching it with her hands when she went through fourth position with her arms, so it seemed to be moving restlessly about her all the time. When she did a large leg movement, it rippled over her leg like a wave, only her little pink slipper protruding from the foam.

Her dancing was a kind of moving textbook. When she did her little pas de chat, both feet disappeared under her tutu skirt and she seemed to be like a flower blowing in the wind. I knew one of her partners later and he said she would never prepare for a jump to help her partner. He had to lift her dead weight unaided. Everything she did had to look effortless or the magic of a Romantic ballerina was marred.

Somehow, that effortlessness made sense of the old ballet. She was so much like a spirit drifting about, you really believed she had come back from the dead to protect her lover. It made perfect sense for those moments she was on stage. Her lover, the impeccable, elegant, blond Erik Bruhn, made it easier to understand.

This was our world, Belle-Mère's and mine. Up to our necks in ballet classes, going to ballets, talking about ballet, and reading about ballet. We cared for nothing else. We soon developed the unshockability that goes with the world of dance. That a ballerina was the impresario's mistress meant nothing. But if she didn't have legs that were fully turned out or if she *had* arches that drooped, we were speechless—*this* was bad! Dance is the most ruthless of disciplines. One can claim to be an actor and never act, and if there is a performance, it is so hard to say if it's good or bad. A singer can claim to sing, and much is forgiven because the voice develops late and perhaps this is an off-day. But a dancer must dance. There's no faking it. Everyone can clearly see how well the steps are executed, how much emotion is expressed.

If you say you dance, you *have* to dance. There are no two ways about it.

Levoy Ping

Even among all the famous names, exotic faces, whippet-slim bodies, and imperious manners, I still found time to be fascinated with a student in the professional class. He resembled some kind of rare bird. Not beautiful, but strange. Tall, with long arms and legs. Red hair stood up in a kind of plumage on top of his head. I don't know how well he danced. Adequately, I suppose. But it was his persona that was so riveting. It was hard to watch anyone else when he was in class. Of course I knew his name. Everyone knew his name. Levoy Ping. He was already famous in the school for his remarks. One day while I was watching, Miss McRae said to a male dancer, "You have terrible hands." As he passed Levoy Ping on his way to the back of the class, I heard Levoy say, not very quietly, "Perhaps you should wear gloves."

He was a protégé of Edna McRae. Because he had red hair, as she did? Because he made her laugh instead of trembling at her acid remarks? More likely because of his attitude. He told me later it was that of a geisha. "One must always try to be amusing and to be amused, and that requires hard work."

Belle-Mère was fascinated with him, too. She saw him passing through the reception area from time to time and asked me one day, "Who is that divine creature with the strawberry-blond hair?"

I had never categorized Levoy Ping as a divine creature. I

wasn't ready to go that far. (Belle-Mère had been reading a lot of Evelyn Waugh at that time, which had had a big effect on her vocabulary.) I told her.

She said, "What an unusual name."

To say the least.

One evening, I had arrived early and Levoy was late for class and we passed in the doorway of the men's dressing room. He looked at me in a manner I later came to associate with Dame Edith Evans and said, "What is your name?"

Transfixed, I said, "Harry Potter."

Levoy said, "Hmmmmm," and swept away, dragging a fortune in imaginary ermine behind him.

Up until that time, I had imagined I was invisible. Who could have noticed me? What did I look like then? I have a few photos, and when I study them, the question still remains. To me, I looked very adolescent, and there is something vague about my whole appearance. Nice hair, but was it dark blond or light brown? A nicely proportioned body without a trace of any budding sensuality. Not much chin, and eyes that had an El Greco look. Sad and imploring for some kind of divine intervention. I know that at the time I was not at all sad and nothing could have been further from my mind than divine intervention. Some kind of physical intervention, maybe.

Perhaps I caught Levoy's attention because I didn't come off the same assembly line as the other little ballet boys, trying to parlay a trim little rear end into a big career.

Several nights later, as I was coming out of the school, he was waiting for me. He said, "I'm Levoy Ping and I thought you might like to have a cup of coffee with me."

"I don't drink coffee," I said.

Levoy looked at me pityingly. "Do you drink Coca-Cola?"

"Sometimes," I said. My mind and mouth were thick with the surprise of having my usual home–school–ballet class–home trajectory interrupted.

Levoy spoke more kindly. "Could this be one of those times?"
"Yes," I said. "Yes, sure."

"Don't ever say 'sure,' " Levoy said. "It always sounds like an airline stewardess. Or a nurse."

So we had coffee and Coca-Cola. I actually wanted a Dr Pepper but was too embarrassed to change my mind. I had almost never had a soft drink before, because Belle-Mère thought they were bad for the teeth. Levoy drew out of me how old I was, what I was studying at my very theatrical school, what ballets I had seen, and what I thought of various dancers. I, of course, asked him none of these things. I found him very profound and sophisticated and at no time noticed that he did not speak at all of himself but only of me.

He had a very gracious manner, styled, he once told me, on Mrs. Calvin Coolidge—the only truly beautiful woman, in his opinion, to have ever been a president's wife. (He admitted he had never seen Mrs. Grover Cleveland or Mary Todd Lincoln.)

As we finished our drinks, he said, "How would you like to sleep with me?"

I said, "Gee, I'm not tired, and besides, it's only nine-thirty."

Levoy gave me a long, level look through his imaginary lorgnette. Then he said, "I'd like to meet your mother. I'll see you home."

Belle-Mère was there when we got to our apartment. Which surprised me. Usually she wasn't, because she took the class immediately after mine. I hadn't seen her at the school and figured she was working overtime at her job checking results for a research company. One of the other older students had put her on to it. The company used part-time employees a lot, and you could come in when you wanted to and work as long as you wanted to. Which was perfect for dancers who went to class in the morning and might want to go to an audition from time to time. Belle-Mère said that almost everyone there was an aspiring actor or a novelist or someone in the arts. She loved mixing with all those people even if the work was incredibly boring and ter-

24

ribly paid. With the little bit of occasional alimony she got, it was enough to pay our rent and my school fees and buy food. Just.

Miss McRae had given me a half-fee scholarship at the ballet school, which helped a lot. And on Saturdays I bagged groceries at the grocery store down on the corner.

Belle-Mère was transfixed when I appeared at the door with Levoy. When I introduced them she said, "Levoy Ping. Levoy Ping. What an unusual name. Where are you from?"

"Chillicothe." Levoy said. "I'm one of the Pings of Chillicothe."

"And 'Levoy'? Is that a family name?" Belle-Mère said. She wasn't being funny.

"In a way. My mother's favorite brother was named LeRoy and his wife's name is Yvonne. I'm a tribute to the two of them."

"How nice."

"Do you think so?" Levoy said. His voice gave no clue as to whether he thought so or not.

"Wouldn't you like to sit down?" asked Belle-Mère.

"I'd like to sit down in the kitchen." Levoy said.

And so we did. Belle-Mère was pretty good herself at the "I'll ask the questions and you'll do the talking" technique. We found out Levoy lived alone with his capuchin monkey, Igor. He was twenty, had been studying ballet for two years, and was sure he could make it.

"I'm famous for my legs and feet," he said. "At least around Chicago. Look."

He sat down on the floor and, removing his shoes, showed us how he could point his toes in front of him until they curved over and touched the floor. Those were some arches, no mistake.

Belle-Mère and Levoy got into a spirited discussion about ballet technique then and there. She asked him whether he pulled up or sat into his hip when he did pirouettes. ("Up, up, up" was his answer.) Was he really able to get his heels down when he did very rapid changements in first position? ("Almost" was the answer.) What did he think of her first position? she wanted to know. She pulled her skirt up very high, showing her garters, and put her heels together. "Quite good" was the answer, but don't force the feet apart too much. It does no good, weakens the arches, and the audience can't tell the difference.

Belle-Mère wanted to see how it felt to be partnered, so Levoy lifted her onto one shoulder, hitting her head a little bit on the ceiling fixture. I sat on the straight-backed chair, by the kitchen table we had found in the street, and was quite surprised. Even more so when, suddenly, Belle-Mère plunged into a fish dive from Levoy's shoulder, ending up with her chin an inch from the floor and one leg locked behind Levoy's left shoulder.

"Mother," I said, "are you sure you should be doing this?"

"Oh, lay off, Harry," my mother said just as a loud rapping on the door stopped her from adding whatever she was planning to add.

I opened the door. Mother and Levoy stood in the middle of the kitchen floor looking a little overheated and flustered. A very strict, very tall woman in black stood in the door. "Mrs. Potter," she said, adding nothing.

Mother said, "Yes?"

The woman went on. Her hair was piled on top of her head. She looked a little bit like Margaret Hamilton in *The Wizard of Oz*. Witchy but tall. And big. Big shoulders. "I'm your downstairs neighbor, Miss Afrodisian, and I must ask, what is going on up here? It's almost eleven o'clock and we people who work must get our sleep."

"Hi, Afro," Levoy said. They knew each other, evidently.

"Levoy, what the hell are you doing here?" asked Miss Afrodisian as she strode into the room. Her voice slid down about an octave.

"Hey, those are great-looking shoes," Levoy said. Miss Afrodisian was wearing spike-heeled patent-leather pumps. (They looked very lethal.)

"Actually, they're very comfortable," Miss Afrodisian said.

"Could I try them on?" Levoy wanted to know.

26

"Sure, why not?" She kicked them off, sitting down on one of our hard, straight-backed kitchen chairs. "Have you got anything around here to drink?" She directed this to Belle-Mère as the lady of the house. She hadn't really noticed me.

"Just some Scotch," Mother said.

"That sounds swell. Forget the ice. Just a little water." She was the only one drinking. "Let's go in the living room," she said. We followed her, Levoy navigating very steadily in her shoes. "You have to press down with the ball of your foot," he said to me. I was not planning to be next.

Miss Afrodisian flopped into our sprung armchair and threw her legs over one arm. She watched Levoy as he marched around the room with the patent-leather pumps protruding from his sagging gray corduroy pants.

"These are comfortable, Afro," he said. Looking at her dangling feet he said, "You should have been a dancer."

Miss Afrodisian then told a story about a young woman who did tap dancing on one leg and classical ballet on the other and between the two of them she made a pretty good living. Mother and Levoy laughed a lot, and I joined in, although it didn't seem to be much of a joke.

Mother looked at me. "What are you laughing at?" she demanded.

"I was only laughing because you were," I said.

"Good," she said.

"For God's sake, Harry's fifteen years old," Levoy said.

"I don't care. When I was his age I was a virgin and I didn't know anything," Mother said.

"When you were fifteen *everyone* was a virgin. Excuse me. Not Loretta Young. That was *before* she was a virgin." This from Miss Afrodisian, whose black dress had now slid up to show the tops of her black stockings and some kind of elaborate garters.

"Pull down your dress, Afro, I can see your garter belt. I suppose you're wearing a Merry Widow waist cincher, too? *And* I think it's time you shaved your legs," Levoy said.

27

Mother said politely, "Would you like another drink?"

"Why not?" Miss Afrodisian said merrily, getting to her feet and heading towards the kitchen, tugging down her dress and whatever she had on under it. We could hear the clink of the Scotch bottle against her glass. Her voice came through the kitchen door: "When you're six feet two in black pumps, you might as well go all the way."

Mother tried to dampen down the hilarity that was in the air. "How do you two know each other?" she said, once Miss Afrodisian was back in the chair, legs waving.

It seemed they had met not too long ago at a company where they pasted real clothes on Godey's Ladies prints, which were then framed in shadow boxes.

"I never heard of such a thing," Belle-Mère said.

"Not a lot of people are good at it," Levoy said. "There's a lot of little ruffles, pleats, and folds to make and then glue in place. And little bits of lace to put around bonnets and parasols. Afro was already working there, and we got along very well. We tried to make Godey's Ladies look as slutty as possible."

"Oh, God. You couldn't make them look *too* slutty. The guy that ran the place loved it," Miss Afrodisian said. "I started pasting sequins on like hoop earrings. He loved that. Then I got the idea of pasting marabou feathers on instead of lace. Very sticky to do. He loved that, too.

"Yeah. We went wild. Levoy had the idea of pasting legs and things from lingerie ads under the hoop skirts. They sold even more of that stuff," Miss Afrodisian said. "Then some minister and his wife out in Indiana got some for wedding presents and the shit hit the fan. And we got canned."

It didn't seem to faze either of them. Levoy now had a scholarship from Miss McRae where he got lessons in exchange for sweeping up and cleaning the mirrors. Miss Afrodisian said she finally had made the break into show business and was starting next week in a musical revue as "the Male Lily Pons."

Before I could ask how this could be, Belle-Mère decided I'd

28

had enough education for one evening. She said we had to go to bed. "It's a school day tomorrow." And thanked Levoy and Afro very much for coming over. "It was really fun," she assured them.

Afro asked us to please come see her show at the Club Whoopee. "I only work Friday, Saturday, and Sunday. And I do a little coat-checking, of course."

That was just the beginning of our life with Levoy. He came around a lot. He cooked for us. He sang for us. He danced for us. But he never stayed overnight.

He often waited for me after class. And mainly talked about how to improve my technique. He dinned into me how important the standing leg was. "You must not relax into it. Up, it has to be up from the arch of your foot through your knee into your hip. Then the rest of it is free to move." Much of what he told me was playback from Miss McRae, but he had quick perceptions of his own. He showed me how to stretch my feet by getting a kind of hammerlock on the lower foot with both hands and pulling that arch over.

He showed me how to do push-ups standing on my head with my feet braced against the wall. "You have to look like a man and act like a man on stage," he said. "If anyone is looking for girls there are plenty of the real thing around."

Levoy was fond of singing, too, but largely from a repertoire of his own. "Violate Me in the Violet Time" often accompanied the evening dishwashing, as did "A Woman Without a Man," which started: "You can roll a silver dollar around the barroom floor." Somehow I loved that image. " 'Twas a Cold Winter's Evening" had a wonderful line, too: "When a gentleman dapper stepped out of the crapper."

This pervasive atmosphere of illegal and immoral sex did Belle-Mère a world of good. She never seemed to worry that it would do me any harm, and she was right. All my attention was focused on my classes. My ballet classes exhausted me, and my regular classes took up all my spare time, what with my homework. Occasionally, we would go to a Susan Hayward movie, Belle-Mère's favorite, but the ballet world was a closed one. It took up all our time, and we wouldn't have had it any other way.

She seemed to have been waiting all her life for this total immersion in a climate of intense, hothouse femininity.

We had wonderful evenings in our dingy little flat on West Roscoe. I would be studying, or trying to, at the dining-room table, slowly picking away at the oilcloth to reveal its webby substructure while trying to memorize something about the Huguenots. Meanwhile, in the background, Levoy would be counseling my mother to let her hair grow longer and tease it "into a huge mane of hair. One can never have too much hair, never!"

Or Afro would be fitting an elaborate dress on Belle-Mère that was being created for his nightclub act. Afro would tell Mother, "You have a perfect figure for couture." Adding, "If I could, I would only wear black." Which was untrue. In fact, Afro had a great predilection for green satin and never entered a room without eyeing the draperies. Scarlett O'Hara had left a deep impression on Afro, but I think the true role model was Brenda Starr.

Lovers

I think sixteen is about the right age to start having a regular sexual relationship. That's how old I was when I started sleeping with Levoy Ping.

I was nearing sixteen when we met at Edna McRae's school, and for the next two years Levoy was a fixture in my life. As he was in Belle-Mère's. I guess that's how he slipped around us. That and the kissing.

Levoy was a wonderful kisser. We were sitting beside each other on the couch watching television. I was kind of cozied up to Levoy, he had his arm around my shoulder. He said something funny, and when I looked up at him, he kissed me. Very warm lips. Just moist enough. Before I knew it, he was lying on top of me kissing me with a lot of tongue. It was fun.

And then we were pressing our groins together. We actually spent a number of evenings pressing our groins together. Well, not *many*, because we were almost never without the presence of Belle-Mère. Where she could have been the evening we started kissing, I can't imagine. Maybe I was home with a cold and Levoy had gotten there ahead of her. The Adult Beginners was the last class of the evening.

Sometimes Levoy would try to kiss me when Belle-Mère was in another room, but I wasn't having any of that. I think I

31

thought kissing was something like swimming: it felt good and it was fun. Of course I was masturbating by that age, but I don't remember conjuring up any images. It, too, was like swimming. Fun, felt good, readily available. More so than swimming.

Levoy and I were probably doing our little dry-humping number for six months or so before he slipped it to me. And even that was pretty modest. Maybe Mother was in class again, but we were sprawled on the couch with Levoy pressing into me. He reached down and undid the buttons on my pants and the buttons on his own and pressed his cock down in between my legs. And came in a jiffy. My underpants were soaked.

After, he lay on top of me groaning for a while, and then like a dead body. I said, "Gosh, Levoy, I have to get up and change my underpants. This feels icky."

He muttered in my ear, "It wouldn't be so icky if I had been up your ass." I didn't answer that one. I just struggled out from under him. Changed my underpants and rinsed out the other pair so Belle-Mère wouldn't see something funny in the laundry. But, of course, it wasn't long before he was up my ass. And I was up his. It was sort of like more fun. But I certainly wasn't in love with Levoy. I had no ideas about that kind of thing.

I was in love with ballet.

Summer Theater

I had only been studying for a little over a year but I was acquiring technique. Because I was growing at the same time that I was studying intensely, my body had changed a lot. Miss McRae's voice kept calling out in class, "Pull up, pull up." And I did. My legs were straight. My waist was thin. My back was flat. But actually, I didn't care so much that my body looked good. What I cared about was that suddenly I could do double pirouettes. I could get up on the ball of one foot, bend my other knee so it formed a triangle with my toe on the knee of my standing leg, and around I went. It was thrilling.

I had good feet. I got them from my mother. We both have good arches and our toes point into nice shapes. We both stretched out our legs and pointed our toes and it looked good. Levoy, of course, had fantastic feet. ("Too supple," Miss McRae declared, but there wasn't a person in the class who wouldn't have loved to have those "too supple" feet.)

I was beginning to jump. My thighs and buttocks were beginning to get larger and stronger, and I had nice arms. Not too graceful. I never felt embarrassed by all those airy-fairy gestures and positions. They kind of made sense to me.

For only a year's study, I was dancing pretty well, when some of the dancers in my class started talking about auditions for summer stock. Chicago had a summer theater, the Music Tent, that did Broadway musicals. Tried-and-true stuff they knew the public would like. Levoy was going, and he insisted that I come along. "But I'm not ready," I said. "I'm just starting."

"You're good-looking and I don't think they care about double pirouettes and entrechats-six and all that stuff. They just want you to get out there and move your ass. Give it a try."

Levoy also insisted I wear a tight little striped top of his. I wore my school tights and slippers with it. I really had no idea if I was cute or not. I was blond. Blondish. That's all I knew.

We went to the Kingsley Studios for the audition. There were a lot of boys there—this was a "boys only" audition evidently—and we knew most of them. Edna McRae's was the best school in Chicago, so anybody who was planning a career went there. There were a few boys who had come in from New York and some older guys, dancers, I guess, who had washed up in Chicago because of boyfriends or other kinds of jobs.

The choreographer giving the audition was a woman. Her name was Sally Ann. She liked me and took the time to show me some of the steps. I had never done show dancing, but it wasn't so hard. Just fast.

They were planning to do *Oklahoma!* evidently, so there were a lot of strutting and legs-apart kinds of steps. Cowboy stuff. *Brigadoon* was being done, too, so we did those sword-dance things. That was easy to do.

Sally Ann took our names and telephone numbers. She said, "Levoy and you have the same phone number." It was a statement, not a question. She was quick.

I said, "I live with my mother and Levoy doesn't have a phone so he uses ours."

"How old are you?" she wanted to know.

"Seventeen. Almost seventeen," I said. Almost was six months away, but who needs to know?

"You look younger. But good. But good," she said. "You must be studying with Edna McRae. I can always tell. Nice sharp positions." I nodded. She was talking to me much longer than any-one else. She went on to talk to others.

That evening she called. They wanted both Levoy and me. Rehearsals started the first week of June. We would be doing two shows and trading around with a sister company in Milwaukee. They were doing *Kismet* and *Bloomer Girl*, I think. We would per-form two weeks of our show in Chicago and then go to Mil-waukee while they brought their show in to our theater. Then we'd do two weeks of *Brigadoon* in Chicago, and so on. Then the summer would be over. We would get $125 a week, would be put in a hotel in Milwaukee, and would live at home in Chicago. After rehearsals, we could go to class.

We were stunned. Belle-Mère was stunned and thrilled. One hundred and twenty-five dollars a week coming into the house? It was a fortune. Maybe we should move. Maybe she should stop asking for alimony. Maybe I should quit school. Maybe we should move to New York. Her head was swirling with plans. I was already the voice of reason in our household. "Oh, Mom, let's just save as much money as we can and I'll study real hard for another year and then we can go to New York." (Which was what we did.)

A lot of the guys in the company came on to me. Most of the singers from New York and all the leading men did, too. The guy who did Curly in *Oklahoma!* was very sexy and really got on my case. In the wings, he was very friendly, but I just did my schoolboy thing. I talked about my mother a lot and how I'd like him to meet her. What was I supposed to do?

Levoy never let me out of his sight. In Milwaukee, we shared a hotel room. So we were really getting at it when we were up there. No chance of Mom walking in, and there is something sexy about second-rate hotel rooms anyway. Who can resist them? Large, emptyish rooms with large, emptyish beds with head-boards, a dressing table, an armchair, and floral draperies. A musty, empty smell. You *had* to take off all your clothes and fuck a lot, if just to liven them up. Otherwise you'd cry. I think they

35

had a fatal effect on my ideas about interior decoration. The other boys in the company probably figured out what was going on, but Levoy and I always acted as though we were just friends. Which, actually, we were. Being older, perhaps he felt differently, but for me it was just fun. I stuck it in him. He stuck it in me. We took turns. One day it was his turn; the next day it was mine. It felt good. Seeing his large penis always got me pretty excited, and we did sixty-nine and that kind of stuff, too. But it was something like going to class. I enjoyed doing it. That was all.

If Levoy had said he was going away forever, I would have missed him. Some. You know how kids are. It's only later, when we know how we're supposed to feel about a lot of things, that we start feeling them.

Sally Ann, the choreographer, was very nice to me. I don't think she had any ideas about me. She just liked me. We talked about what we were reading. I was going through a premature fascination with F. Scott Fitzgerald. She was very big on writers like Pearl Buck and Louis Bromfield, whom I had never heard of. I remember she was reading *The Rains Came* that summer. I think she found it in her hotel room. She wanted to go to India and be covered in emeralds and rubies by some prince. I told her he might be pretty dark. She didn't care.

Anyway, I danced in show business, but I was never crazy about it. Most of the dancers loved it. Loved the admiring faces out front. The men waiting at the stage door. Always men, whether they were waiting for the girls or the boys. Sometimes goofy people or kids waiting for a diva or a ballerina for autographs, but otherwise men, men, men.

Later, when I was studying at the Opera in New York with Margaret Craske, a student named Betty Ann Paulin was smiling and "projecting" in class as she danced. Pretending she was right down on the footlights as she did her glissade, assemblé, changement, changement. Miss Craske gestured at the pianist, Helen, to stop. "What are you doing, you wretched girl?" she said. "I'm selling it, Miss Craske," Betty Ann replied. "Well, you can just go sell

36

it somewhere else," Miss Craske said in that high, fluty, fruity voice of hers. And motioned Helen to start playing again.

That's how I felt. I wasn't particularly interested in "selling it." I loved the mathematical precision of classic ballet. The music played and it all unfolded. The body turns inward, then outward, then pauses. Then poses on the tip of one foot while the music goes on, then catches up. Somehow it was so meaningful, so useful to me.

I didn't look forward to curtain time, to spitting in my mascara box and wiping the gluey black mixture on my lashes with the sticky little brush. Or painting my face. We still used greasepaint when I started dancing. It did have a peculiar sweet smell that always smelled hot somehow. Maybe I just associate it with bright dressing-room lights.

I loved going to class the next day. Seeing my leg go higher, my foot more pointed, my knee steadier. Day by day. Suddenly feeling myself higher in the air when I jumped. Having more time in the air to beat my ankles back and forth, like birds trying to escape. Suddenly *really* turning twice in the air when Miss McRae shouted, "Spot, Harry, spot!" Finding that if I snapped my head around twice, holding the window across the room in focus, my body followed. Also finding myself in plié when I came down, my feet neatly facing in opposite directions. It was like Newton discovering gravity.

Everything Miss McRae had been teaching us was true. You repeat the exercises, you change your body, and suddenly your body is obeying you. Creating new shapes. Letting you accomplish new trajectories through the air, new patterns for your feet, legs, arms, and head on the stage.

Homosexuals *are* men finally; and the thrill of your body accomplishing hugely complicated physical things is the same whether you're throwing somebody out at third or managing three double tours en l'air without falling down. Which is to say, I guess, I never really got into being a pretty boy, spoiled by adult male attention. I liked earning the money. I liked being a grown-up and paying the rent for Belle-Mère. But most of all, I liked dancing itself.

The dancing we did in the shows that summer was sort of silly. Easily done and no challenge. I always thought that choreography had a lot to do with how well the choreographer could dance. *Oklahoma!* was choreographed by Agnes de Mille. She only gave dancers things to do she could do herself, and she didn't have a lot of technique. So her steps were easy to do.

Miss McRae understood this and stopped me after class one day. "You're doing very well, Harry. You have good concentration. I know you're already working, but I hope you'll study with me for another year. I think you could become an excellent dancer and partner. I think you could become a danseur noble. You have the right proportions, and a good face, and you're a hard worker. Your mother knows she's never going to dance, doesn't she?"

What a good egg Miss McRae was. She undoubtedly saw Belle-Mère in her leg warmers and sweater tied at the waist going into class every night as my class came out. Nice body. But obviously far too old to dance professionally.

"Yes," I said. "Yes, I think she does. It's just that she loves it. Like I do."

Miss McRae said, "She loves the idea of it. You love it because you can really do it."

We left it at that.

I stopped sleeping with Levoy, if you could call what we were doing sleeping. It just seemed silly. He began hanging around with another red-headed kid who had just arrived from Green Bay. Maybe all that red pubic hair going at it at the same time was stimulating for both of them.

I didn't miss it, sleeping with Levoy. It was ballet that held my attention. Miss McRae was teaching me the Bluebird variation from *Sleeping Beauty.* And Estelle Fairweather and I were learning the second-act pas de deux from *Swan Lake* in partnering class. We were going to do it with the Oak Park Civic Ballet. Little girls running around in swan outfits and us.

Levoy and Belle-Mère came to see it. Estelle didn't have great points, but nice arms. She could really get that swan thing going. And I had been going to the gym twice a week in addition to class, so I could get her up there on the lifts.

Belle-Mère made my prince's tunic: black velvet with a little ruffle in the neck and silver braid down the front. She'd seen a picture of Erik Bruhn posed at Elsinore in a tunic like it—as Hamlet, I think—and she copied it. It was her Christmas present to me. I got her new pointe shoes. She got me new tights, too. Black. I got my hair cut like Erik's. I think the resemblance ended there. But Estelle and I did creditably. I wasn't really nervous. All those shows at the Music Tent helped me with that. But I got nervous afterwards when we were taking our bows. I saw Miss McRae sitting behind Belle-Mère and Levoy. She'd arranged for us to do this production and even arranged for us to get paid—fifty dollars each. But she never mentioned she was coming to see it.

The next day in class she said afterwards, "Not at all bad. Not bad for a first performance. I was proud of you, Harry. You hadn't even danced two years ago. We got you in the nick of time. For seventeen, not bad at all."

I never knew where Miss McRae had learned to dance. And learned to teach. She seemed to have sprung full-grown into life as a portly ballet teacher. With nice feet. She must have danced beautifully upon them at one time. They were her only gesture towards a ballet background. She wore big black dresses like slipcovers, but on her feet were little pink ballet slippers. Always immaculate.

I never knew if she had a husband. Had had a husband. Or a boyfriend. Or a girlfriend. Nothing. And very probably there *was* nothing. Ballet is very fulfilling. She probably went home at night, just tired. Not missing a lover or fame or a glamorous past or any of the rest of it. For her, ballet was like three good square

39

meals a day, I'm sure. Although I think she had three good square meals a day, too.

Belle-Mère began to get serious as my high-school graduation started looming. "I think we should go to New York, Harry," she said to me one night when she came home from class. Belle-Mère wasn't dancing better, but she was dancing stronger. She was in great health, even if she couldn't do a double pirouette.

"I think that's a good idea," I said.

She looked at me a little surprised. "We can't hang around this town forever. Levoy will be twenty-two his next birthday. You've finished school. I think now is the time to strike out," she said.

"Fine. When do you want to go?"

She ignored me.

"And I think I need a new teacher," she said. "I'm not really improving. Levoy feels the same way. Oh, someone called Sally Ann called you today. Who's Sally Ann? There's no Sally Ann at the school."

"You remember her. She was the choreographer and the dance captain at the Music Tent last summer. She probably wants us back."

"Me, too?" Belle-Mère asked.

I let that go by me and went to call Sally Ann. It was a New York number. I knew they stay up late in New York.

It wasn't for the Music Tent. It was for Saint Subber's summer theater in New Jersey. She was going to be the choreographer there. She said it would be a full season of shows. No traveling to Milwaukee. They were going to do *Carousel* and *Paint Your Wagon,* and they were also going to do *Brigadoon.* That's why she wanted Levoy and me, because we already knew the show. She thought she could get me the sword dance solo. One hundred and fifty dollars a week and a lot of work.

I was pretty excited, but I asked her if there was maybe something for my mother. "What does your mother do?" she said.

40

"Dance," I said. "Sort of."

"What does your mother look like?" Sally Ann said.

I appreciated that she didn't ask how old she was. Belle-Mère was sitting in a nonchalant manner in the easy chair across the room, reading. But she wasn't turning any of the pages of *Dance Magazine*.

"Good," I said.

"Does your mother do anything else? Does she sing?"

"She sews," I said.

"Good. Let me see what I can do. Saint has a costume department. Maybe we can get her in there. Auditions are next week. Can you be here? I'm sure you're dancing even better than last summer. Zachary Solov is the choreographer. I'm the dance captain and his assistant. He's the choreographer at the Met and I want him to see you. He'll love you."

"The Met?"

"The Metropolitan Opera," she said.

I thanked Sally Ann, got the details as to where the auditions were being held, hung up, and explained to Belle-Mère that we had to move to New York the next weekend. My high-school graduation was a farce anyway. All those silly noodles. *They* were all staying in Chicago. *I* was going to New York with Belle-Mère and Levoy. Levoy had to leave Igor the monkey behind. Which made me feel sad. I used to go over to Levoy's and Igor had learned he could ride on my shoulder as long as he didn't pee. Now he was going to the zoo to be with other monkeys just when he had learned to control his bladder.

We took the Greyhound. With Edna McRae's blessing. She said we must go immediately to Ballet Arts in Carnegie Hall and not miss any classes. We should try to get into Vladimiroff's classes, or failing that, take class with Vera Nemchinova, the last of the Diaghilev ballerinas.

"I think she drinks too much, but you'll never notice," Miss McRae said. "She did *Les Biches* for Diaghilev in one of the last

41

seasons. Nijinska, Nijinsky's sister, did the choreography. It was never performed in this country. She's one of the last ballerinas trained in St. Petersburg. You'll learn a lot from her."

Were we green. We got off the bus at the Forty-second Street terminal like refugees from the Ukraine. Someone in Chicago had mentioned the Chelsea Hotel, so we went there. In a taxi. We never took taxis in Chicago.

This was long before Andy Warhol, but the Chelsea was just as bad then. A collapsing red-brick ruin with Virgil Thomson somewhere upstairs and alcoholics everywhere else.

I called Sally Ann. Auditions were Tuesday.

Sixteenth Street

Our apartment. It seems impossible to think of now: four rooms for twenty-five dollars a month. The address was 248 West Sixteenth Street. One of a short row of ruined store-fronted tenements on a street with some cared-for buildings but largely pretty ruined itself. It was mostly Hispanic. I think I could safely say it was the worst block in Chelsea. Our neighborhood was called Chelsea. To this day, Chelsea has resisted being up-graded to the level of its name.

Our street even had the worst whore. Other streets had slim, tight-assed Hispanic girls. Girls with a certain tautness and chic, something like racehorses jockeying for position at the post. But our whore was fat, slovenly, and not even Hispanic. She used to stand with one foot on our lower step, her elbow leaning on the iron stair-railing, watching the short dark men who walked by. Occasionally, she threw back a wave of greasy unwashed hair. A large rhinestone bracelet was her only gesture towards beautifi-cation. She turned her back on our building. There was no busi-ness there. Too poor.

They all said it, our dancer friends who came to visit. "Your whore, she's really bad." We were ashamed and longed to have one of those flighty little Spanish fillies patrolling our block. But no such luck. The best we could do was Tony Perkins out cruising once in a while.

Our building was filthy. Garbage was strewn in the halls. Urine stained the stairs and its smell floated in the air. Children ran down the stairs peeing. The contest, it seemed, was to see who, starting from the top floor, could reach the front door without running out of urine.

All three of us carried a candle and matches in our dance bags, as the lights were often out when we got home and the stairways were pitch black. We were more afraid of stumbling than being mugged, though muggings weren't out of the question. Breaking and entering was more the style of our building, and it was usually our neighbors who broke and entered each other. Why wander far from home when it's all right here under your nose? To put it mildly.

Later we also took to carrying a brick in our dance bags, too—to fend off unwanted advances as we came down the street. It was some neighborhood.

The apartment itself? Someone we met at a rental agency put us onto it. Belle-Mère hesitated in front of the building; the worn stone, the light scattering of lettuce leaves, cigarette wrappers, and scraps of paper down the steps and onto the street daunted her, I suppose. The windows looked as if people had spit on them to clean them. "Twenty-five dollars a month," she said. We went in and up to the third-floor front on the right. We opened the door with the key the agency had given us.

It was a railroad flat. The first room was the kitchen. It had a small iron cook stove. A bathtub with an enameled lid in two liftable sections. A sink. Built-in cupboards, and two straight-backed wooden chairs. It was the sort of place where Little Annie Rooney would have lived when she was down on her luck and on the run from Mrs. Meanie.

The next room was smaller, with a small mirror hanging on the wall by the window. (I still have that mirror.) There was a second small room with a window on the air shaft and then a rather large front room.

"We could make this into a kind of practice room," Belle-Mère said.

"And then we wouldn't have to furnish it," Levoy said, looking out the window.

There was a fireplace on the wall that had been sealed up with a small gas heater in front of it. It never worked, though we often tried it.

"There's no toilet," I said.

"It's in the hall, I think. For everyone to use," Belle-Mère said.

She sounded so hesitant I had to say, "This is fun. It's like going back in time."

So we took it. We painted it all white and furnished it from the Salvation Army. It was our home.

One little room in the middle was Belle-Mère's, with a single bed in it. We bought a cheap printed Indian throw for the bed. With a little end table and a lamp, both painted black. It was our sitting room, too.

In the next little room, we had a double Salvation Army bed where Levoy and I slept. Our sex life was definitely over, so I didn't have to worry that Belle-Mère would wake in the night to slurping sounds.

We put up a dance barre across the front wall in the big room, crossing the windows. We rarely used it except to hang wet dance clothes on it. That room was always too cold to be used in the winter, and in warmer weather, our Puerto Rican neighbors had frantic, noisy dancing parties that penetrated that room so it was uninhabitable. There was no rest or relief in that room, but having it empty and luminous at the end of the other rooms kept us from feeling confined.

The odor of that building was unique, quite separate from the urine smells in the hallways. From the endless cooking in our neighbors' kitchens there was a sweetish, sour, sickening kind of smell. A smell of cooking vegetables, but I never knew which vegetables. Some mixture of the small, tortured tubers I saw outside the Puerto Rican stores in the neighborhood. Maybe with a bit of goat mixed in. Like body odor. Or dried vomit. Perhaps there *was* dried vomit in the halls that mixed with it. Does it sound disgusting? It was, but it didn't really disgust me.

It didn't disgust any of us. We were focused on our dance careers. We were soon off to Saint Subber's Lambertville Music Tent anyway and a summer much like the previous one.

The auditions were easy. Zachary Solov's choreography was a step forward from our season in Chicago and Milwaukee, but show business is show business: kick, step, twirl, smile. I saw Sally Ann point me out to Mr. Solov. He had curly hair, a turned-up nose, and a big grin. That merry Russian look. He tried to be a temperamental star but he was really just a good egg.

Belle-Mère was sent way up Eighth Avenue somewhere to help the costumers with fittings. Everything that could be was rented from Brooks Costumes. (I didn't even know there was a Brooks Brothers, so I never confused the two.) A lot of new costumes were being made for *The King and I*, which had been added to the repertoire at the last minute, since all the good costumes had already been rented out.

I suppose all summer stock is the same thing. First, all the other male dancers check you out, to see if you're fuckable or competition. The ones in the mood sleep with each other and get it out of the way early in the season. Then the singers make their moves. And the stars pass through, picking and choosing bed partners here and there, like a quick shopping trip to the supermarket: "Oh, this looks good . . . and this . . . and this. . . . Let's get the hell out of here." And male and female, they'd be gone to another summer theater and another company.

Then there were the shoals of people in the company management and from the audiences and from the neighborhood of country homes in Bucks County and New Jersey that surrounded the theater. The dancers were something like a party of pioneers crossing the country while the Indians raided them. Except our Promised Land was autumn, when the season would be over.

When you're seventeen, I guess your self-concept is that you are supposed to capture someone else's fancy. At least when you are a seventeen-year-old male dancer. It never occurred to me to select someone for myself. Levoy had selected me, and now I had deselected myself. Levoy did have good manners. He didn't try to crawl over me in the night.

Harry Is Left Alone

She was too old to fuck. Levoy? He didn't like women. Why was he fucking my mother? Why wasn't he fucking me? Even though I didn't want him to. It was a weird mix of being incredulous and jealous and not knowing of whom exactly.

I started backing out of the room. I'll just leave, I thought. They'll never know I was here. Belle-Mère's eyes popped open and looked directly into mine. She had the same "Am I hallucinating?" expression on her face I'm sure I had on mine. Then she did try to get out from under Levoy. He only pumped harder, misunderstanding what she was doing. He thought it was passion. I ran back through the kitchen and into the hall. I slammed the door hard behind me so they could hear it.

I went down and sat on the front steps, my dance bag between my feet. I felt sort of shaky. Surprising, surprising things had just happened.

I heard someone running down the stairs and into the front hall. I turned. Belle-Mère. For someone usually so scatty she was pretty composed.

"Can you just forget about all this? It won't happen again. It hasn't happened very much."

I said, "I feel like a betrayed whore." I had just been reading *The Berlin Stories* and had been pretty impressed with Sally Bowles.

48

"Why 'whore'?" my mother said. I didn't answer. I decided not to tell her that I had been sleeping with Levoy, too. That would be all too much like Isherwood's book.

"Actually," my mother said, "I was just trying to save Levoy from a life of perversion."

"Fat chance," I said.

"We can't put all this behind us, I guess," Mom said, and sat down beside me on the steps.

I told her I couldn't really imagine the three of us living cozily together in our cold-water flat anymore. I was thinking that every time one of us came home there would be the expectation that someone would be in bed with someone. Not my mother and me, of course, but you get the picture.

I'd been so excited when I rushed in. There were going to be auditions for the opera ballet company next week. Levoy wasn't going to audition. He was still studying at Carnegie Hall at Ballet Arts. As was Belle-Mère. They were suspicious of Cecchetti technique, which was taught at the opera school. The teachers at Ballet Arts said it took too long. So I had been studying at the opera school by myself. I hadn't seen much of Zachary Solov, since he didn't teach. But when I came out of class that day, he had been in the ballet school office and, seeing me, was very friendly. "Be sure you come to auditions, Harry, but don't worry. I get to pick one of the three new boys we need. You are definitely my choice." He smiled. Patted me on the back. Not on the ass, I noticed. So he was truly being friendly. I was so excited I didn't stay for the second class I usually took. But rushed home. And made my discovery.

I let myself in, went to my bedroom, and there they were. Not even under the covers. Like two naked praying mantises. Not until I saw their naked bodies, Levoy pressed down on my mother, did I realize how much they looked alike. You could hardly tell where one appendage left off and another one began.

I immediately thought of that joke about the little girl asking her mother if people went to heaven feet first. Her mother said,

"No, darling, why?" The child replied that she had just passed the maid's room and the maid was lying on her back with her legs in the air shouting, "Oh, God, I'm coming." And the little girl added, "And she would have gone, too, if Daddy hadn't been holding her down."

It did look like Levoy was holding my mother down while she was trying to escape from under him. But of course she wasn't.

What a lot of emotions. My mother. Mothers don't fuck.

So the good news and the bad news all came on one day. I was going to go into the Met ballet company and my mother and best friend were going to move out. And set up housekeeping together.

They did just that. Right next door, in the building just to the west of ours. Another cold-water flat like ours was available on the fifth floor and they moved there. Over the roof. It was shorter to go upstairs in our building, cross the tarpaper roof, and go down one flight to their new place. I was never in it and I didn't help them move. I sat on the front steps and as the sun was setting went upstairs to my apartment. My apartment which was now all mine. My mother had taken my lover and departed, which was certainly the most melodramatic way to put it.

They didn't stay there very long. They found a bigger place up on Twenty-second Street near Ninth Avenue. My mother would call from time to time, so I learned that they had needed a third roommate and had invited Afro Afrodisian to come live with them. Afro took her/his Male Lily Pons act down to the Club 84 and went right to work.

It was kind of strange being in my own apartment. Taking out the laundry. Ironing (very occasionally). Shopping for food. Cooking (also very occasionally). Fortunately for me, I was so busy at the opera that I was hardly ever at home except to sleep. And not always alone. But more of that later.

Dancing with the Danish Ballet

Stupid me. I didn't even know there *was* a Danish Ballet. I'd heard of the godlike Erik Bruhn and I guess I knew he'd come from somewhere over the sea, but it never dawned on me there was a whole company full of godlike men like that. But there was.

It was in the fall. I'd been accepted at the Met for their ballet company and had gone in to sign my contract and there was a hullabaloo of dancers going in the stage door when I arrived. The Danish Ballet had just arrived from Copenhagen and were in rehearsal for their season at the Opera, which would finish just as the opera season began. A man at the door said, "You here to audition for the extra dancers?"

"Do we get paid?" I said.

"Peanuts," he said.

"Well, peanuts are peanuts," I told him. "Where do I go?"

I went where we always went: the rehearsal room on the fourth floor. A very cute, short, dark man was looking everyone over. Fredbjorn Bjornsen. Perky. With sparkling eyes and his dark hair combed straight back and glued down. Quite a cutie, indeed. He looked at me and I guess thought my blond hair made me look kind of Danish. "Could you stand over there?" he said in perfect English, gesturing to the corner down by the mirrors where a few other tallish and blondish boys and girls were standing.

"You don't have to do a dance audition," he informed the dozen or so chosen ones after he had made his selection. "It's just for *The Flower Festival at Genzano*. You'll be peasants, wandering around in the background."

They were doing *Flower Festival* on their opening night, so I was able to see the company pull out the stops. Margrethe Schanne and Fredbjorn did *La Sylphide*, the ballet from the early 1800s that made Marie Taglioni famous. (She was the first to dance on pointe, you know, after her father whiplashed her to the peak of perfection.) Margrethe wore the white tutu, the flower wreath, the pearl bracelets and necklace, but she didn't seem particularly fragile and fairylike to me. She wasn't particularly pretty, so maybe that's where the critics found a comparison to Taglioni.

Fredbjorn, on the other hand, in his brown plaid kilts, was pretty dashing. Leaping and jeté-ing here and there, leading his troupe of other kilt-clad boys in lots of aerial stuff. Those Danish boys could jump. They wore little black slippers with a white "V" over the toes, so with their tights it looked as though they were wearing particularly tiny slippers, and had particularly pointed feet. Seeing those darting feet shoot forward through the air, strong thighs and flapping kilts dashing after them, was pretty exciting. The audience thought so, too. Of course, a large part of the audience was only too thrilled to see those skirts fly up and reveal a well-packed pair of little black shorts.

Henning Kronstam was their great beautiful male, now that Erik Bruhn had left to seek international fame, and Henning was quite something. Taller than the other men, dark, with a sort of Robert Taylor face. Very handsome, but romantic and fragile, too. Not a Heathcliff but a Chopin.

He danced *Night Shadow* with Margrethe Schanne. Mona Vangsaa was in it, too. Very beautiful, too, an elegant brunette. In *Night Shadow*, a poet is in love with a married woman, who sleepwalks. At the end, her jealous husband stabs the young poet, and the sleepwalking wife, in her long white nightgown, comes upon the body. She walks off, carrying the body in her arms,

52

Pietà-style. Henning Kronstam was much bigger than Margrethe Schanne, but she must have been very strong, because she did cradle him in both arms, walked off slowly into the wings, his beautiful head dangling. The audience was very struck with it. Me, too. It was touching in a way I hadn't been touched before. Mother/mistress caring for her lover/child. It gave me chills.

In the last ballet, we finally got our chance to go on. I wore a short jacket, knee pants, and black felt hat with a wide brim. I took the hat off and waved it over my head a good bit as we huzzahed the dancing.

Inge Sand danced *Flower Festival* with Fredbjorn Bjornsen. They were an adorable couple. She must have been somewhat older and was a dainty little blond Danish doll. He was her boyish and adoring suitor. They also did *Coppélia* together, I was told, and I could imagine her impersonating the doll and he as Frantz, the village boy who falls in love with her.

"Perky" was the key word for the Danish Ballet. And cute guys. The women were pretty, but except for Inge Sand, they had no real zip. Whereas the guys had all the zip you could ever ask for. This company had been founded by the famous Bournonville, who had been trained in Paris, around the turn of the nineteenth century.

I read later that he and one of his pals used to practice with one of them playing the violin and the other improvising madly around the room. Dancers who hoped to teach had to play the violin also, as they demonstrated the steps to their own playing. They often earned their livings teaching ballroom dancing to wealthy folks' kids and probably the wealthy folks themselves. Even poor Taglioni ended up this way, after being heaped with jewels by the Czar and living on Lake Como in great style with her husband, the count. Probably a no-account count, as she eventually lost it all and wound up in London teaching people to waltz and do the schottische. The polka, too, I suppose.

Anyway. Bournonville favored male dancers, and his training primarily had to do with jumping, doing beats—all the bravura male stuff. Which is why that company has all those exciting guys leaping their way into your heart, while the pretty women sort of noodle their way around as second-class citizens.

So that was the Danish Ballet. Charming ballets we hadn't seen before, pretty people, and those thrilling, jumping, handsome guys. It taught me a lot. I'd never before seen a company that wasn't dominated by a ballerina and lots of *Swan Lake* and *Sleeping Beauty*. They did do one three-act ballet, which had to do with a kingdom under the sea, but it went on interminably and I think was a revival of some famous thing that had been done in the late nineteenth century. It *was* very Victorian, and they didn't do it again, once they realized the public was far more interested in those leaping boys. Essentially, this company was something else altogether.

We hadn't seen the last of them, either. Fredbjorn Bjornsen was around town a lot for the next few years staging some of the Danish ballets. And Stanley Williams, with such an un-Danish name, finally came over and established himself as a teacher. He taught Edward Villella from the New York City Ballet. There was a lot of talk that he had fallen in love with Villella, but then, who wouldn't have? Such a sexy guy. Such a sexy body.

As soon as the Danish Ballet season ended, the Met season began, and I was thrown into my new life. And my new loves. I was excited but I wasn't a sap. Which was lucky for me.

The Met

It was wonderful working at the old Met. They tore it down, you know. It was the last desecration. They were planning to tear down Carnegie Hall when they came to their senses.

Time-wise it wasn't so ancient. The building wasn't a hundred years old, I suppose, when I was there. The stage looked like it had a million nails punched into it and pulled out again. We used to laugh at Alexandra Danilova, who was still dancing, and the way she had of tiptoeing out on stage studying the floor in front of her as she came out. We always said she was looking for a good place to dance. At the Metropolitan Opera it wasn't such a bad idea. That stage floor was rugged.

Anyway, to bring you up to speed: I had auditioned for the Met. I had been accepted by the Met. Now I was a dancer at the Met. Living alone on Sixteenth Street, seventeen years old.

I hardly ever wore real clothes. I struggled out of my cold-water flat in a pair of corduroy pants and a gray sweater every morning. Got on the subway at the Eighteenth Street entrance.

We called it the Seventh Avenue Subway. The names IRT and the IND never really sank in. We were never going to Queens anyway. Alfred, one of my new friends at the opera, was asked if he had ever been to Canarsie on the Fourteenth Street shuttle. He said, "No, but I hear it is very beautiful." He told me he had

55

one cardinal rule: "Never go anywhere you can't get home by subway." He made that rule after waking up in a taxi in the Bronx wearing pink panties and a cross. And he was Jewish.

The subway stations were Twenty-third Street, Twenty-eighth Street, Thirty-fourth Street, and Forty-second Street. The Forty-second Street station had an exit right at the stage door of the Met. Fortieth and Seventh. Right by the fruit stand. You bought an apple and rushed in the door right there. A jolly-looking man sat by the stage door. I never learned his name, he never learned mine. He knew I was one of the dancers. I'm sure that anyone with an air of self-confidence could have raced through the stage door at any time.

Straight back was the elevator. Room for four, six maybe at a squeak. The elevator was old and shaky, with a lightbulb right in the middle of it. The ballet school and rehearsal room were on the sixth floor.

The stars had their dressing rooms directly off the stage. The dancers' dressing rooms were on the third floor, on the other side of the stage, but we didn't go there unless we were performing.

Usually we walked up to the sixth floor because the elevator was so slow. The halls were stacked with wicker trunks with costumes from ancient productions: *Lakmé, The Girl of the Golden West, Thaïs, The Flying Dutchman*. The names of the operas were stenciled on the sides of the baskets none too neatly, operas that hadn't been performed in years.

The first time I walked up the last short flight of stairs, behind the mirrors and up onto the strange high walkway that ran along one side of the room under the window, I recognized it immediately. I had seen an old photograph of Pavlova in rehearsal. She was wearing one of those very full tulle tutus, a bodice with puff sleeves, the neckline gathered with a ribbon, and her hair plastered down over her ears with another ribbon. The photo had been taken right there. Right in front of a slightly tilted big mirror with a battered gilt frame. She was in that fourth position dancers always fall into, knees back, feet flat. It was the very same mirror still standing there in its huge gilded frame. I can imagine Pavlova looking into it and saying, "Look, tonight I'm only going to do a double pirouette at this point in my solo. I'm tired." What do you suppose she spoke? French, probably. Maybe she learned some English in all her touring. She lived in England in Golders Green, where everyone Jewish lived. She was Jewish. I wonder if she ever thought about it. It's not the sort of thing a dancer would think about very much, not when you're longing to have a piece of cake and knowing you can't.

God, it was exciting. Me, dancing right where Pavlova had. Nijinsky, too. He did *Tyl Eulenspiegel* at the Met when he was on the American tour. Diaghilev, the company impresario and Nijinsky's lover, was afraid to go on the tour because a fortune-teller had told him he would die on the water. So he never crossed the ocean and sent Nijinsky with the dreaded Romola when the company went on a second tour to South America. She was Hungarian and a terrible dancer. He was Russian. When they married in Rio, they couldn't speak a word to each other. And this was where Nijinsky had rehearsed *Tyl Eulenspiegel*. A ballet no one ever does now. It just lives on in those grainy, browny pictures they loved to take in those days.

I know my ballets. Belle-Mère had *Beaumont's Book of Ballets* and I read about every one of them. I'm a good student. Maybe too good. I can't help learning from my mistakes.

On our first day, Zachary Solov gave us a little pep talk. He didn't introduce the dancers to each other. Obviously a lot of them were in the company already and knew each other well. There were only about half a dozen of us, the new dancers, in a company of maybe thirty-two altogether. Eighteen girls and fourteen boys. (We were "girls" and "boys." No one talked about "women" and "men.")

In his pep talk, Zachary Solov told us that the Met had agreed to an evening of ballets as part of the repertoire. Perhaps we would do *Les Sylphides,* and certainly a new ballet of his own devising but, for the time being we would rehearse the ballet from

57

Faust. I gathered that Mr. Solov had choreographed this as a guest artist the previous season and that most of the dancers already knew it.

As soon as we started rehearsals, I got the picture pretty clearly. The opera company was divided into real dancers and not real dancers. Some of the not real dancers were very nice-looking, but when you got close you realized they weren't very young anymore.

Among the real dancers was a redhead named Maggie. A real Maggie: all common sense and grit. Maggie could really dance, and she was strong. I knew I was going to like her.

And there was Joy. Joy was brunet and kind of lavish-looking. At first glance I thought she might be a not real dancer, but she surprised me. She could really whack out those pirouettes and beats.

There was Anne Thatcher, also very good technically. Like me, infatuated with dancing itself.

One fantastic-looking Russian girl had incredible legs and an incredible head. What is it with those Russians? That long neck, the kind of square head with a long-nosed profile finished off with a strong, wide jaw, and those tippy-tilty eyes. Not to mention those slippery, curvy legs. Not straight but really curvy, with super-curvy feet. One look at those legs and feet and you knew straight off where *Swan Lake* came from. Her name was Asia. Pronounced like a Southerner saying "I see you"–"Ah see ya." Quite exotic. I was going to have to keep my eye on her to see if she could really dance.

There were also Nancy and Luellen and several other little baubles in blond and brunet. Very pretty; pretty bodies. I came to think Zachary Solov was a genius for using those people so they actually looked like they could dance.

The boys fell into the same two categories. Clifford and the other Harry were nice-looking: dark brunet, light blond. But I don't think they ever went to class—didn't want anyone to see what they couldn't do. There was Don, the bodybuilder. He told me once, "When I see myself in the mirror I start to get a hard-on." That says everything, doesn't it? Steve was his counterpart. Imagine Jack LaLanne doing double tours en l'air. Pretty trippy.

There was a cocky kid named Tony, who wasn't a bad dancer. He was Italian and wanted to be a choreographer. I guess he thought that once he wasn't a dancer anymore, people would stop conjecturing that maybe he was queer.

There was Alfred, my new friend, who resembled Jean Cocteau and had the most splendid feet I have ever seen on a human being. He was a particular favorite of Miss Craske's. Perhaps his 1920s looks brought it all back to her.

There was Siegfried Ilquist, the Norwegian god. Illy wasn't the greatest dancer on earth, but he had a superb dancer's body. The first time I saw him in the dressing room stripping his dance belt off that fantastic body, I felt something zing through me. Can a person be in lust? I don't think I was in love with him, but he was the first man I ever pursued. I slept with him many times and I never didn't feel like it. That has to say *something* for the power of beauty and lust.

And then there was Rex Ames. The bad boy of ballet. Rex could really dance. He was certainly our best male dancer. Black leather, Elvis Presley pompadour and all. Sex on a stick, that was Rex. He was very hot. Everybody wanted to sleep with him and everybody did. He ignored me, thank God.

And why not? I was just this green kid from Chicago. Some technique. A hard worker. A ballet teacher's delight. I was called "the White Virgin" around the dressing room very shortly. Later, Rex Ames said to me in a fit of bad temper, "You always reminded me of Grace Kelly. And that is not a compliment."

In the Dressing Room

I was riding around with Tennessee Williams in Key West and he didn't want to fuck me. I said, 'Tennessee, pull over.' " Someone named Robby was staring into the mirror putting gummy mascara on his upper lashes as he talked. Siegfried Ilquist was sitting next to Robby, studying his own face in the mirror. I had just come in. Siegfried looked at me in the mirror and said, "You're over there," gesturing with the back of his head at the long table on the other side of the room. My new pal Alfred was already there, looking at a jar of greasepaint with an unhappy look on his face. I had to admire Siegfried's take on makeup. He just had on light pancake and a line over and under his eyes. No Sophia Loren doe-eyes look for him. He stood up. He was just wearing a dance belt. Some ass.

I went over and sat down next to Alfred. "You don't have to put that stuff on," I said. "Where'd you get it? That drugstore in Times Square?" I picked it up. "Leichner's. It's too messy. I'll let you borrow my Max Factor No. 22, and you can get some tomorrow. It's a lot easier. That Leichner stuff gets all over everything. If you have to lift somebody, it's everywhere except on your face." I had learned about Max Factor in summer stock.

Robby said, "I make up for the first two rows. Fuck the rest of them."

A voice from somewhere said, "Well, you've certainly tried."

Robby swept out haughtily. Over his shoulder he said, "I never sleep *down*."

As he left, someone else said, "What a little cunt."

Siegfried said, "Oh, his heart is in the right place."

The voice in the back of the dressing room—it was probably smart-aleck Tony Compostella—said, "Yeah, but his cock isn't."

Everyone laughed.

We were doing *Faust*, and Mattiwilda Dobbs was singing. I could hear her on the intercom. Really nice voice. I was beginning to learn something about singing, too. We were in rehearsal for *La Gioconda*—the Dance of the Hours. A real ballet. Zinka Milanov was singing the lead, with Leonard Warren. They called her the Queen of the Met. She was everything you think is ridiculous in an opera singer—big, old, and she never moved. But when she was having a good night, her voice was more beautiful than anyone else's. That's what we'd been doing today. Tonight was *Faust*, which was easy. More like folk-dancing. We wore knee britches, leaving the boys like Robby no chance to show off their ass.

Faust had already started downstairs. We weren't on until the second scene, so we had a longer break after our last class. Siegfried came over to our table and stood behind us. "What are you guys doing when we're done here?" he said. "Want to go to Tad's Steak House for something to eat?" He was already in his knee britches. We didn't have to experience those powerful thighs in the dressing-table mirror. Alfred and I looked at each other. "Why not?" I said. Alfred and I would have probably gone to the Bickford's cafeteria right behind the theater anyway. Alfred lived with his parents on the Lower East Side in a housing project, but they were used to his being out wandering around in Manhattan for half the night. Alfred had just graduated from the High School of the Performing Arts and he'd been out on the streets of the city for years. Elegant and slightly dazed, but knowledgeable. I think everyone thought he was a foreigner.

After the performance, neither of us said anything about

Siegfried's invitation. Obviously, he was interested in one of us. Maybe both of us. Robby walked behind us towards the dressing-room door. In a very good imitation of Bette Davis, he said, "Tad's Steak House—what a dump," and vanished out the door.

It wasn't that bad. It had blinking lightbulbs outside surrounding the name. It was right on Forty-second Street, in among all those sleazy movie houses with all the action in the balconies. (How does one know this stuff so fast? I don't know. But one does, like osmosis.)

Tad's looked like a bar, but they did have a steak and a large baked potato and salad for $3.98. Can't beat that. In the few weeks we'd been working, Alfred and I usually had Salisbury steak at the cafeteria. Sometimes we went to a White Castle for those little hamburgers, but usually that was even beneath us, and we didn't go there very often. Only sometimes on a Saturday, between shows, when we did two shows.

"I'm choreographing a modern-dance piece for the Ninety-second Street Y and I thought maybe I could get you guys to be in it," Siegfried said after we got our steaks out of the way. We had all decided to spend another thirty-five cents on apple pie à la mode. Alfred actually wanted rice pudding, but that wasn't in the Tad's repertoire. Or his favorite, prune pockets. Tad's wasn't kosher.

"When would we rehearse?" I wanted to know.

"Sundays. Joy said she'd work in it. There'd just be the four of us. It's a Young Choreographers Night in December. I figure we can get it together in about eight rehearsals. Long ones. I know exactly what I want to do. I'm just going to do it to the sound of falling rain."

"Do you *have* the sound of falling rain recorded?" Alfred inquired politely. I think his mother must have been reading Virginia Woolf when she was pregnant with him. He always looked and talked like a Sitwell at a tea party somewhere. "Perhaps you should use Chopin. You know, many people think George Sand

62

fucked Chopin to death. He weighed hardly a hundred pounds, even in good health." We didn't know that. Alfred went on, "Do you ever have the impression that life is something like climbing a mountain in the fog? You know, one of those days when the sun is shining through the fog so it's all bright and white and you can see where you're going right around you, but no further? Something like a Caspar David Friedrich painting." Siegfried and I looked at each other. Neither of us had ever heard of Caspar David Friedrich. I admired Alfred for striking out so boldly without considering whether Siegfried would be interested in his sudden riff on life.

Siegfried was a real professional. How old was he? Twenty-two? Twenty-four? Older. Very glamorous, very sure of himself, and very sexy. He was all that. Blonds aren't usually very sexy, but he was sort of a bigger, stronger Erik Bruhn who looked like he might really like to fuck. That's not so common among Scandinavians, you know.

"You're climbing with other people and you just assume they know where they're going," Alfred continued. "But maybe they don't. Maybe you're walking along the edge of a precipice. Maybe they'll disappear into the fog and leave you alone."

"That's a good idea for my piece," Siegfried said. "I think that's what I'll do. By the end I'll be all alone. My idea is that Joy and I will be lovers and you two will be aspects of myself."

Which aspects, was what I wanted to know.

"Harry will sort of be my happy, eager, childlike side. And you will be my doubting, depressed side," he said to Alfred.

Alfred said, "I love my role already. Did I get the depressed side because I'm brunet? And Harry got the happy side because he's blond?"

"No," Siegfried said. "Because you're taller. Besides, how could Harry play the depressed person?"

"Oh, you should see him when he can't get his pirouettes to the left," Alfred said. "He can be suicidal."

"You guys are fun," Siegfried said. "Let's get out of here." I wondered what was so fun about me. I hadn't said ten words all evening. "Where do you go?" Siegfried wanted to know.

"Alfred goes downtown on the Broadway local. I take the Seventh Avenue down to Eighteenth Street," I said.

"Oh, good, I'll go along with you." Underground, Alfred scuttled off towards his platform and Siegfried and I walked over to the Seventh Avenue local track.

Nothing brings back my past like the subway stations in New York. High-rises come and go, but the subway is as unchangeable as the Pyramids. That night on the Seventh Avenue local platform must have been exactly like the first night the station opened. Maybe not the first night, but about a week later. In the 1920s? Gloomy lights, gum ground into the cement platform, the tile on the walls across the tracks already greasy, and that smell of hot metal in the air. It was like that the night Siegfried and I stood there, two blonds, about the same height. Brothers, maybe. Dance bags slung over our shoulders. "We're just going to wear practice clothes," Siegfried was saying about his dance. "Maybe street clothes. Maybe just like the clothes we're wearing. No set. This new guy, Tom Skelton, said he'd do the lighting for me free."

If I were to take the subway this very evening and get off at Forty-second Street, it would be exactly the same as it was that night. Siegfried may be dying at St. Vincent's. Me with my doctor's bag instead of a dance bag. But there would be the same gray light, gray smell, and battered gray cement on the station platform. Only the black man playing the drum made out of a big oilcan would be different.

Siegfried got off with me at the Eighteenth Street station. "Do you live around here?" I asked him. "No, actually I live in Queens, but I thought I'd walk you home. Maybe come up and talk for a little while." Home run, Siegfried. Your plans for your modern-dance piece got me completely off guard. I was very excited. Was I going to be in bed with that great Scandinavian body yet tonight? Feeling those smooth chest muscles? Running my hands down over that flat, flat stomach? Maybe being kissed with those curved lips, just like a statue's?

Siegfried didn't like to kiss, it turned out.

Siegfried walked into my cold-water flat, looked around, and said, "I think I'll stay overnight. You don't mind, do you? It's a long way out to Queens. You've got two beds." I guess I mumbled something. Siegfried didn't want to have a cup of coffee. He asked for a glass of water. And started undressing in the little bedroom where Belle-Mère used to sleep. I went into the kitchen and brushed my teeth and when I came back Siegfried was in the double bed. He didn't have anything on. I could see his underpants on the chair—Jockey shorts. I undressed, trying to be nonchalant. As nonchalant as you can be with a hard-on.

Siegfried didn't say anything. He was just lying there with his eyes closed and a smile on his face. He had that kind of Attic smile—turned up a little bit on the corners, like the smile you see on the faces of those early Greek statues. They're amused, but you don't know what about. Probably at how easy I was. At least he wasn't looking at my hard-on.

As soon as I got into bed, wearing pajamas, Siegfried opened his eyes, reached over and turned out the light, and reached over for me. "Let's get you out of those things," he said, unbuttoning my pajamas. When he felt my hard-on, he said, "We'll have to do something about that." I felt for his penis. It was up and felt very big, circumcised. That was good. (I've never liked uncircumcised penises. Like eating endive.) "Why don't you poge me and then I'll poge you," he said once he got me undressed. I had just lain there, pulling my feet up when he pulled my pajama pants off.

I didn't say anything, but just pulled him on top of me. He fitted his penis between my legs. "Not romantic enough for you, huh?" he said. It felt good. Large. He pressed into me. I put my

65

arms around his neck and kissed him. I felt like kissing him. His mouth was sort of dry and he didn't open his lips. He pressed into me again and I came.

"Sorry," I said. "I guess I'm just overexcited at being in bed with you."

"It's okay—it's kind of flattering. Got any cards?" I did, actually. Belle-Mère and Levoy and I used to play hearts a lot. I reached over and turned on the lights and got out of bed to get them.

"Nice ass," Siegfried said.

"Same to you."

We sat on the bed with nothing on and Siegfried taught me how to play gin rummy. I never had before. "It's getting late and we have to rehearse *La Traviata* tomorrow," I said. "What's to rehearse?" he said. "And we're young. We'll be fine if we don't get any sleep at all."

Which is pretty much what happened. I was laying my cards out in front of Siegfried, sitting cross-legged on the bed, and I noticed he had a half-hard-on. So I laid the cards right down in his crotch and leaned over and slipped my mouth over it, in among all the cards. "Oh, hey," he said, and leaned over backwards onto the bed, his winkie just popping right up among the cards. Did you ever notice how the penis fits so exactly right into the mouth? Perhaps you haven't.

Before we got done, those cards had pretty well had it. (I tried to iron some of them out a few days later, but they were pretty crushed up.) He finally came between my legs. I was afraid of that big engine of his. Really big. Is that a Scandinavian thing? I never heard that it was. I came at the same time he did. Just from him flailing around on top of me. It can happen. "Hold me very tight," I said in his ear and he did. He did, and then we slept for a while, all sticky. Then we got up and took a bath together in that funny tub in the kitchen with the lift-up lids. I don't know what got into me, but I pushed him down on the daybed when we were going back towards the bedroom and gave him a blow job. I guess I felt like I couldn't get through the whole next day

66

without having sex again. One more time just to hold me for a while. He enjoyed it a lot and kept running his hands through my hair.

"Nice hair," he said in a dreamy kind of way.

"Mmmmm . . . bummm . . . mmmmm," I said.

And then he came all over the place. Sexually he was kind of a lavish guy in every way.

On the subway back to the opera house that morning, he told me that he lived in Queens with someone who was a clerk at Bloomingdale's. They had been lovers last year. Last year was Siegfried's first year at the opera. He was from Minneapolis and had been trained by the Esterhazys there. He said his roommate wasn't his lover anymore. "Oh, well, once in a while," he said.

"Do you want to move in with me?" I said. I had fallen in love with Siegfried for the moment. You know how it is. Somebody good-looking pops it to you and you think this is it for life. Many a marriage has gotten off the ground just that way, I'm sure.

"Oh, no. I'm fine where I am. But we'll have lots of fun this winter, I promise you." He reached over and patted my knee. When we walked up the subway stairs, he fell behind me and reached up and grabbed my crotch from behind between my legs and gave me a reassuring squeeze. That was Illy Ilquist's gesture of affection.

I was glad it all happened with Illy so soon after my mother left. I had someone to be close to, even if it was Illy's rather cool idea of closeness.

Robby gave us quite a look as we came into the dressing room. I just ignored him. The stage manager came in and said, "Callas wants two boys to escort her in for the first party scene in *La Traviata.* She said she wanted the two blonds. I guess she meant you guys—Illy and the new kid. What's your name?"

"Harry," I said. "The new Harry."

And that's what they called me that season: "the new Harry." Thank God they didn't call the other one "the old Harry." He was blond, too, and I'm sure would have worked with Illy if I hadn't been on the scene. But he was always nice to me.

Robby wasn't. As we headed out to go down to the stage, he said, "Oh, those tall, bad-tempered blonds. They always get everything their way, and we short brunets just get our brains fucked out."

"You should be so lucky," Tony said.

It's curious, Tony showed up in my office a year or so ago. While we were at the opera, he had decided he wanted to be called Antonio, and for some reason people actually did. He recognized me. "You used to dance at the opera, didn't you? Just for two seasons, as I remember. I'm still there in the new house. I'm old as hell. Which doesn't seem to matter. I must have had a yard of cock in me in the last two weeks. I've got this really shitty cold."

He was rather admiring of the fact that I had become a doctor. "You shouldn't have quit dancing, though. You were good. Didn't Balanchine want you at the New York City Ballet? I seem to remember that."

He was right. They did want me, sort of. At least they were interested. But I didn't want them.

He looked around my examining room. "Do you ever fuck anybody here in the office?" he said. "Get them right up on that examining table and sock it to them?"

"I don't, but what a good idea," I said. I didn't say anymore, in case he thought I was coming on to him. We said good-bye and I never saw him again. I guess he got over his cold. Of course, it could have been early symptoms of AIDS. I hope not. I never go to the opera, so I've no idea if he's still in the company or not.

Norma and Other Operas

J ust come right over here, Mary, and hit this gong," Dino
Yannopoulos said. He was talking to Maria Callas. They were
both Greek, and I guess he must have known her in her previous
life as Mary Somebody from Brooklyn. Maria didn't cotton very
much to being called Mary. She was very fine now and was getting what the dancers called "high tits" from having to hit a gong
in the third act of *Norma.*

"I can't do this with all these people watching me," she said im-
periously. She *was* imperious in her new nonfat incarnation. Very
thin and tall, with a head like one of those figures on the early
Greek vases. All nose and eyes. "There will be just as many people on the stage when you do this next Thursday," Dino said.

She repeated herself. "I can't do this with all these people
watching me," she said again. Have you ever noticed that stars do
not enter into dialogues with people? What you have to say is
not important. They just repeat themselves until they get their
own way.

"Okay, everybody, back into the wings," Dino said. "You're
not on stage yet in this scene." There were about one hundred of
us on the stage with the chorus, the dancers, the extras, and the
rest of the cast. Fedora Barbieri was already in the wings. She was
shorter, squatter, and had a very reliable voice. She knew what

69

she had to put up with and what she didn't, as far as Callas was concerned.

We all went into the wings. We weren't really in costume, but some people were wearing Druid helmets with horns on them. *Norma* takes place in France in the time of the Druids. How's that for an unlikely plot location? Was Mario del Monaco the Roman centurion? I think so. He was very handsome, with a large, hovering prison-matron of a wife.

"I can't do this with all these people watching me," we heard Miss Callas repeat. There was a very long silence. There wasn't any real battle of the wills. She was the one with the big mallet in her hands. She was the one that had to hit the gong.

"All right, everybody. Go into the halls," the director called out. There were narrow halls leading off on each side of the stage. We obediently packed our bodies into the halls, trying to avoid getting our eyes gouged out by the horned helmets. On the other side of the closed door we heard some feeble sounds of the gong. "Norma is calling the Druids to her aid," Alfred said in my ear.

"That's us, I think," I said.

"Well, let's go aid her," he said as the door was flung open, and we all poured back onto the stage.

As the rehearsal ended and we left the stage, we saw a woman in a pink suit with a strange kind of pink stovepipe hat tilted on her head and an immobile, masklike face standing on the step that led to the star's dressing rooms. "That's Marlene Dietrich," Alfred said. He seemed to always be hovering somewhere near my ear. The figure looked more like a life-size Marlene Dietrich doll.

"Are you sure?" I asked him.

"It's the hat," he said. "Only Marlene would wear a hat like that. Would dare to wear a hat like that."

Maria Callas greeted her. They kissed on both cheeks and disappeared towards her dressing room.

"I guess they're going to have lunch," I said.

"I don't think they're going to bump pussies," Siegfried said into my other ear. "I never heard that about Maria."

As we went up to the dressing room, he told me that when Marlene was first in Hollywood she was having affairs with Gary Cooper and Maurice Chevalier at the same time, which neither of them objected to. But when she added Mercedes de Acosta, a Hollywood personality, to the mix, they drew the line. So she told both of them they could go fly a kite and hung out with Mercedes. That improved her standing with me.

That evening Siegfried said, "When I first came to New York, I was walking down Sixth Avenue at night and I looked across the street and there was Marlene Dietrich and Noël Coward, just walking along. He was wearing white tie and tails, she was wearing a long white gown and white fox. I thought, This is it. This is why I'm here. A town where Dietrich and Coward walk down the street and nobody even turns around to look."

"Oh, Illy, I love you so much," I said.

"Well, I want to thank you," he said.

He was lying on his back with his legs spread around my waist. I was kneeling between them, masturbating him. He had his arms behind his head and was good-humoredly regarding the wonder of his own cock. It took two hands.

It turned out that Illy really liked a long massage session finishing with me masturbating him. Sort of worshiping at the shrine of his penis. It was sort of worth worshiping.

He loved bodies. He said to me once, when my legs were on either side of his head, "I could never get used to men who don't have nice feet."

Sometimes when Siegfried and I were having our sex sessions he would want to have me slide my penis into him as I knelt between his legs. "Don't move," he would order. He certainly enjoyed his own orgasms, running his hands over his body and pressing down around the base of his penis. Once a friend called while we were in the middle of one of our sessions and I talked and then sucked his cock while I listened to my friend rattle on. This made Illy uneasy that the person on the other end of the line would hear slurping. "He wouldn't know it was you," I told him when I hung up.

He had something with his brother, because once we had flung ourselves onto the floor while I was working him over and his brother called and Siegfried took it. He got really hard while I was sucking on him and he was talking to his brother. Makes you think, doesn't it? All these little clues that no one ever pieces together.

We were having an afternoon off and we were at my place. They were setting up the stage for *Aida,* so we couldn't rehearse on it. The sets for *Aida* were so enormous that they couldn't get them all into the theater. There were giant two-story doors on the back of the theater and the second- and third-act sets were left on the street while the first act was being set up. Which meant that whatever the temperature was out on Seventh Avenue was the temperature on the stage.

In the winter, it was so cold that the dancers in the triumphal scene were allowed to stay in their dressing rooms until time to go. We had so little on they called us "the Sex Squad." Both Illy and I were in the Sex Squad. The best bodies were chosen, because all you wore was a tiny bikini, body paint, a headdress, and a lot of bracelets. The girls had a little bra top, too.

That night we sat in the dressing room, bright orange with body paint and naked, until we heard Stanley, the stage manager, shout "Sex Squad" down the hallway, and out we came. We always liked Stanley the best of the stage managers. A slight little dark-haired guy with contact lenses. He always looked at you with his head tipped back, the light glinting off his contacts, trying to get you in focus. One of the other stage managers was an always confused man of vague foreign origin who wore a wig with the net hairline attachment clearly in view. Alfred angered

72

him one day by cutting a strip of netting and gluing it along his own abundant, natural hairline and walking ostentatiously in front of him.

Then there was Patrick, the younger, red-haired manager, who always projected that he was too good for this job. He was probably right. He was sort of good-looking and that never hurt at the Met. Patrick was much too dignified to shout "Sex Squad" down a corridor. He would have come to the door of the dressing room and said quietly, "You're on."

There was always something wonderful going on at the Met. Because we did repertory, we were always rehearsing something new; there were always new stars appearing for rehearsals. Lily Pons was one of the most exotic. It was her last season, and she was fitting in her rehearsals with her busy life as a socialite. She was married to André Kostelanetz and was a BIG star and had been a big star for many years. We were fascinated as she always showed up for rehearsals in couture dresses and furs and all her jewels. She was really major-league.

I wasn't in *Lucia di Lammermoor*, but I was passing the stage late one morning when she was rehearsing. Miss Pons was getting irritated, waiting at the head of the staircase for her entrance in the third act—the mad scene, as if you didn't know. She waited, dressed for lunch in a navy-blue dress, lots of jewelry, and that famous turned-under pageboy bob. She still looked as she had for years in the magazines and newspapers. Belle-Mère would have been thrilled. The rehearsal had been seriously dragging on.

Maestro Stiedry seemed to be only interested in the chorus that day. They would rage up to Lucia's entrance and then he would tap his stand, stop the orchestra, and ask the chorus to do it all over again. They had done this about twenty times. Miss Pons was looking at her Cartier watch, tapping the toe of her high-heeled Bally pumps.

Suddenly the chorus got themselves all worked up, the orchestra didn't stop and swept into Miss Pons's entrance. She appeared at the head of the great stairs, paused a moment, and started down. Maestro Stiedry tapped his baton, stopped the orchestra, and said, "Mees Pons, Mees Pons, what are you doing? You are singing the Bell Song from *Lakmé*!" She glared at him and said, "After all, Maestro, I am mad!" And rushed towards the stage door, grabbing up her mink from a chair as she ran.

Neighbors

The only break from rehearsing, performing, and fucking seemed to be parties. When I look back, there were always lots of parties going on. Impromptu parties, beer-drinking or wine-drinking parties. I don't even really remember a lot of drinking going on. Lots of smoking, though. Dancers always smoked a lot, to keep from feeling like eating. At the old opera house there were always red-painted buckets full of sand sitting about where people could douse their cigarettes.

I had neighbors on Sixteenth Street who were frequent party-givers. Bill and Dave. Bill was blond and a painter. Dave was dark and wrote plays. They seemed thrillingly professional to me, so self-assured in their careers. Bill did work practically full-time as a temporary secretary to support himself and Dave. Dave didn't do much but sit about looking like a cross between Humphrey Bogart and John Huston.

Bill and Dave were from the University of Texas and all their friends were from the same school. They had all known Jayne Mansfield there and were astounded at where her bosom had carried her. Evidently she had graduated summa cum laude. Something she learned in Texas must have kicked in when she hit Hollywood. Cathy Crosby had been in their class, too. She opted to marry Bing Crosby and get out of the running completely. They seemed to envy her slightly more than Jayne.

I thought they were all terribly interesting and exciting. I had read *My Sister Eileen* and expected New York to be full of strange people and strange goings-on. I was never very fond of campiness and the kind of Tallulah Bankhead–style bitchery that was social life in the dancers' dressing room at the opera, but I loved the kind of wild and rowdy evenings at Bill and Dave's. I suppose it was what I imagined bohemianism was going to be like, and it was.

Bill and Dave were what they now call "out," and nobody they knew cared in the slightest. They evidently had been completely out at the university, had lived together, and nobody cared there, either. They had a beautiful, voluptuous friend named Nora, whom everyone expected to become a big star. There was a couple named Ted and Valerie. Ted did make it later. I saw him on Broadway in that Tommy Steele musical. What the hell was it called? *A Pocket Full of Sixpence*? *Half a Sixpence*? Who knows? It was terrible. Valerie was ahead of her time. She looked something like Demi Moore. A desperate Demi Moore. She was the only one that usually got very drunk and sang, "He May Be Good Fucking but He's No Fucking Good." I always thought she was sort of desperate because hubby wasn't good fucking. How should I know? It can't be any fun hanging around with a crowd of homosexuals who are getting theirs good and proper and at very regular intervals when you're not. Probably feels very unfair.

Bill and Dave had an open relationship. Could they have called it that? Probably not, but they both slept around a lot. Dave more than Bill. I think Bill would have liked Dave to stay home and sleep just with him, but Dave had a kind of drinkin'-and-smokin' Hemingway-style manliness about him that also, I suppose, required a lot of screwin'. The homosexual Hemingway. Or Norman Mailer. There's certainly plenty of them around.

Dave told me once that it was best to have six lovers that you were sleeping with regularly. That way, when one of them dropped you, he really wasn't missed all that much. You could replace him by going out trawling the streets regularly. Dave liked to trawl the streets. Greenwich Avenue, in the Village, and Third Avenue were the big cruising grounds in those days. Dave told me that Washington Square Park on the west side along the railing had been the big pickup area when Bill and he first came to town a few years before. The men just sat along the iron-pipe fence on that side of the park, their heels hooked over the lower railing. Others would patrol up and down looking for what was good. That was the origin of the expression "the Meat Rack." There it all was, bulging out of worn denims, and not even for sale. It was being given away.

I never did that. It always seemed so embarrassing, going to bed with someone you didn't know. Like, wait a minute . . . where did you go to school? How old are you? What's your favorite ice cream? All that stuff. No wonder those guys were always hungry, when they skipped to the dessert right away. Just think, you might meet Mr. Right, hop in the sack with him, and he's gone and you never even knew it. Just another one-night stand. I think they all come to that conclusion after a while.

Of the men I've known who were the most sexually active, it seems to correlate with how successful they were in other areas of their lives. When they haven't got much else going on, they seem to pride themselves on their fucking. Just fucking one person very often doesn't count. It has to be a lot of different people. It's not so much being famous or powerful or rich, it's more how busy you are in some area of your life and how much you like it that keeps you off the streets. As long as you're doing something you like regularly, you don't seem to be compelled to boff every other stranger who comes along.

I think Dave secretly suspected that his writing plays was going nowhere, was not going to go anywhere, and that sitting around in a cold-water flat on Sixteenth Street letting Bill support him wasn't exactly making it. So he felt like fucking a lot. Have I stumbled on some kind of new sex motivation that has nothing to do with testosterone?

At the parties Bill and Dave gave they frequently lit their little string of rooms with candles. The shadows seemed brown and gold, rather than black. In the bedroom that you passed through to get to the living room, the wall you walked by was covered with many small wooden frames filled with photos of their idols and icons, people like Greta Garbo and Marlene Dietrich and Thomas Mann and Eugene O'Neill and John Barrymore and the Lunts and Noël Coward and George Gershwin. Sarah Bernhardt wasn't there, but Eleonora Duse was. Of course, I knew hardly any of these people. I had to have them identified and explained to me. Ethel Merman wasn't there—they weren't fans of commercial Broadway theater—but Lupe Velez was. The Mexican Spitfire. The actress that picked up Gary Cooper after Clara Bow dropped him and, after committing suicide, was buried wearing a wedding dress. She was supposedly pregnant at the time. Is all this possible? Probably not, but Bill and Dave admired her "work," as they called it. I wonder if she called it that.

Then, after this cave of flickering shadows over the dim faces of the glamorous great of the theater and movies, there was a warm, noisy room full of good-looking people who all liked you, who were glad you were there, who laughed a lot, cussed a lot, and said wild things people never said in Michigan.

One of the neighbors was a fat boy from Texas who'd known Bill and Dave at school. He had taken an upstairs apartment on the top floor—the same one Belle-Mère and Levoy had for a while. I used to go see him by going up to the roof and crossing

78

over and going down the stairs. The front doors and roof doors were always open and people roamed freely about. The fat boy's name was Nick. He worked as an assistant to Helen Menken. I think he worked for her free. She had once been married to Humphrey Bogart, which counted a lot for him and for us. What he did for Helen I have no idea, but his Texas family was rich and could afford to keep him going while he found a place for himself in New York.

Nick gave parties, too, with much the same crowd of Texans that Bill and Dave invited. I used to go there sometimes after a performance. In those days, the kind of mascara we used was hard to get off. Some always stuck at the base of your lashes. Nick always accused me of not trying to get it all off, so I could arrive at his parties looking all wan and smudgy-eyed. I wasn't there trying to pick somebody up, so I don't know what he was worried about. I certainly felt wan, and I was there largely to see if there was something to eat.

Nick was a great cook, and when he awoke in the night and felt anxious, he would get up and cook an elaborate meal. Even if it was ready to go on the table at five in the morning, he would sit down and eat it. Often he would call in the night and ask me over. I was always game to eat, even in the dead of night. I did ask him to please not call me until it was ready to serve. Then I would put a raincoat on over my pajamas and climb the stairs to the roof, beaming my flashlight ahead of me, and descend to big, fat Nick, already at the table. He was like something out of Dickens: napkin tied around his neck, a knife in one hand and a fork in the other, ready to tear into whatever *cordon bleu* delight he'd concocted. We never made small talk—not at five in the morning. We just downed it; then I returned up over the roof to get a few hours' more sleep before going to the opera.

Often I took my friend April with me to parties at Bill and Dave's. April was a dancer who had been in stock at the New

Jersey theater with me. She was something like a spirited squirrel. Her name was April Orjune. She had a sister, May. She told me that her parents had absolutely no sense of humor at all but had chosen both their names without realizing that they were covering a quarter of the months in the calendar: April, May, or June. Introducing those girls at parties was always a problem. People always said things like "What's your brother's name? August?" But April and May didn't rile easily. They said things like "No, Dick," putting a lot of emphasis on the word. That was usually May, who was older and bigger and heavier and more lethal all around. She would say, "No, Dick . . . head" to the inquirer if it was a man, the "head" slightly under her breath.

I learned so much from the Orjune sisters. They were real Greenwich Village girls. The kind that must have sprung up in the early days when Edna St. Vincent Millay lived there. They took no shit. You didn't see that a lot in Michigan, either.

We were at the White Horse Tavern one night and May was seated by some man who proceeded to get drunker and drunker as he spilled out the story of his life. She sat there patiently until he said, "I don't know why I'm telling you all this, you don't even know my name." May said, "No, but it ought to be Schmuck." We left.

The Orjune sisters lived over Slongo's Garage on Hudson Street and had a large apartment for which they paid seventy dollars a month. It was filled with tables covered with letters they were planning to answer, circulars they were planning to read, and bills they were planning to pay. And they had closets, hampers, and boxes full of clothes they were planning to iron. When I had nothing better to do, I would drop in and iron. I once ironed for eight straight hours. The closets were jammed with blouses, shirts, trousers, pajamas, and skirts. I'm sure that was the only time in their occupancy over Slongo's that the ironing was ever fully done. I love to iron. All part of that female side of me, I suppose.

I don't remember Illy ever going to any of these parties with me. He would have thought they were boring and the people weren't sexy enough. Like many homosexuals, he preferred all-male parties, which I never liked all that much. Also, I don't think he wanted to parade me around in public. It would have cramped his style.

I did go to some all-male parties. I remember one party in what they call a "garden apartment" in New York—actually, a basement with a little light filtering in from the windows in the front at sidewalk level. It was after the theater and it was mostly boys from the opera. Vincent Warren was there. We were about the same age; maybe Vincent was a little bit older—a beautiful guy from Florida. I always envied him because he could do the splits very easily. I heard he was Frank O'Hara's lover later. The great thing about being a poet's lover is that you get eulogized a lot, but I don't think Vincent cared that much about being eulogized.

I supposed Vincent thought I was very inexperienced and uptight, a typical midwestern twit. He said, "What you need is to be really fucked hard by somebody like Steve." That was one of our tough-guy bodybuilders in the company. Illy was talking to somebody right beside me. I turned to him and said, "Do you think that's what I need, Illy? Do you think I need to be fucked hard by Steve?" Illy in his most Scandinavian manner stared at me as though I had gone completely out of my mind. To his credit he didn't say, "Why are you asking me?" He just turned away. But we left together and he did fuck me hard that night. Marking his territory, even if he wasn't going to say anything about it.

I don't know quite what I thought about things in those days. I guess I wanted someone to say they wanted to stay with me the rest of their life and make plans to buy a house in the suburbs and all the rest of that stuff. Nobody did then, but many guys do nowadays. But deeper down I think I knew that I didn't want that. What I wanted was to love somebody so much that where we lived and what we did really didn't matter. I was too young to wonder about what the next steps were.

How I Loved to Dance

D ance is the only thing I ever loved that wasn't another person. I *did* love it, really loved it. Now it's amazing to me that
I was able to dance and be in love with another human being at
the same time.

In comparison, being a doctor is a job, my job. It's not really
a career. *That* ended when I stopped being a dancer.

My theory is that you are only capable of really feeling, really
fully enjoying yourself for about an hour and a half per day.
That's all we really have the emotional stamina for. So the rest of
the time we might just as well keep busy. Sleep eight hours, eat
a couple of times, take a shower, and get a haircut. Chances are
that there are another eight hours left over where you might as
well work. It doesn't have to be particularly meaningful as long
as it pays the bills. Just as long as you're getting in that hour and
a half of living fully and deeply every day.

When I danced I always had my hour and a half of class to
really feel that thing. Something like Zen meditation. Just you
and your body and the music: concentrating, concentrating,
concentrating.

Miss Craske used to say in that high, fluting English voice of
hers in the ancient high-ceilinged rehearsal studio on top of the

old opera house, "Leave your problems outside the classroom, my dears. Leave your problems outside the classroom."

It was like that. You put aside whatever was bugging you and did your class. When you went back to your life, you could somehow handle things better. Perhaps they weren't solved, but you were stronger. Eventually they solve themselves, don't they? You don't solve them. Your problems just wear themselves out if you hang on long enough. You only have to make sure that by the time they do work themselves out, you are still in command of your senses and still look good.

In the studio, Helen would be at the piano wearing her green eyeshade. Everyone took a place at the barre. Shoulders square, heels together, feet turned out, eyes straight ahead, one hand on the barre, elbow relaxed, the other arm down and slightly curved. Helen played a chord on the piano and you raised your outer arm through first position, your hand moving in front of your body to your chest, out to a straight line from your shoulder, keeping that elbow up and relaxed. Down you went into plié as the music played, knees opening to the side, as low as you could go.

Miss Craske calling out: "Don't force. Don't force. Do *not* roll over on your arches. It accomplishes nothing, my dears, nothing."

And the unfolding of the pattern again. The loosening of the hip sockets, the turning out of the thighs so you can move laterally across the stage from side to side. Sort of like a Picasso, or an Egyptian fresco. The audience seeing your upper body from the front, your legs from the side, all at the same time.

Freedom, I think that is what it was all about. Freedom. Ronds de jambe, your leg pointed out so just the tip of your pointed toe touched the floor, and you make the shape of half a pie. To the front, to the side, to the back. Brush through with a flat foot past your standing heel, and around again. Then reverse it. So your hip sockets get very loose, yet your legs stay taut and strong.

And there were grands battements, your leg lifting as high as your nose in front, then high as your ears to the side, then high as your ass behind. "Do not tip forward." Miss Craske would warn, walking about to inspect our grands battements en arrière. "It accomplishes nothing, do you hear me, nothing." But we did.

We worked so hard, sweat pouring from our bodies. Stretching our muscles as much as possible; tightening them as much as possible. All so we could dart around the stage later, legs whipping front, back, lifting, lowering, yet always in complete control. Strong bodies that move fast or slow, as the legs and arms make their patterns. Heads stationary, arms moving slowly in their own separate orbits while legs did quicker, completely separate activities. All of this just so you can dance better. All of this training is not really learning to dance. This is just training the body to execute steps.

The Russian ballerina Natalia Makarova said, "Dance is not training. Dancing is something you do after you have been trained." You felt that, you felt that inside you. Inside was the urge to float through the air, turn and twist your leg high, point your feet down to make sharp, pointed shapes like arrows to lead your body through the air.

With your teacher's help, and your own concentration on which muscles did what, looking in the mirror to see if you were creating the shapes your body was capable of, you create a new body. Tight, lean, and trim. Legs made to open high and wide in any direction, arms to hold neat, fine lines extending your shoulders or framing your head.

You go to the middle of the room for "center," as they call it, after doing the barre exercises. Slow movements, standing on one foot, your supporting leg immovable as you do slow patterns with the other leg. Slowly you revolve in front of the mirror, lean forward, your leg lifted in arabesque or attitude. You bend the knee of the leg you're standing on and reach one arm forward and the raised leg back into first arabesque. Then change arms slowly into second arabesque, then slowly change legs into third arabesque. Dipping lower, stretching your body to its longest extent. Mesmerized by the fulfillment of your body's potential.

Then, finally, the last half hour of the class: the allegro section, where you are set free, your body primed and ready to fly. Pirouettes in the center, little jumps, big jumps, entrechat quatre, whipping those pointed feet back and forth as you leap into the air, back and forth, back and forth.

Miss Craske then gave us combinations of steps. Across the room on a diagonal, one by one, as Helen bent over the piano, trying to give us the surge of music to lift us even more. Stepping back, lifting your leg in front of you in a pose, looking up towards where the imperial box would be if there were any such thing, holding your pose just one moment, smiling as incandescently as you could, the Tchaikovsky races on and you lift out of your pose. Rush across the floor to catch up with the music, racing forward in a glissade, tossing your front leg sideways into the air, pulling the after one with it, ankles meeting before you land neatly, feet together in fifth position. A grande assemblée. If you're advanced enough your feet flutter back and forth in entrechats like flames flickering. From your locked-in position, feet side by side, toes pointing in opposite directions, a quick pointed toe to one side and around to the back, you're off into a perfect double (shall we say triple?) pirouette. Up on the ball of one foot, twirling around, the other foot's toes pointed and touching your knee, like a weathervane in a high and prevailing wind. And you stop . . . up! No slopping into a fourth position like a sandbag heaved into a corner. But up, perfectly placed, smiling, completely controlled. Miss Craske calls out, "A double pirouette is enough. But stay up. Let them see you. . . ." You sink down into your fourth position like a feather coming to rest. Then further, until your knee is on the floor behind you. You make a grande révérence to your invisible audience. In your head, you hear them applauding you, loving you. You rise in one movement to the ball of one foot to take a first arabesque, one arm extended in front, your leg lifted and foot pointed behind, a perfect and classic profile, you are looking into the wings. You lift leg and arm slightly as though you are about to fly away, and you are gone into the wings. In the thunder of their hands beating upon each other.

You imagine someone else appears upstage from the opposite wing. Your partner on pointe, fingers just touching the edge of the circle of her fragile, platterlike tutu skirt. The music shifts and ripples, and she's off in her own magical floating and rippling and darting around the stage.

Oh, it was wonderful. Dancing—the perfect art. Consuming itself as it happens. Leaving you only with the feeling of having seen . . . or felt . . . moments of actually doing what you once only dreamed of doing.

For it is like a dream, one of those weightless dreams, where you are hovering in the air, quickly moving here, hovering there. So much faster and lighter than an ordinary movement. Lifted by the music. It's no wonder that you become obsessed with making your body more aerodynamic, ridding it of excess weight that holds you earthbound.

This was the fantasy in class. Preparing for performance. Then imagining, in the brief moments of performing at the end of the class, that you were there: dancing in St. Petersburg or Paris or London, on stage with Karsavina or Massine or one of the baby ballerinas—Toumanova, Baronova, Riabouchinska.

I was never interested in modern dance, though we had a class in it at the opera from the beautiful Mary Hinkson. So beautiful you almost became convinced there was something in it. But none of us wanted to throw our bodies to the floor like Martha Graham, or strain our bodies up from it. We hated turning our thighs in, clenching knees together, when we had spent hours straining them apart.

We always said that modern dancers were people whose thighs were too large to do ballet. Though Mary Hinkson was there to show us differently. But there *was* something to it. The great goddess Graham never showed her legs, only outlined under tight-stretched skirts. I'm sure she had Oriental blood, with a kimono body and a Javanese princess's head.

I saw her dance in one of her last performances. Could she have been near eighty? She flung herself to the stage. I felt sick. Surely she would not rise again. But she did. Only to fling herself down again. This is not good, I thought. But it was the apogee, the pinnacle, for someone whose body loved to dance but whose legs precluded classic ballet. She had created an entire way of dancing all her own, and many followed her.

But Martha was never to know the thrill of the orchestra playing, your cue coming, and out you went, whirling and spinning through the air, only lightly touching the stage with the ball of your foot or the tip of your toe.

The Yellow Opera House and the White Virgin

If it can ever be said that one loved a building, I loved the old opera house. And it wasn't even beautiful. It was rather ugly. It was yellow for one thing, the old Metropolitan Opera. It was built of yellow brick and really didn't have an imposing facade on any one of its four sides. It was rather like Carnegie Hall in that respect. You got the feeling that the architects had decided upon all the things that had to be inside, arranged them, and then slapped brick on the outside of all these cubes and squares and horseshoes of opera boxes. There was a large flat front on Broadway that looked like one of those unfinished churches in Italy, the ones where they spent all the money on the lavish interiors and never had the money to finish the facade. The Metropolitan had a glass-topped Victorian carriage entrance along all of the ground floor of this facade, and an even more important one on the Thirty-ninth Street side. It was at the Thirty-ninth Street entrance that all the high-steppers and big spenders of the latter part of the last century arrived. There they swept in, with trains, piled-up hair, and lorgnettes. That was the women, of course. The men were in top hats, white tie, and smelling of bay rum and violet toilet water, with their hair slicked down tight and collars standing high.

You could easily imagine you were back in that past when you scurried down Fortieth Street in the late afternoon to the front of the building where we took our extra classes. We entered a door that led up to the rehearsal studios in that part of the opera house. In other studios, sopranos would be rehearsing *Così fan tutte*. The floors were covered in shiny brown linoleum, and the walls were a kind of beige that must have been customary at the turn of the century. The dark brown woodwork, the transoms above the doors, the building fairly reeking of the days of Evelyn Nesbit and the Red Velvet Swing—of brunettes in high pompadours and tight corsets, the swing of their skirts showing off a little foot, tightly booted.

This was the decor of a bygone era, still living on in the 1950s. Watching over us as we slipped off the raincoats we had flung on to run down the street, still in our ballet slippers even if the streets were wet or icy or packed with hard snow. We had little time to get ourselves around the corner from the rehearsals that ended at four o'clock and take our place at the barre for the 4:15 class.

Alfredo Corvino was our usual teacher. We all loved him. He was small and dark, solidly but beautifully built, with a classic but slightly rounded profile. And the gentlest of natures. He never raised his voice, and only when you looked hard into those eyes—so brown you couldn't even see the pupil—did you see that he was deeply amused by the pretensions and folly that flowed around him: the students and dancers, all determined to get their legs and their careers higher with every passing day, and the singers swaggering through, their legs buckling under the weight of their stomachs and their egos.

Alfredo had been slated for an important career. He was being noticed in solo roles by the critics. Then World War II started and he was drafted. When the war was over, his hopes for a career were also. He was married and had two small daughters, and he inevitably turned to teaching. There was never a clue as to whether Alfredo was disappointed in the hand the game of life had dealt him. Like a Zen monk, he accepted cheerfully his daily round. Teaching class after class after class. Like most dancers, he actually loved dancing and loved seeing his students improve. I wonder if he was from Argentina originally. He wasn't from Italy, and I don't think he was born in the United States. You rarely see very masculine men with such a quality of sweetness and gentleness. He had to have been foreign—Americans are never like that.

While we were doing our pliés and ronds de jambe, the cleaning ladies were getting ready to leave the opera house, having prepared it for the evening performance. Down in the lower corridors, lights shone over the paintings of the stars of earlier days. Almost like a votive light, there was a single illumination shining down on Amelita Galli-Curci, Caruso, and Rosa Ponselle, stars who had made their names in this house. Our own stars were not there yet, though we heard that Zinka Milanov's portrait was being done. We had seen pictures of her in the *New York Times* after opening night. She had appeared in the Grand Tier smothered in white fox to see how Maria Callas would be received by "her" public. Zinka was Yugoslavian. I always thought she was pleasant and untheatrical at rehearsals, though she clearly knew that respect was due her. She had an imperial manner—something like Queen Marie of Romania or the Queen Mother of England. Always smiling and pleasant, but unbending.

The red velvet staircases swept up to the upper corridor where you entered the boxes. Everything was red velvet and gold leaf, as you might expect in an opera house, but the lighting was very discreet. Small lights above the doors; golden, shadowy lights in the corridors. Even on the grand staircase there were no blazing lights to show off gowns and jewels. There was something very confidential about the opera house, as though you were in a jewel case, which was even more pronounced when you entered a box, or took your seat in one of the tiers above, to find yourself on the edge of a cavern of space.

Music flowed through these boxes, perfectly and clearly. Even when you were seated among hundreds, the yearning quality of the tenor's voice in *Il Trovatore* was very personal. It made you remember what yearning was all about. And made you feel like crying.

The opera house was rather narrow for the depth of the space. The house occupied the entire block bounded by Broadway and Seventh Avenue, Thirty-ninth and Fortieth Streets. It was big. When you pass the ugly green-and-maroon skyscraper that now occupies the space, you can't ignore that there was a lot of floor space there. But much of the sides were taken up with corridors, spacious boxes, and rehearsal rooms, so that the distance from the boxes to the stage was accentuated by the fact that the sides weren't all that far apart. It was probably created in that way so that operagoers could observe what others were wearing and what appropriate or inappropriate people were accompanying their friends.

That was the atmosphere of the old, ugly yellow Met. Outside, the look of a beer factory. Inside, a hushed, vast, murky, low-lit jewel box just waiting for the lid to go up and reveal the glittering jewels on the stage.

Which could be both symbolic and real. For some reason, I was out front one night when Lily Pons was doing her Lucia. In the first act, she wore her own real diamonds. It was amazing. Under the spotlight, her diamond necklace ringed her neck in fire. It blazed as she sang. I have never seen jewels perform their role so burningly bright, perhaps to make up, in some way, for Lily's diminishing brilliance in her last season.

Backstage, there was no muted anything. Everything backstage made you realize that the theater was made of wood. The pockmarked and beaten wooden stage itself: could it have been the original, after millions of nails had been driven into it and pulled out again? It hardly seems possible, but then again, nothing else had been changed since the opera house had been built.

The hallways and dressing rooms smelled of old wood. The old mirrors had reflected thousands of faces, and their old wooden frames had been repainted many times. They were encrusted like the frosting on a birthday cake, paint dripping here and there.

Many of the sets were originals from productions as long ago as the 1920s. The sets for *La Gioconda* were painted with realistic views of Venice, with no attempt at all to resemble fine art. The most beautiful sets of all were the Eugene Berman creations for *Don Giovanni.* They were enormous paintings, actually. One between-scenes drop was orange with a sharply painted black wall of ruins, foliage sprouting from the crumbling pillars. Acres of orange and black. How wonderful it would be to have a house so enormous that such a painting could be hung in the living room.

Eugene Berman was nowhere to be seen during the rehearsals for *Don Giovanni,* but Cecil Beaton was very much present when the sets were put up for *Vanessa.* Eleanor Steber was Vanessa, in large black hats with sweeping plumes. Beaton had done the sets in the style of Aubrey Beardsley. There was one brilliant ballroom scene, where the set was the entrance to the ballroom, with the effect that an enormous room swept away to the left, through a huge arch. You really did have the feeling there was a vast room through that arch, one that reached all the way to Thirty-eighth Street. As I recall, everything was in black and white and orange in this set, too. Cecil shouldn't be underestimated. He was like one of the great designers and set builders to Louis Quatorze. He knew his profession well, and when an effect was needed, he knew how to create it.

In comparison to these sets, the dressing rooms were squalid. They smelled of greasepaint, even though no one was using greasepaint anymore. Also, the dressing rooms had low ceilings, turn-of-the-century low lighting, and long tables with yellowish lights around the mirrors. When you looked into them and saw people moving behind you, it was always as though they were against black. Their bare bodies, trussed in with dance belts that made the waists smaller and the buttocks and crotch bulge, passed to and fro behind your bare shoulders as you daubed shadow over your eyes, glued your lashes together with sticky mascara, drew your eyebrows on above your real ones.

Minda Meryl

Was it strange, my friendship with Minda Meryl? She was a big star. Well, almost.

I was just a kid in the corps de ballet, one of the least important people in the opera company. Mr. Bing had just brought her in from Europe to do the Risë Stevens roles. She was a sensational Carmen and evidently had set all Vienna ablaze with envy. At least that was the way she told it. She was going to do *Orpheus and Eurydice* and *Der Rosenkavalier* the first season I was there. Octavian in *Der Rosenkavalier,* a "pants" role.

We met because I was going on as part of her entourage in *Der Rosenkavalier* on her second-act entrance. We had done our rehearsals with Risë Stevens, so I had never seen Minda.

She and I were dressed almost exactly alike. White satin knee britches, long white satin coat trimmed with silver braid, a lace jabot, a very white wig. She was in a white carriage being drawn by a white horse. A real one.

I was rehearsing in my head the little thing I had been given to do with two other boys in *Faust*. Could it be called a solo? If something that took two minutes and was danced with two other people could be called a solo, it was a solo.

Suddenly, just before the music cue, the profile in the carriage turned, looked at me, and the voice said, "What number makeup are you wearing?" I said automatically, "Max Factor 22." We went on. There was no time for a "Thank you."

When I came out of the elevator after the performance, she was standing in the back corridor. A tallish woman with short light-brown hair, in a sort of Audrey Hepburn style. Not a really beautiful face—Minda's eyes were a little small—but she had a great nose. She still has it, as far as I know. Like a Greek coin in profile—very straight, starting almost between her eyes.

As a group of us burst out of the elevator she said, "Which one of you gave me our makeup number?"

"I did," I said.

"Thanks. I thought it looked so much better than mine. Sorry to just yell out at you."

"That's all right," I said.

We were all standing around, sort of impressed that one of the stars was chatting with us. They did, of course, but we were always aware of that star aura.

"What's your name?" she said.

"Harry Potter," I told her, reaching out for the hand she was holding out towards me.

In Michigan women didn't introduce themselves and shake hands. Men did. Women just smiled and hung on to their purses.

I said, "These are my friends Alfred Houston and Tommy Corrigan and Robby Schmidt." I always used full names, even then. I hate introducing people by first names, as though they're disposable.

"You've got a lot of *ee*'s there," Minda said as she shook their hands.

"That's because we're boy dancers," I said. "Everybody is Robby and Tommy and Harry."

"Harry doesn't fall into that category," she said. "You've been saved. Though it doesn't sound like you'll want to keep it when you're a big star. Harold Potter, more likely."

"Who knows if that will ever happen?" I said. We were beginning to clog up the narrow passageway to the stage door, and the other dancers were pushing past us as they went out, hating us for talking to a star.

"Oh, I think so. I think so," Minda said. "You've got the look." Her attention wandered. She turned and took a very large red fox coat out of the hands of a tall man behind her. "This is my husband, Josh. Josh Meryl. I got my name legitimately. Everyone says I never got that name in Dayton. They're right."

Mr. Josh shook hands all around, said they had to go, and they went out right ahead of us. There were no fans waiting for Minda Meryl. She wasn't that kind of star yet. They were waiting for Lisa Della Casa, who had sung the Marschallin that night. So beautiful, really beautiful. She looked exactly the same offstage as onstage. We would much rather have chatted with her. For us, that was a *real* star. Of course, Minda Meryl is a real star now, and if she still chats with the ballet boys as she leaves the new opera house, I'm sure they are suitably thrilled.

I had actually noticed Minda before in a rehearsal of *Carmen*. A dress rehearsal. She was stepping in for some imported soprano who was sick. I loved her more later but I liked her a lot at the rehearsal.

The costumer had decided that Carmen would enter with her friends swathed in yards of black veiling. Carmen, that is. Not the friends. As they came swaggering in, Maestro Stiedry stopped the rehearsal and said, "Mees Meryl, you are not on the music!"

In a perfectly ladylike voice she said loudly, "I've got so goddamn much veil, I can't even see you!" The offending veil was removed and the rehearsal went on.

In the dressing room for days afterwards you could hear someone or other saying, "I've got so goddamn much veil . . ."

All of us got to know Minda better when we did *La Périchole* together later that season. She was doing it with Cyril Ritchard, the English music hall's answer to Noël Coward. It was an Offenbach *opéra bouffe* from the Second Empire, something about some Spanish viceroy in Peru who falls in love with a beautiful street singer. The steet singer was Minda, La Périchole.

97

Minda shared the role with Patrice Munsel. They were both a lot of fun. We danced in a kind of street circus that entered with La Périchole in the first act. Bulky Don was the weight lifter, and I was a hat seller. I wore a stack of six hats and did a little dance. I guess that was a real solo.

Minda kidded around with us in the wings while we were waiting to go on. One night as we were leaving the theater at the same time, she said, "Are you going somewhere to eat?" Josh wasn't waiting for her. "Mind if I go with you?" she said.

We were thrilled, of course, and so we all traipsed across Seventh Avenue, Minda in her red fox. Together we had trays and shiny tables at Bickford's. She wanted to know all about us, where we were from, where we had studied, what we planned to do. She acted more like an older sister. Not motherly. She's actually one of the rare stars who wasn't all that thrilled with herself. Maybe fighting her way out of Dayton and through the drafty halls of opera houses in Leipzig and Darmstadt did it. Later, she was to be a real friend. I was appreciative at the time, but we never saw each other after I stopped dancing.

Minda had a way with words. When I was discussing the boys in the dressing room, she said, "It's called promiscuous. It's called sleeping around. It's called being boy crazy. It's called high school."

I told her about Henry Right, the young man in the opera management who was so in love with one of our budding choreographers in the corps de ballet. Mr. Right was trying to help launch the boy's career, and was rewarded with an occasional bit of nooky. Minda said, "The fucking he's getting isn't worth the fucking he's taking."

When I wondered whether one of the ballet critics was hallucinating when he eulogized a really bad male dancer in his column, she said, "He writes his column with his cock."

"More like his ass," I replied.

"You're getting to be quite a witty lad," she said admiringly.

I loved Minda. I've never been so outspoken since.

On dieting, Minda recommended, "When you feel like eating, fuck instead. If that's possible, of course." The Minda Meryl lifestyle should have been made into a book.

One of my favorite remarks was about a new contralto who was making a big hit at the Met. "They're just trying to slow her down enough so she can be a nymphomaniac," she said.

After a while, she and Josh used to invite me to go places with them. I became a kind of surrogate kid brother. I never discussed my private life with them. I was happy to go to parties and the movies with Josh and Minda.

One night, we were at a party that turned out to be more of an affair than they had thought it was going to be. Everyone was rather stuffy and all dressed up, so Minda drank more champagne than she should have. When a very Fairfield, Connecticut, kind of couple introduced themselves, Minda said, "This is my husband, Lester, and my lover, Mitch," giving us make-believe names. The woman looked at me in a patronizing way and said, "Did you say 'bitch'?" Minda said, looking her very squarely in the eye, "Not to him, I didn't."

They had a comfortable apartment in the West Seventies, and some Sundays when I didn't have a modern-dance rehearsal, I would go there for brunch. We would read the Sunday *Times* together.

In Michigan, we didn't have anything like the Sunday *Times*. It overwhelmed me a bit. I often thought that if you had absolutely nothing to do and all the money in the world, you still couldn't do everything that was in the Sunday *Times*. The plays, the concerts, the art exhibits, the movies. So much to do. Selecting what you wanted to do was what made you into a New Yorker. New Yorkers decide "I only do *this*," narrowing their lives down to John Cage concerts, movies from Yugoslavia, and George Bernard Shaw plays. Then you knew who you were and so did everybody else.

The Sex Squad

There were ten of us in the Sex Squad. Ten boys. There were ten girls, too, but they didn't really count in our minds.

Being in the Sex Squad didn't mean you were among the ten best dancers, it meant you were among the ten most fuckable dancers. Let me make it clear that when I say "fuckable," I mean desirable. There were some of us that didn't fancy some guy jumping our bones but much preferred jumping his.

Let's see. Who exactly was in the Sex Squad?

Illy Ilquist: Tall, blond, a handsome face and a sumptuous body and not a bad dancer at all.

Rex Ames: Shorter than Illy. Strongly resembling Tyrone Power, he probably had the strongest technique in the company.

Robby Schmidt: Our *enfant terrible.* Very sexy, short, a good jump, but not as much technique as he thought he had. And a complete slut.

Tony Compostella: Later Antonio Compostella. Dark, not particularly handsome. Not a bad technique, but a long body and shortish legs. In training to be a slut.

Tommy Corrigan: Red-haired, cute, again a long torso and shortish legs, but on him it looked good. He would have liked to be a slut but was too Catholic.

Clifford Fearing: Our Heathcliff. Very dark and handsome. Not much of a dancer and never pretended to be. From somewhere in the Caribbean. Famous for his self-introduction, "Suck or fuck?" Hung out at the YMCA a lot.

Todd Weinstein: An excellent dancer. Blondish with slightly protruding eyes. A Margaret Craske favorite, although he danced in the Antony Tudor manner.

Bobby Ferrett: I think he was from the Philippines actually, despite the last name. He really couldn't dance at all, but he was handsome and had a nice body and his family was very rich. The Met knew a good thing when they saw it.

Robert Rhodes: I never knew him very well. He wasn't bad-looking and could actually dance with a lot of style and presence. He was a Craske favorite, also, and left the company mid-season because he had supposedly sat on some broken glass while taking a bath. Who knows? Of course, everyone in the dressing room thought he had definitely sat on *something* in the bathtub that had put him out of commission.

And then there was me: God knows how I would be described by one of the other dancers. Probably like this: Kind of blond. Kind of a hick. Beginning to develop some real technique. Seems very innocent, but there has to be more to it than that. And they would have been right.

My great friend Alfred was not in the Sex Squad, and I'm sure to his great relief. He was really too noble-looking for the sexy contortions Zachary Solov had contrived for us to dance. And he would have hated being painted orange and then having to wash it off in the company of others. That was not Alfred at all.

Just because we were in the Sex Squad didn't develop any particular esprit de corps. It just reassured us all that in the evanescent world of ballet, we were among the season's most admired butterflies. Probably something like the *Ziegfeld Follies* used to be. Beautiful and very admired. But loved? That was another story altogether.

Alfred Thought
He Was Jean Cocteau

One of my best friends at the opera was Alfred. He looked like a French refugee. The truth was much plainer. His parents, Sally and Ed, lived way downtown on the Lower East Side in a housing project. He lived with them when I first met him. They regarded their son with awe. It was as though a peacock had deposited its egg in the nest of two sparrows. "What have we wrought?" could be seen in their eyes as tall, elegant, very European Alfred passed before their wondering eyes.

Alfred was a particular favorite of Miss Craske at the opera school. Partly, I think, because of his elongated and articulate body. He looked like the illustrations in a "How To" ballet book with his high-arched feet, his slender thighs, his strong-beaked face with the swept-back hair. His body looked like it was capable of any ballet position. Which it was. However, energy and attack and expressing his emotions through his body were not his. Alfred once said to me, "With those legs they shouldn't try to make you dance. They should just let you walk around." Which was actually more true of himself.

Another reason for Miss Craske's attachment to Alfred is that he was something of the *beau idéal* of a ballerina's partner from the 1920s. In photographs of Pavlova being partnered, her male companions had the same long, slender limbs and blade-like profile as Alfred. I think he brought back the dear, dead days when Miss Craske was frolicking in the back row of the Pavlova company, as it hauled itself from Canberra to Perth, Vancouver to Quebec, Buenos Aires to Bogotá. Miss Craske, it was rumored, had also danced travesty roles—male partnering roles in which she dressed as a boy. Evidently, this was very common in the early part of the century. Once I did find a picture of someone named Craske in a kind of romantic-chevalier outfit. Large plumed hat, knee britches, with long hair. It could have been her. Miss Craske, gray hair in a bun and tan slacks, lived wreathed in the mysteries of her past. She never reminisced.

What she did do was involve favorite students in the mysteries of her love for an Indian guru called Baba. There seemed to be an ashram somewhere in Miss Craske's past. Her pet students seemed to favor Baba themselves. Those of us who were not pets of Miss Craske believed that they were sucking up to her, feigning interest in her living Indian deity, when actually their primary interests were getting her attention and getting laid. Wasn't everyone's?

To his great credit Alfred never displayed the faintest interest in Baba or any other Oriental mysteries. Even though among the leading Craske favorites, he sailed serenely along pursuing his own internal destiny and ignoring all else. Miss Craske respected that, I'm sure. I once asked him about Baba. He said, "Mama and Papa may be gaga for Baba, but I'm not."

Alfred's internal destiny was to live as though it were the 1920s and he was in France. His head of a hawk did resemble Jean Cocteau's, and he did nothing to discourage this comparison. When not studying dance, he drew, in the style of the Russian expatriate artist Pavel Tchelitchev. Tchelitchev had a studio on East Fifty-fifth Street, and Alfred sometimes hung around in that neighborhood, hoping to run into him by chance. Perhaps attract his attention. He was not physically unlike Tchelitchev either. Tchelitchev might think of him as a son, but that was unlikely.

Tchelitchev's longtime lover was Charles-Henri Ford—perky, adorable, and full of cheek, absolutely the other end of the spectrum from Alfred. True, Tchelitchev had discovered Nicholas Magellanes lounging about on the sidewalks of New York and had sent him over to Lincoln Kirstein and George Balanchine at the School of American Ballet. He was now one of the premier danseurs of the New York City Ballet.

But more, Tchelitchev had come from the 1920s art world of between-the-wars in Paris. I knew nothing of this scene, but I learned all about it from Alfred: Picasso, Derain, Tchelitchev, and other artists designing sets for the Diaghilev ballet company. *Les Six,* the French musical avant-garde, created scores to be danced to. Alice Nikitina, the fragile young ballerina, was the mistress of Lord Beaverbrook. This was glamour, certainly as Alfred saw it.

During our first year at the Met, Alfred moved to a little topfloor cold-water flat on Bank Street in the West Village. It could well have been in Montmartre: the walls an ancient gray plaster that must have been painted white before the First World War. A narrow iron cot. Paintings leaning their faces towards the walls. Small plaster works on the fireplace mantel. No curtains. A fire escape outside the windows. I don't think I was ever there in the evening. I remember no lamps, only limp New York light filtering in from the courtyard behind the building. There was absolutely no color. Even Alfred's eyes were the color of dust. In this little enfilade of small rooms it was forever 1928. Alfred even dressed it, in his black pants and long-sleeved white dress shirt with the sleeves turned up a few times. Not too long ago, I saw an early photo of Vladimir Nabokov rowing on a lake somewhere in Germany in the 1920s that looked exactly like Alfred in the 1950s.

Alfred drew elongated male nudes as though they were floating overhead or drifting off towards the horizon, stunted children dressed in gigantic leaves, figures already much explored by Pavel Tchelitchev. His paintings, however, were much more his own, and often showed a figure closely resembling himself. Sometimes he was a man waiting on a lonely train-station terrace in a country that was clearly not the United States. Or a figure with his face plunged into a vase of brilliantly red flowers. Loneliness, torment, beauty of a magical sort were Alfred's stock in trade. I was entranced.

I was equally entranced with his stories, recounted in his cracked, old-man's voice in a drifting, matter-of-fact manner. He told me this: one afternoon, as he lay resting in the gloaming on his narrow cot with no lights on, he heard a noise. He looked up. A man was on the fire escape trying to jimmy the window open. Someone else would have leaped up shouting or run to the door to escape before the man could enter.

Alfred rose and silently glided across the room and pressed his pale face with the large, staring gray eyes to the window, just above the burglar's lowered head. The burglar glanced up, saw the spectral face, and leaped back, shouting. With a clang, his tool fell the five stories into the courtyard. Clinging to the flimsy fire escape railing for a moment, he gathered himself and fled up the fire escape to the roof. Then Alfred drifted back to his cot and resumed his nap.

This is his story, anyway. I loved it particularly because it was unplanned. This is how Alfred responded to an emergency—as he thought Gertrude Stein would have liked him to.

He also had a favorite story about his father. He was seated in a park near their housing development one afternoon when he saw a woman approaching he was sure he knew. As she came closer, he became ever surer that she was among his acquaintances. But who? Finally, when she arrived directly in front of him, stopped, and said hello, he knew who it was: his daughter.

Alfred never commented on his relationship with his parents, but stories like this suggested he realized that his family was not without their own personal quirks.

Alfred also sang. In his quavery voice, he sang, "As I sit alone each lonely night/Counting out my cards from left to right," and finally reaching something about how he was all alone just playing solitaire. His voice sounded like a recording reaching the modern day from long ago, something like Ruth Etting's. A fine, slightly whiny voice rising above a band that played like Paul Whiteman's while men in white pants and women in cloche hats two-stepped around the hotel terrace. Everything in Alfred's life seemed to have happened a long time ago.

Alfred didn't have a lover, but I knew he wasn't averse to being picked up by adventurous strangers on the bus or in the subway. His pale, languid, poetic air must have appealed to many. I'm sure that although he would never be aggressive seeking romance, he would not place many obstructions in the path of someone seeking it from him.

Our dancer friend Robby had been in some kind of detention home for boys with Alfred when they were teenagers. It was never made clear what they were doing there, or what they had done, but there was a kind of complicity between the two of them. They spent little time together, but they had the air of survivors of a long crossing of the Great Western Desert by covered wagon. They had seen things and survived events we could never know. Alfred and I were already too old to be able to replicate the experience as friends.

Alfred's stories of the reformatory conjured up visions of tall, uncurtained windows looking out over endless snow plains scattered with an occasional pine tree. Within, all was chill and empty. He hinted at abuse and neglect. It was all very *Jane Eyre*. Robby and he considered escape, but how and where across those snowy endless fields? This was in New York State somewhere. He made New York State seem very romantic, if unpleasant. Again, all of this was in black and white, accented with shades of gray. And dark-blue night skies. Just like many of the Joseph Cornell boxes.

Later, Alfred was to work with Cornell, and the interiors of those boxes must have seemed like coming home for him. He already had inhabited the vast, empty spaces Cornell confined in those small, handmade wooden boxes. Full of stars and snowflakes and the feeling that something important once happened here but is now gone. All of Alfred's life was like that. He was the last and sole witness to a once amusing and vibrant world. But it was clear to me, even enchanted as I was, that this world had never been here on the North American continent, and most likely not here in the time and space of this planet. Even when and if it had, Alfred had not been there. Disliking the world of Sally and Ed in the projects, he had imagined a lost world and then gone there to inhabit it.

I had never met anyone like Alfred in Michigan or Chicago. I don't think there was anyone like him to meet. I enjoyed coming into his lost world, and there I learned a great deal about the Magic Realist painters and the Paris of the 1920s and '30s. There I first heard about Djuna Barnes, the details of life with Gertrude Stein and Alice B. Toklas, of the cosmetics queen Helena Rubenstein's early attachments to and patronage of Picasso and his circle. All the backstage gossip of the Diaghilev ballet and its tours between the wars were common exchange between Alfred and his pals over tea. I learned that Nijinsky was followed by Massine in Diaghilev's bed, and Massine in turn by Serge Lifar.

This was my world. At one end of the spectrum, tangled in the hot bodies and sprawled legs of my lovers in my almost sordid apartment on Sixteenth Street; through the brilliant lights and exhausting days and nights on the opera stage; to the almost ghostly and never quite real atmosphere of Alfred's Paris–in–Greenwich Village flat. Not dusty but not clean, always stale smelling, that little top-floor apartment.

Have I caught the atmosphere a little for you? Even in the kaleidoscopic possibilities of the varieties of life in New York at that time, this must have been a unique one. Now gone. Other people live in the apartments where Alfred and I once lived. My building now has a new brick facade and hints at respectability and normal life within. As does my own life. True, Alfred remains, and he is far more unchanged than I. The last time I met him it was on the steps of the Metropolitan Museum with my daughters. He was with Robby, who is now a wizened and drug-raddled gnome. Completely unrecognizable from the sensuous, rosy-skinned, dark-eyed, arrogant boy who used to swing his buttocks about the dressing rooms at the opera.

They both, despite the daughters, addressed me as though we had just thrown our dance belts and ballet slippers into our dance bags and were heading for Bickford's. They had been visiting the period rooms because they thought the English library with its huge desk had a cheerful air, with the permanent electric sunlight pouring a yellow haze into it. They liked the pink French drawing room with its abundance of roses embroidered on the upholstery and the great ruches of the pull-up pink taffeta draperies. "Now we are braced for the subway again," Alfred said. "And modern-dance concerts at the 92nd Street Y, where I'm sure at this moment, someone is dancing something called *My Sacrament* and rolling around on the floor hanging onto a large log."

Robby's eyes were empty as he looked out over the students sitting on the museum steps and the yellow taxis loitering along the edge of the pavement. I wasn't sure he knew who I was. He turned to my daughters and said, "When your father was young, he was very cruel to people." My daughters said nothing. They seemed neither to hear him or to understand him.

Alfred said nothing, either. He shook hands and smiled in that dry manner. "As usual, you leave as though you are going somewhere more interesting," he said to me.

"I assure you that is not the case," I said.

His hooded eyes looked as though they didn't believe me. Robby's line was down again and he left wordlessly with Alfred, walking down the stairs. Alfred turned and said, "You know

109

where we'd be today if we had been successful in our dance careers? On a truck-and-bus tour of *Bye Bye Birdie* in Milwaukee. If we were lucky."

My daughters and I went down to where a taxi was waiting. They didn't ask about Alfred and Robby or how I knew them or about my days as a dancer when I explained I had known them at the opera. But then they never have and never do.

The Supers' Party

A short, dark young man with a bath towel wound about his head like a turban was standing in the middle of the room shrieking in a high falsetto when I came into the room. "It's Schrieber," Alfred said. "He thinks he's Risë Stevens. I suppose that's the hell scene from Gluck's *Orpheus and Eurydice*."

"How'd you guess that?" I said.

"All those people writhing around on the floor. Like all those extras crawling around on the staircase when Orpheus descends into hell, remember?" he said.

I did remember. And I wasn't very happy about it, either. When we rehearsed it, Mr. Bing, the director of the Met, stopped the onstage rehearsal and came up onto the stage and came directly over to me. "You have to do something about your hair," he said. I stared at him. "You're too blond. I can't see anything but you on the stage." And he walked off.

We took a break then, and Stanley, my favorite stage manager, came up to me. "We'll spray it brown," he said. "It's nothing. I'll meet you up in Wigs when we're done rehearsing."

Harold up in Wigs found no problem. "I'll just buy some of that temporary spray-on stuff," he said. "It'll wash right out."

"This is my natural color."

"No one thinks it isn't, honey," Harold said, patting me on the behind. "Nice little ass you got there."

"It's natural, too," I said.

"Oh, I'm sure it is, I'm sure it is," he said, glancing after me as I walked out.

I didn't stride out, but I gave it as much as I could. Everybody was patting your ass at the opera. The ballet girls did it absent-mindedly when they were talking to you, as though they were petting a dog or something. The dressers did, and some of the stagehands, too. They were all just being affectionate. They didn't really think it was going to lead to anything else, and if patting my rear end gave a little lift to their long, hard day, so be it.

In the elevator going back down to the stage level Stanley said, "I think Mr. Bing was just trying to call himself to your attention."

"You're kidding. What about Mrs. Bing and all the little Bings?" I said.

"There aren't any little Bings," Stanley said as he pushed open the creaking grille that closed the open side of the elevator. And left me to think about it.

At any rate, I was still thinking about it when I went to a party that night with Alfred. He didn't want to go alone. "The supers are giving it," he told me. "They've invited some of the boys from the ballet. One of those supers is really good-looking, and I want to go, but I don't want to go alone."

"What's wrong, can't you get home by subway?" I asked him, remembering his number-one rule: "Never go anywhere you can't go home by subway."

"I can walk home," he said. I visited Alfred once when he still lived with his parents on the Lower East Side. I tried to be nice and homey with them. Alfred said later, "You're the only person most gay boys in this town know that they can introduce their mothers to."

The supers, or supernumeraries, at the Met were a kind of raffish crowd that never varied. The same boys and men reported in every evening for their pittance and a chance to carry a spear or a sedan chair or be in a crowd of citizenry. We got to know them pretty well, because our scenes often involved a crowded stage and they were on hand. Many of them were out-of-work actors, and some were the younger boys from the ballet school of the Met, in training to join the company. Most of them, however, were great opera buffs and knew every detail of every star's history, performance schedule, and eating habits. The stars knew them, too, and were very friendly. Only Maria Callas was haughty. Her great rival, Renata Tebaldi, made a big show of being warm and gracious with her backstage admirers, to point out the contrast. But Lisa Della Casa was everybody's favorite. She kissed and hugged her fans back in the wings. One night, in *The Marriage of Figaro,* we were going on at the same time she was. She turned and looked back at us in her eighteenth-century white wig and panniers and said, "Let's go, kids." Really adorable.

Eleanor Steber was more one of the boys. She hung around with the stagehands a lot, backstage. Sort of a larger-scale Mae West. Once I went out into the audience to watch her rehearsal in the new Eugene Berman–designed production of *Don Giovanni.* She was Donna Anna, the wronged woman. No one was in costume yet, but she threw herself down upon the body of her slain father anyway, the minute little Cesare Valletti. Her bosom came tumbling out of her low-cut black dress, covering Mr. Valletti's fine little features. She seemed unaware of it. The conductor's hand trembled a little, but he struggled on. We could see Mr. Valletti's eyes opening and staring hard at the flow of flesh over his nose and chin. The maestro stopped the orchestra; Miss Steber sat up and calmly tucked her bosom back in. Signor Valletti sat up too, smiling. She pushed him back down with one hand and the rehearsal went on. Backstage I heard her say to some laughing stagehands, "Aw, he loved it. That's why I didn't move for a while."

Because of this one-big-family atmosphere onstage, it wasn't out of the question for Alfred and me to go to a supers party. We didn't know all their names, but we felt friendly towards them. And as far as finding new friends, lovers, or one-night stands, probably everyone onstage thought anyone else onstage was fair game.

It must have been a Sunday night—the only night the Met was dark and nobody had to work. I stepped through the crowd rolling around on the floor and went out to the kitchen to get something to drink. I had no idea who the host was or whose apartment it was. Nobody seemed to know. I didn't really drink, so I took a paper cup of punch from someone, ladling it out of a big metal cooking pot on the stove. I was just noticing that there was something in it when two older men met in the door-way, expressed pleasure at seeing each other, and kissed on the lips. That was new to me. Kissing in bed was one thing. Men kissing in public I hadn't seen before. Alfred appeared on the other side of them in the door and saw me looking. Goggling probably. As they broke apart, he came towards me, followed by Ronald, the super he had come to see. Ronald was tall and dark and good-looking. Older.

"It's European," Alfred said. He'd noticed my surprise at the men kissing in public.

"I don't think Frenchmen kiss on the lips," I said.

"Oh, sometimes, surely," Alfred said in his best Jean Cocteau manner.

I don't think he'd seen a lot of it, either.

Back in the living room, there seemed to be a lineup of older men around the walls while the younger ones mingled and pa-raded in the middle.

"I don't remember seeing these guys at the opera," I said to Alfred.

"They're just here to see what's new and good," Ronald said. "What are you here for?" I asked him.

"I'm here to see what's old and bad, actually," he said. "No, I'm just kidding. I'm here to meet the love of a lifetime. Aren't we all?"

The *Aida* Christmas

On Christmas Day, we did *Aida* in full body paint. Two men with buckets of orange glop marched into the bathroom and each of the Sex Squad took turns standing between them to be painted. We had already made up our faces, and wearing only a dance belt, we stood with legs apart while, with wide brushes, they slapped orange paint all over our bodies as though they were applying wallpaper paste. I never thought to ask who the professional body painters were. Two Italian men who were related to someone in the dressers' union, I'm sure.

Then we dashed back down the hall to the dressing room to put on the little wraparound skirt and the armbands that made up our costumes. We also had little helmets to cover our hair. We originally had rather tall headdresses, but the moment the choreography required that we bend forward, the headdresses went rolling. So helmets had been substituted. I guess somewhere in all those Egyptian frescoes there must be something that suggested our attire—lowly slaves most likely. In ancient Egypt, if you had any kind of social standing at all, I'm sure, you had a headdress. It was so hot, you didn't want any extra robes.

The girls had Cleopatra wigs, little black curls dripping down on each side of their faces.

The dress rehearsal had been quite an event.

We didn't have to wear body makeup for the rehearsal, which was a godsend. Everyone was afraid of getting smeared by us. One touch and you were orange from one end to the other. Fedora Barbieri was singing Amneris in this production, and she was particularly afraid of us, because her new costume cost a fortune. When she appeared on cue at the rehearsal, the orchestra had stopped playing, they were so amazed. Her wig was Cleopatra style, but all in rhinestones. Dripping chains of rhinestones all over her head. Her robe was scarlet, and over it she wore a long cloak of gold lamé. Long. Dragging yards behind her. On her chest, two giant wings sprouted forth, gold, well above the level of her head. She was wearing gold platform sandals. Nor had she stinted in the makeup department, either. We were used to Fedora because she had sung with Callas in her debut in *Norma*. Fedora was a real trouper, and when Callas got into vocal trouble in their duets, she always supported her and tried to make her sound good instead of blaring forth to make sure the audience understood there was nothing wrong with her voice. I think she felt that she had been overshadowed by Callas in *Norma,* and here she was going to shine. Zinka Milanov had the title role, and Zinka never overdid it. Secure in her position as Queen of the Met, she wore the same kind of vaguely Grecian robes that she wore in almost any period opera.

The stage manager let Fedora rehearse the second act in her finery, but I noticed him talking to her quietly in a corner of the stage after the curtain came down. She had gotten rid of the wings when she appeared on stage in the performance, but the rhinestone wig was still in place.

Christmas Day evening it was well below zero. It was cold on that stage, and everyone stayed in their dressing rooms until the last moment. If you walked behind the looming sets you could look out the gigantic Gothic-arched doors standing open on the back of the theater as the traffic zoomed by on Seventh Avenue. *Aida* is so loud that it drowned the noise of the passing cars.

Not only was *Aida* done on Christmas Day but on New Year's

Day also. New Yorkers like to go to the theater on the holidays. Taking the whole family to the opera on Christmas Day probably dates back to the time of Queen Victoria. We really didn't mind that we had to work—what were we going to do instead? Almost no one had a family that lived nearby, no one knew how to cook, and no one wanted to eat that much anyway. We were just as happy being there all together in the theater, covered in orange paint. There was something almost gala for us, too, on the *Aida* days. The orange paints sloshing around the showers, the running up and down the halls almost naked, then the sprint down to the stage where the onstage temperature would make your skin bubble up into goose bumps under your orange covering, the blatant blaring of the triumphal march, and you were on. The Sex Squad was displaying their near-naked bodies for all to see. Briefly, but thoroughly.

We fled the stage as quickly as we descended upon it, and dashed back into the showers to get rid of the orange. We were all in the communal showers together, and you really never got it all off, even though the tile walls were covered with the splashing paint as it washed off our bodies. It was fun, these naked young bodies, jostling and splashing and laughing.

Homosexuals as jocks. It happens.

After the performance that Christmas Day evening, I was with Illy and some of the other boys having supper at Bickford's. Alfred was with us. And Fabian, a boy who wasn't usually in our crowd. He was small, with very dark hair and sapphire eyes—sort of that Paulette Goddard look.

Illy said, "Let's go to Staten Island on the ferry."

We arose as one, went to the subway, and took the train to South Ferry. We ran into the terminal to dash through the big doors on the upper level and straight on to the upper deck of the boat.

That was the old green Victorian ferry terminal then. The new one wasn't built yet. The old one was much more in keeping with boat travel. You could imagine the ladies with their long swishing skirts and umbrellas, holding their piled-up hair and towering hats as they hurried aboard. The men accompanying them in derbies, with high, hard collars and a *New York Times* rolled up tightly under their arms. This was their terminal, with that late-Victorian look and smell—narrow windows, buff plaster, linoleum floors, and mahogany woodwork. The peculiar smell that old plaster and old wood gives off. There was something sexy about it, too. It suggested rendezvous in second-rate hotel rooms, white thighs, thick pubic hair with a large, dark penis thrusting out of it, clothes half dropped off, dark and woolly, white and starchy. No slim, fit, suntanned bodies for these folks. Theirs was sex as need, desperate and groping, and soon over, to be forgotten and lied about.

We stood on the front deck and froze our butts. You know how the Staten Island ferry is. The rounded ends, front and back, with the folding metal grilles to let people on and off. The open side decks with the benches. The big inner room with all the benches that look like they came from the old Pennsylvania Station or a church somewhere. Right in the middle, that snack stand with the coffee and the big greasy doughnuts. I loved those doughnuts. I never eat anything like that anymore, but then I could eat twenty of them and never see the difference.

We stood on the deck looking up at the night sky. So navy blue and full of stars that night. It was very clear, and the lights of Manhattan didn't dim the skies out here on the harbor waters. The few lights of St. George were tossed over the rising hill of Staten Island. There were very few other people on the boat. No one was coming home from work on Christmas Day, only a few people who had been visiting in Manhattan for the day.

We were planning to just get off the boat and circle round the terminal and take it right back again. You weren't allowed to just stay on and ride it back. They had a little man in a navy blue uniform and cap to shoo you off. I'm sure if you were determined, you could hide in the bathrooms—but the fare was only five cents. We could afford that.

119

As we walked into the terminal, a voice was squawking over the intercom, "Last train to Tottenville. Last train to Tottenville." Right there, before us, was a little train. A cartoon name and a cartoon train. We really didn't even look at each other. We just ran and jumped on the train. The doors slammed. We were off to Tottenville. We knew it couldn't be far away, because Staten Island wasn't very big. Would we even have enough money for the tickets? We did. When the conductor came around, we dumped all our money together and bought round-trip tickets. We knew we had to come back. We had one dollar left. Enough for the ferry and the subway for four people on our return: five cents and a dime, respectively, for each of us.

Our miniature train chugged through the snow of Staten Island, stopping at towns none of us had ever heard of. It could have been Vermont, or Ireland, twenty or thirty years earlier. There were very few lights out the train windows. It was one o'clock in the morning, very late on Staten Island.

We were the only passengers to descend at Tottenville. The train station, Victorian to match the terminal, was as miniature as the train, but there was someone on duty behind the ticket grille. We asked when the next train returned to St. George and the ferry terminal and the agent said five-thirty. We asked if there was a coffee shop or a restaurant open. He seemed to sense that we were on some kind of moonlit escapade and told us that there was nothing to do in Tottenville but take a stroll and see the sights until the train left. Tottenville was a beach resort. We had crossed the island and were on the Atlantic shore.

I just recently read a biography of Aaron Burr. That strange man who killed Alexander Hamilton, Burr would most probably have been the emperor of Mexico if he hadn't been apprehended in New Orleans on his way there. His name was linked with his own daughter's, which may have been why he challenged and shot Alexander Hamilton. That same daughter disappeared at sea when the boat that was bringing her back to her father in New York from her failed marriage in the Carolinas was captured by pirates. (I had always been fascinated by the idea of walking the plank. She was someone who actually had.) There was always talk about Aaron Burr's effeminacy. He was a small and pretty man, who after all his trials married a former whore. Previously, she had married a wealthy wine merchant and was very rich when she and Burr wed. This was the apogee of her career, married to a famous, or infamous, man, but they soon split up. Not long after, just before he died, he insisted on being taken to a boardinghouse on Staten Island, near the Atlantic, perhaps here in Tottenville. In his final moments, at his request, his mattress was carried to the beach. He died there on the sand, as close as he could get to the waters that had closed over his daughter. Was that it? Was that why he wanted to die by the edge of the sea? There was something magical about Aaron Burr that has never been fully explored by the historians who want to tramp around over his story and force him into place beside Washington, Madison, Jefferson, and the rest of them. I've read Washington was very much in love with Lafayette, a slim, young French officer with pink cheeks when he arrived to help in the Revolutionary War. There are certainly many undercurrents to history that have been ignored. Washington married a widow and never had children. Am I on to something or not?

We tramped all over the hard-packed snowy streets of little Tottenville. Wooden Victorian houses. Big, bare trees. Clear sea air and cold, not too cold. But we four ragamuffins in our dark clothes, hunched down, hands in pockets, braced ourselves and were brave as we trudged down the middle of the streets. Tottenville had single bulbs strung overhead at each intersection, throwing long black shadows as we crunched away from them, heading towards the next intersections. As we passed under them, the lights flickered and swung in the night wind. The streets were lined with empty trees, lacing their branches together against the blue-black sky. Through them we could see little diamond stars. In the Middle Ages, people thought the sky was a bowl and that at night, when the sun was down, you could see the little holes in the bowl letting the light of an even more brilliant world shine through. As a child in Michigan, I could easily imagine that at night. I could imagine it again in Tottenville.

A timeless world lit only by the streetlights at the intersections. All white and bare, under the navy blue light of the night. We four black figures, travelers, seekers, pilgrims crossing the snow in the cold, cold night, but not complaining. None of us knew quite why we had impetuously run off to Tottenville, but we were artists—or so we believed. Looking for new experiences and exploring our emotions. This was before drugs.

We slowly crisscrossed Tottenville in the night. There were no cars out on this cold Christmas night. Only one light shone from an upstairs window in all of the town. It must have been a bedroom window. High in a tall, square, befurbelowed Victorian house, dripping in porches and wooden gingerbread, like a damp cake with the single large candle of a wooden tower. Someone was in the house and that someone was up. Reading in the night, perhaps drunken in the night, maybe not able to go on one more minute with his or her meaningless, frozen life. I imagined it all in a moment. A leftover, once-monied Tottenville family. The last child who never left home (a man, a woman?), well-read and lonely in their upstairs room. Knowing that nothing was keeping them there but having no idea of where to go. Not for me, I thought. That will never be me.

Illy was enjoying his adventure. The snow, the dark blue light, the swinging streetlights. Almost golden crystals themselves in the crystalline night. Alfred was probably imagining it all as a ballet set or a box by Joseph Cornell. Small images of dark nights, snowflakes, lacy trees. It was exactly the kind of night when the ballerina Taglioni might have descended from her carriage into the snow to dance for bandits, in exchange for being allowed to keep her diamonds. Alfred would have loved the night for these things. Tottenville was a kind of ballet decor.

Sapphire-eyed Fabian would have enjoyed it only because he was with dancers from the opera he didn't knew well in a place he knew not at all. He was adventuresome. All dancers are adventuresome. Perhaps even more so then, when most people in the United States had never seen a ballet dancer, let alone a ballet.

Finally, we returned and sat in the train station, keeping warm, for about an hour. Then the conductor walked along the slippery platform swinging his lantern, the lights went on in the train, and we were ready to return to New York.

It was beginning to get light as we recrossed on the ferry. We had no money left for even a cup of coffee. What we had would be required for our subway fares. We were so honest. None of us would have dreamed of jumping the turnstile, even in desperation. We would have walked first.

On the boat and during the snowy walk, Illy never touched me. It would have been quite out of character for him even to throw his arm over someone's shoulder in camaraderie. I wasn't surprised, and *would* have been surprised if he had made some kind of affectionate gesture. Which he never would have, particularly in front of Alfred and Fabian.

On the staircase going down to the subway at South Ferry, we were behind Alfred and Fabian, and I said to him, "How about a sleepover?" He looked at me with those sly, almost Oriental, Genghis Khan eyes and said, "How about a fuck-over?" and reached over and pinched my ass. Quite out of character. Illy couldn't easily be affectionate, but occasionally he could be pretty cute.

Alfred got off at Fourteenth Street and we left Fabian on the train to go to the Upper West Side, where he shared an apartment with some other boys. We offered no explanation to him as to why we were getting off the train together. I'm sure he thought we were going to go sleep together somewhere, which wouldn't be really discussible news in the dressing room. That we were lovers of a kind would be. But he wouldn't draw conclusions without more evidence. I knew he would gossip. All ballet boys do. But we were limiting the damage and having a fuck-over. It was a good one.

Harry Thinks About
Antony Tudor

There was something reptilian about Antony Tudor. Snake-like. He was one of those people you can't care about. No matter what terrible thing you might hear had happened to them, you wouldn't care. He was very unlikable. He probably wanted it that way. He didn't like me.

Our paths never crossed except in partnering class. He taught regular class once a day, but I never took his class. I only took Miss Craske's. He had a kind of movement style that I really didn't want to develop: a really erect spine with the legs under it, going this way and that. All on one plane. No leaping or turning. Something like someone balancing a broom on the tip of their finger. You know how that goes? The broom swaying slightly and the person under it lunging in all directions to keep it upright. That was sort of the way he put dance steps together.

In partnering class, he taught the classics: White Swan, Black Swan, *Nutcracker,* sometimes something from his *Lilac Garden.* Only the last had some of that skidding backwards and forwards.

I took one regular class from him and I didn't like it. He had an annoying trick of placing his hand between a boy's legs and demanding that they hold it there with the strength of the inner thigh muscles. Of course, the boys who were sucking up to him, trying to get into the company or thinking he could get better parts for them, smirked and flirted. I just stared him in the eye when he tried it with me and clamped down real hard so he had a hell of a time getting his little pink hand out. He even seemed a little embarrassed, which was unheard of in his case.

He was bald with fringe in the back, rather like Mr. Bing, the director of the opera. They both had a kind of bald-eagle shape to their heads, their noses a bit beaklike. Mr. Bing had a kinder and more open look in his eyes, which were dark. Antony Tudor's were blue and hooded, like a snake, with the same dead, cobra gaze. He always seemed slightly drugged. Maybe he was.

Whenever I took his partnering class, he always affected that he couldn't remember my name, although he knew everyone else's. One day my partner Irene and I were doing that lifting part where the White Swan pas de deux starts and he wanted to correct something. "You," he said, "Umm, umm, umm . . ."

"Harry," I said, spelling it out across the chest of my T-shirt with my finger: "H-A-R-R-Y. Not such a hard name to remember."

He blushed and said, "I'm sorry." But he never called me by name after that, either.

It wasn't a problem, really. We rarely saw each other, and I'm sure I never occupied his thoughts. One night, as I was coming into the theater, he was at the stage door, beautifully dressed, to accompany someone to the performance, I guess. He was wearing a navy blue suit and the vest was double-breasted with little curving lapels. Very English. Very smart, actually. It made me like him a little better.

One of the older dancers in the company, who had been with Ballet Theatre, told me they had been in a rehearsal of *Undertow* with Tudor's former lover Hugh Laing in the lead role. At that time, Hugh Laing had been Tudor's lover for umpteen years. Evidently Tudor was lashing out with his viper's tongue, telling some dancer how hopeless he was when Hugh Laing broke in and said, "Oh, fuck you. You're all washed up. You haven't choreographed anything in years." In a voice that could be heard all over the theater.

Tudor said nothing, just hung his head and walked into the wings. The rehearsal was over. As I said, you might have felt sorry for someone else, but never for him. There was something so lethal, so mean, about him, you would have felt you were really overdoing it by feeling any sympathy for him.

There *was* something of a cobra about him. You always felt he was coiled to strike and you'd do best to stay out of reach. Except for those gullible guys who thought a few minutes in the sack with Mr. Tudor might pay off career-wise.

I found out Illy had slept with him when we were lying in bed one night having just done the Big Nasty. He was lying there stretching those beautiful thighs and calves and feet. Illy had great feet, much better than mine. It made me think of the White Swan pas de deux, which we'd been practicing that day, and I said, "I hate Antony Tudor."

Illy said, "Oh, he's okay. I slept with him to make sure I got into the company. He was on the audition board and asked me to go to dinner afterwards. Was I going to say no?"

I didn't scream or throw up. But I was indignant. "How could you?" I said. "He's so old and so horrible."

"He wasn't so bad. He's in pretty good shape. A whole lot better than Vernon Fly." Mr. Fly was my neighbor on the top floor of my building on Sixteenth Street. We often compared his physique to the Pillsbury Doughboy. The fact he always wore white didn't do anything to help the situation.

I didn't want to say, "God, you'd sleep with anything." After all, he was sleeping with me. But I couldn't imagine it. "What did you do?" I asked.

"I fucked him. He wanted me to fuck him. He didn't want to fuck me, and I wouldn't have done that anyway. What was funny is that they called me the next day. Mattlyn Gavers, you know, the ballet mistress."

"I know Mattlyn Gavers, I see her every day, for God's sake." Sensible Miss Gavers was the only one in the entire Met ballet operation who seemed to be totally sane.

"Anyway, she called and said they'd decided they wanted me right after I auditioned. It was a done deal before I ever left the theater. They just waited until the next day to call. So I didn't really have to sleep with Tudor after all." He laughed and reached for a cigarette.

"Of course Tudor knew that when he asked you to dinner. He figured now or never," I said.

Illy looked at me admiringly. "You're right. Any other night I would have turned him down. You're quick, Harry, you're quick." He looked at me as though he was noticing something about me for the first time.

But later, after I left the opera, finished medical school, and had come back to New York, I went to see Ballet Theatre's production of *Lilac Garden,* probably Tudor's best ballet. (Who could have been dancing in it? Scott Douglas, I remember. Perhaps Nora Kaye was still dancing then. Maybe Eleanor D'Antuono. She was a beautiful dancer and a beautiful woman.) I was very moved. All that stiff-backed movement made so much sense. The young man whom the older woman really loves. The older man whom the older woman is about marry, whom she really doesn't love. The whole network of everyone loving the wrong person and keeping quiet about it. Just moving formally through the garden and their lives, not resisting where society was sweeping them.

And I forgave Antony Tudor everything. He must have been like someone who had survived a great war where they had been forced to do horrible things. His emotions were dead. I have no idea what the battle was that killed him off internally. Maybe it happened when he was very young. I know he came from humble beginnings. Was his father a fishmonger? Something like that.

I didn't feel sorry for him; we all are responsible for what happens to our emotions. But I admired him for having at least extricated something wonderful and made it come alive in a ballet, even if he couldn't make it come alive in his own life. I forgave him for being the sinister despoiler of the not-so-innocent. He

128

had put something on the ballet stage that Petipa and Massine and Balanchine never could have.

Balanchine was never interested in anything except the way bodies move, never emotion. Martha Graham was interested in emotion but couldn't make bodies move using ballet movements. Tudor managed it. Shithead that he was, he made something new and beautiful and rich for us. Then he lost it, and lived on a long, long time in the shipwreck of his life.

Perhaps that was why he was so automated and stunned and lost in petty sensuality. It wasn't that he had lost Hugh Laing. He had lost "the thing." He couldn't make beautiful ballets like *Lilac Garden* anymore.

A Trip to Far Rockaway

Illy and I were leaving a party late. Probably over in Chelsea at Dick Baer's. Nobody was there trying to get laid, just the usual crowd. Illy and me, Alfred, Tommy, and some guys we didn't usually hang around with, like Fabian and Vincent Warren. It was late, getting towards five o'clock. We were heading towards my apartment on Sixteenth Street. Illy said, "I'm not sleepy." He never was. He generally had to fuck himself to sleep. "Let's go to Far Rockaway." He dragged me down into the subway entrance at Seventh Avenue and Fourteenth, an express stop.

The next train through went out to Queens, where we changed for the Far Rockaway train. It was March. New York is cold in March. Gray.

It seems to me now, when I look back, that everything was gray outside the theater. The gray streets of New York under the gray sky. Our gray, colorless clothes we wore when we weren't rehearsing or performing. Our colorless apartments, worn with all the lives that had passed through them. The color of our lives was under the lights at the theater; the reds of *Aida,* the orange and black of *Vanessa,* the blues of *La Forza del Destino* and *The Magic Flute,* and the brilliant yellow of Eugene Berman's sets for *Don*

Giovanni. There was the energy and excitement. Away from the theater, the only color was in our sex lives. The ivory and umber and rose and white of other people's bodies, forcing their way onto us, into us, exciting us past all containment. That was colorful, too. But a color that was more felt than seen.

The color of having Illy near me warmed the leaden skies that were slowly becoming visible as our subway pulled across the marshes of the bay behind Far Rockaway. As it curved on its tracks, I could look back and see the train behind us. So out of place in the gray dawn, its bright lights, its empty cars rattling over the brown-and-green marsh grass turning its back against the sea wind. The last stop before the Rockaways was a small fishing village. Inlets full of tiny, tired boats, low tide. The houses not much more than shacks, looking much like the boats, only overturned. A surreal station stop for a train I only knew crawling through the black tunnels of midtown Manhattan. Here the train was almost like some kind of centipede that had been stripped of its shell. A long, crawling kind of crayfish, vulnerable and out of place in a world where there could be wind and rain and sunshine. A kind of environment it never had known.

Often, in Manhattan, I sat on the train and thought how bizarre and wonderful it would be if it just chugged and whizzed underground to places like Des Moines and Spokane. Making all the local stops. Just on and on and on. Much slower than the above-ground trains because of all the little close-together stops. But you could sit there, your ankles crossed, and ride on without end. The shorter, darker, more smartly dressed people of New Jersey giving way to the thicker, fairer people of Pennsylvania, making just short runs between places like Morristown and Bucks County. The Pennsylvanians giving way to the really big, bluff farmers of Ohio, who in turn would be exchanged for the thick blonds of Iowa. You would see thousands and thousands of different people, all making their little runs from one part of their own homeland to another, while you forged on, day after day. In the bowels of America, seeing all of America pass through your underground train.

But Far Rockaway had nothing to do with that world. This was where it all began. Where subway trains were born and lived in the real world before they dipped below the surface of the earth.

The sun was truly coming up as our train made the local stops along the length of Far Rockaway. This was the narrow strip of sand that reached back towards the city and formed Coney Island. It stretched to the east to become the long emptiness of Jones Beach, and after that the many miles of Fire Island. The bay getting ever broader and deeper as this offshore sand barrier reached further into the ocean. Here, in Far Rockaway, were the cottages of the turn of the century. Built shoulder to shoulder in little ranks at right angles to the subway. On the other side of the tracks, towards the mainland, were larger, four-story apartment houses, mostly in brick. At the far end of Far Rockaway were housing complexes of much taller buildings. We got off at a favored stop for Illy. He came here frequently in the summer. He loved to swim and sunbathe, and Far Rockaway required no complicated logistics or weekend invitations. Your bathing suit and a subway token did it.

A long walk on the boardwalk at dawn in March on Far Rockaway: this was as romantic as Illy got. For someone as open as Illy was sexually, he was very gun-shy about sharing his emotions. The fact that he liked to walk on the beach at dawn was a big admission for him. Something that half the retired people in Florida were doing daily was very personal for him. I realized this and tried to keep quiet. We had once made an outing to the countryside for a long walk and I had sung a lot while we were walking: "Blue Moon," "I'll Be Seeing You," "How Deep Is the Ocean," "Over the Rainbow." Songs my mother had liked and used to sing around the house in Michigan. Later Illy, in one of his rare accusatory moods, had said that I had missed the pleasure of the walk entirely and had ignored it by singing. Why explain that when I was happy I sang? Evidently Scandinavians don't. So, as we walked along the drenched boards through the air, gray with damp, I kept quiet. I was enjoying the fact that Illy was enjoying himself. I appreciated that he had wanted me to come with him. He didn't love me, but I was being integrated into his life as a trusted companion. Perhaps that was as far as Illy was willing to go.

We went down between the big piers of heaped-up boulders that separated sections of the beach and sat on the sand, after sweeping the damp upper layer away to reveal the dry underneath. It was good and made me think of Michigan, of living someplace where the outdoors was in your life as a daily occurrence. I didn't particularly miss it, but this was the first time I realized that nature was completely absent from our lives. Aside from the shifting levels of outside layers of clothing, jackets to sweaters to T-shirts and back up again towards winter jackets, there was no real indication of seasons in New York. We were just going from one indoor place to another. The life we led indoors was always the same.

As it became true daylight, we became tired and headed back through the little rows of dilapidated cottages towards the elevated subway tracks. Once we were aboard with all the local cleaning people and early risers, it took an hour until we were back at the Seventh Avenue station where we had embarked. It was nine o'clock on Saturday morning.

"It's *Die Meistersinger* today," Illy said. "We're not on until the last act. We don't have to be in the theater until four. Let's go get some shut-eye."

We didn't make love. Neither of us was in the mood.

After the theater, Illy went home to Queens to his department-store boyfriend and I went home to sleep. I love to sleep. I always have. I didn't feel lonely. Illy and I weren't interwoven emotionally. Being away from him didn't tear away a piece of my heart.

Illy Remembers
George Platt Lynes

Illy's lover/roommate/ex, whatever you wanted to call him, worked at Bloomingdale's in the necktie department all day, so Illy felt comfortable making bamboola in his own bed on Saturdays. Don't ask. I was eighteen by now, but I still went along with what older people decided in those days.

After he clambered off me, I stayed in bed while he took a shower. He liked to take a shower before ransacking my body and again afterwards. He probably wanted to take showers at my place, but I only had that tub with the double enamel lid in the kitchen. It was a full bath or nothing chez moi.

I love sleeping in someone else's bed. At least I did then. The different smell, the different texture of the sheets and blankets. It was comforting somehow, to be in the warmth of someone else's cocoon, instead of always in the home I made for myself. You have to remember I *was* eighteen.

After I snuggled and snoozed for a while, I pulled open the drawers to Illy's bedside table to see if there was anything to eat in there. A chocolate bar, some hard candies, gum? (Dancers are always hungry. You hear people talk about dancers being anorexic. They should be so lucky. I ate nonstop in those days and weighed 173 pounds. I'm tall, and was never skinnier. But at-

134

tractive, I guess.) No candy, but I found a large envelope. Dirty pictures? I wondered. Illy and the roommate/lover had separate bedrooms and probably dragged many an irregular through those bedrooms when they went out trawling. Illy said they never slept together anymore. "Never" usually means "not very often." I avoided thinking about the other people Illy might be sleeping with. Of course, AIDS didn't exist then. The clap, yes. Syphilis, too. But people went to Dr. Brown in the East Nineties and got rid of it. I knew that much, although I never had to go.

The envelope had proofs of Illy in it. Small photographs, about twenty-four to a page. No negatives. I could hear Illy still in the shower, washing, washing, washing that fuck away.

In some of the pictures, he was wearing a black ballet costume. A tight jacket with a standup collar enclosing a little white ruffle. The prince's costume in the Black Swan pas de deux. Like that. Some others were naked with a towel tucked around his waist. They were taken with the light from behind to set off his strong thighs. He had his arms crossed over his chest to make them look stronger. Illy didn't have a powerful upper body; it was slender. It made it easier to jump. Nobody went to the gym in those days. Well, a few did, but it wasn't a common thing. Still, a couple of the boys in the company bulged. Don Martin. His friend Steve. But we thought that dancers shouldn't look like bodybuilders. Erik Bruhn was our ideal—all streamlined and whippetlike. Royes Fernandez, too. Slim, trim, and fleet of foot, that was our ideal.

Illy had that look with strong thighs and buttocks. The perfect classic profile. Some of the photographs were of his head and shoulders. The face in profile. He was younger in those pictures, softer-looking. A little less handsome, but angelic in his blondness.

"What are you looking at?" Illy dropped on the bed still damp, hair wet.

"You'll get the quilt wet," I said.

"I don't care," he said. "My mother sent it to me. Let's wear it out. Oh, that's my George Platt Lynes shooting I did. He died last year. Young. I never got any prints. What do you think?" He took the proofs out of my hands and fell back on a pillow, holding them over his head to look at them. "I was studying at the School of American Ballet then. I had just got here from Minnesota. I studied with the Esterhazys in Minneapolis. They sent me there."

"You were quite a cutie in those days," I said.

"It's only two years ago," Illy said. "Do I look a lot different?"

"Handsomer," I said. I snuggled up against him and reached up for the pictures. "I like the towel pictures best," I said.

"I didn't want to do those. I don't know if he was trying to get into my pants or not. He didn't. Maybe I was too innocent for him. Lincoln Kirstein sent me to him."

I knew who Lincoln Kirstein was. Vaguely. George Balanchine and he headed up the New York City Ballet. I didn't like the New York City Ballet. All that "go here, go there" stuff, and the girls got all the best things to do. The boys were just there filling up space.

"Balanchine didn't care about me. He never even looked at me. Allegra Kent, Allegra Kent, Allegra Kent, that's all you ever heard over there. But Kirstein noticed me and told me I should go see Platt Lynes and get some pictures done. He was nice and good-looking but kind of scary."

"Was he English?" I at least knew that English people often had a couple of last names.

"I don't think so. No. Definitely no. New York. He was one of those real New York people. Almost a piss-elegant queen, but not quite. But good." He looked at the pictures, leaning over me. "He did all the famous people. Famous dancers. Maria Tallchief. All the New York City Ballet. And movie stars. His studio had pictures of Burt Lancaster, Rory Calhoun, and Gloria Swanson."

"Gloria Swanson?" I said.

"Yeah, I had to ask, too. He said she really wasn't all that old."

"Neither is Mount Rushmore," I said.

"Anyway, after that I ran around with him a little. He was a really nice guy, white-haired and handsome. He was really famous once and knew all these famous people. He had lived in France and knew Gertrude Stein. His best friends were these kind of weird guys, Glenway and Monroe. Do you know Christopher Isherwood?"

I said I had read him.

"Yeah, he's a famous writer. I met him at a party at George's with his little boyfriend. His boyfriend was only sixteen, and looked younger. Fourteen. Do you like that?"

"Not at all," I said. "I don't get it. Why would anyone want to fool around with kids?" I was one myself. I certainly didn't want to sleep with one.

"Christopher Isherwood told me a really funny thing about George's friend Glenway, Glenway Wescott. He had been a famous writer. He was a piss-elegant queen. Christopher Isherwood said to me at this party, 'Glenway Wescott isn't just an old bag, he's an old beaded bag.' "

Illy cracked up and laughed at the ceiling. He didn't crack up often. He must have liked Christopher Isherwood.

"Parties. Lots of parties. They had parties all the time. Lots of old guys trying to pick up young guys. It wasn't my thing. I heard George say something at a party I didn't like. Someone said, 'Why all these dancers, George? Aren't you getting too old for all these dancers?' George—I suppose he was drunk—said, 'I like dancers because they fuck like minks.' I thought, he never came to see me dance. He wasn't really interested in dancing and he wasn't really interested in fucking. He wanted to be surrounded by people who were fuckable, that's all, so all his old friends could see him. I figured that out and I got out of there. Then he died. He never seemed sick when I knew him. But I called one day. It was snowing. His brother answered and said he had died the day before. He was the first person I knew well who died. It shocked me.

"Let's get out of here," I said, throwing back the covers.

"Aren't you going to shower?" Illy said.

"I don't like showers. I like to run around smelling of you. Smelling of come, smelling of sweat. Can I borrow your blue sweater?" I was running around his bedroom buck-naked. Kind of crazy. I never knew George Platt Lynes, but it made me sad.

I said, "I want to go to St. John the Divine and then I want to go to Greenwich Village and eat at the Blue Mill. Then to Chumley's and laugh a lot. After all that, I want you to come home with me and stay overnight. Can we do that, Illy? I have to rehearse a modern-dance concert tomorrow with Ronald Chase, but until then let's go have fun." Illy's modern-dance concert had never happened, but there was always some choreographer who wanted dancers from the opera to work.

I was pulling on my underpants and my jeans and my sneakers. I pulled Illy's blue sweater over my head and put my gray one into my dance bag. I'd give him back his sweater tomorrow.

Illy said, "Okay, but you have to take a bath before you get into bed tonight." I promised.

Illy didn't like to loan his clothes, so I knew his letting me wear his sweater was a big deal. It meant he really liked me. Today. And tonight.

I loved St. John the Divine. I had never been to France. I'd never seen Notre-Dame or Chartres, those vast, dark spaces. I loved the light filtering through the stained-glass windows. And the fact that no one was there.

Illy had been there before and liked the gloom and that smell, the cathedral smell. Old wet stone, is that it? We used to go to church in Michigan and everybody talked as though they were in a bus station. Soon God would be pulling in from Grand Rapids. Then, everybody all aboard.

St. John the Divine was really churchy. If there is a God, he's more likely hanging around somewhere mysterious.

As we were leaving St. John's I said to Illy, "Jesus never seemed to have much of a sense of humor, did he?"

Illy said, "Maybe he was German."

We went on the subway. The E from Queens, transferring to the D at Fifty-third and Seventh, then on to the A at Columbus Circle.

Then back down to Columbus Circle from the cathedral all the way down to the West Fourth Street station in the Village.

The Blue Mill was right next to the Cherry Lane, a gay bar with a big sign out front that said OFF LIMITS TO MILITARY PERSONNEL. We loved that. You could dance in the back room at the Cherry Lane. I liked the idea of being locked in the arms of a short, husky sailor, doing something illegal.

The Blue Mill was full of Village people. Not *the* Village People but Village people—these people never change. The painters, the writers, the Village girls who always have short hair and long skirts and no makeup. So cozy. Nobody judging anyone else. Nobody even noticing anybody else. Noisy, rowdy, laughing people loading themselves with spaghetti, stuffed cabbage, and cardboard fish. This was my town. After, we went to Chumley's on Bedford Street. Right around the corner.

Mrs. Chumley was there—Violet Chumley, the owner. Chumley's had been a speakeasy. There's a kind of turnstile, where you go up a little flight of stairs and back down again, to keep the police busy, I guess, and a back door, where you can run out into a little courtyard, onto Barrow Street, and disappear around a corner. There was a Chinese bartender, who always seemed drunk. And Violet Chumley in a corner nursing a drink, with a little pair of white gloves on the table.

She was a small woman who looked something like one of the Seven Dwarfs in a white wig and a neat little dress. She was always rather drunk and talked incessantly. Except, because she was drunk, she didn't realize she wasn't projecting and no words were coming out. I sat at her table occasionally to keep her company and I always pretended to hear her. Her little mouth opening and closing, with lots of smiles and chuckles. I certainly didn't keep saying "What?" Once I leaned in very close to see if there weren't some words perhaps that were audible and I heard, as though on a very bad connection from far away, her voice saying, "I've got a terrific sense of humor." And then she chuckled. She certainly always seemed to be very satisfied, smiling and nodding and talking to herself through the long evenings.

The same Village people we had just seen at the Blue Mill were also at Chumley's. Not the very same people, but the same crowd of red-faced writers who drank too much, the women in long skirts who were older than the average girl, the fat men who might have been Irish claiming to be poets in the hope someone would buy them a drink, and usually some men in uniform mixed in. Chumley's was not off limits to military personnel; it was anything but a pickup bar. It was more of a sound-of-your-own-voice bar. They did serve food, but I never knew anyone to eat there. Illy would never have gone there by himself; he went with me because I enjoyed it. I thought it was exactly what Greenwich Village must have been like in the 1930s, still living on in 1957.

Sometimes, to please Illy, I would go with him to Mary's, the gay bar on Eighth Street, or back to the Cherry Lane for a little dance or two. But usually not with Illy. I used to go to the Cherry Lane with Alfred, who liked to dance with me. He led, I could follow pretty well. It was never sexy. We certainly didn't cling in one another's arms. Men in suits and ties used to dance together there and I thought that looked silly. Like a Charles Demuth drawing.

I never liked gay bars, because everyone was obviously there to meet someone but the pose always had to be that they were not there to meet someone, and in fact couldn't care less. In further fact, *didn't* want to meet someone. It always made me uneasy, because I only went with my friends and really wasn't there to meet someone, so everyone wanted to meet me. Somehow they could sense it. Weird thing about men, isn't it? They only want what they have to pursue. I wonder if the hunter-gatherer culture is ever going to end.

At Chumley's, Illy said, "I never came to places like this with George Platt Lynes. We always went to real nightclubs, like the Bon Soir on Eighth Street, or the Blue Note, or the Page Three, places like that. I didn't really know there were places like this." I guess he was still thinking about our conversation this afternoon.

"Was it fun?" I asked.

"It was fun because everyone always looked at us. George and his bevy of beauties. He was good friends with Jimmy Daniels, who managed nightclubs. We were late getting to a Jimmy Daniels club one evening and the place was packed. Jimmy insisted on putting another table in the front and squeezing us in. As we sat down, I heard a woman at the next table say, 'Who's that?' and her friend said, 'That's the photographer George Platt Lynes.' The woman said, 'It's like docking the *Queen Mary*.' "

"And then he died," I said.

"And then he died," Illy answered.

He didn't seem sad, only reflective.

"Do you miss him?" I asked.

"No. Not really. You know I'm not witty. I didn't understand a lot of the things he said. It was sort of like a Noël Coward play. Very stylish. But if you didn't care about stylishness, there wasn't much there for you. I was there to meet people, but it was always older guys trying to sleep with you, hoping it would be for love. They were really never any help. After a while you just wanted to say, 'Let's just go upstairs for twenty minutes and get this over with. Then maybe we can talk about something.' No, I don't really miss all of that. It was exciting because it was a world I knew nothing about. Then I knew about it and it wasn't exciting anymore."

"Will you miss me?" I asked.

"Are you going somewhere?" he asked.

"No. Not particularly. But someday I'll be a George Platt Lynes chapter in your book, won't I?"

Illy said, "I hate this kind of conversation. Of course you'll be a chapter in my book, and I'll be a chapter in your book. I'll be old and fat and disgusting and trying to get young men to go to bed with me. Everybody has to take their turn in the barrel."

"I don't know that that's true," I said. "I think you could like somebody and stay with them a long time."

"Let's get out of here," he said, and stood up.

I could see he had a hard-on. I guess that was his way of expressing affection. He was more affectionate with me that night. He didn't want the lights on and held me and nuzzled me a little bit. That was going a long way for him. It honestly embarrassed me. It wasn't the slam-bang show-off kind of fucking he preferred. I had to admit I preferred him like that, too.

Dancing with the Royal Ballet

Could you call it dancing, really? Wandering onstage holding a bow and arrow in a silly green hat with a feather in it? I was in the first act of the Royal Ballet's *Swan Lake*. Or *Lac des Cygnes*, as they were fond of calling it. The Royal Ballet from London.

Their season opened the day after ours closed. It was that tight. They had come from London short of enough dancers to cover the little stupid roles—the prince's pals in *Swan Lake*, lords and ladies of the court in *Sleeping Beauty*,—so they had auditions in our rehearsal room and I went. Why not? Illy was above that sort of thing, but I had never seen this company, and what better way?

Leslie Edwards conducted the auditions. He picked me right away without my dancing a step. Size, I guess, and nice legs.

Margot Fonteyn was the company's real ballerina. With no opposition. I guess on the company's first visit everyone wanted to see Moira Shearer, because she had just made *The Red Shoes*. But somehow, Margot deposed her. Probably by sucking up to Ninette de Valois, who ran the company. But who knows, and who cares? She was a true ballerina—particularly by Edna McRae's standards. Edna always said, "The ballerina is the person who sets the atmosphere on stage in which the rest of the

143

company dances." That was true of Margot Fonteyn. The company would be galumphing around, doing this and doing that, all nicely executed and perfectly acceptable. A little pas de chat here and a little tour en l'air there. Then the music would signal the approach of the ballerina and she was there. You could feel the electricity in the air. The dancers stood straighter and the audience moved up to the front edge of their seats. Something was about to happen.

Fonteyn was a lovely dancer. She moved lyrically and had a kind of unified way of moving all in one piece that was unique to her. No one leg here and another arm following there. Each movement seemed to be all of one piece. She wasn't gangly. True, she had no real attack, which I think is a highly overrated quality, but there was this enormous force of personal charm. Like that moment when the prettiest girl at the party arrives. Suddenly everything is different. Partly because she is there, and partly because we know she is there and we think differently about her than we do other people. Star quality—part of it comes from the star and part of it comes from us, so desperately needing something different from ourselves. Something better, more beautiful, more exciting. We aren't even jealous. We don't want to be *it*. We are content to regard it and be thrilled.

I have always been disappointed that I never saw Gaby DeLys, the French music-hall star. She evidently was all star quality and nothing else. James Barrie, who wrote *Peter Pan*, worshiped her and wrote a musical for her to perform in when she first came to London from Paris. They were in rehearsals and Barrie was sitting in the darkened orchestra frozen in horror at what he was seeing on the stage as Gaby rehearsed. She realized he was there and came down to the footlights and said reassuringly, "Baa-ree, I know, I know, I know. I can't sing, I can't act, I can't dance. But it will be all right." And it was. She simply came out of the wings in one of her outlandish getups, feathers flying in all directions, and the audience loved her. So much so, they never noticed her singing, acting, or dancing. And couldn't have cared less if they had.

Fonteyn could dance beautifully, but there was nothing particularly thrilling about her dancing. *She* was what was thrilling.

With Fonteyn, you saw the ballerina concept in action. She led her company like a princess leads her court, and they responded to the magic of her presence. They were proud to be the possessions of someone so wonderful. They were right.

Of course, Margot didn't dance every night, but when Svetlana Beriosova or Rowena Jackson or Violetta Elvin or Nadia Nerina danced one of her roles, you knew they were trying to live up to the legend.

Backstage Fonteyn did not kid around. Her magic began at the dressing-room door. No one came near her as she stood in the wings, all powdery white in her feathers, those Asiatic eyes glittering. She was already a swan. All you could have offered her was a handful of golden grain, perhaps. Only her partner Michael Somes could approach her, and he did in a big, kindly way. He didn't dance brilliantly, but he was big and very handsome and dark. Like Laurence Olivier. A movie star. He had a noble presence, too. I've seen pictures of a younger Fonteyn when she was partnered by the embarrassingly made-up and mannered Robert Helpmann. He always looked like a drag queen at the Folies-Bergère. I can't imagine the two of them onstage together. Margot must have heaved a sigh of relief when Michael Somes came over the horizon.

Margot took forever to get out of her makeup and into her street clothes after a performance, but her loyal fans would wait patiently at the stage door no matter how long it took. Not so much for autographs, but just to see her. When she finally did come out, sometimes after midnight, they would gaze adoringly as she moved slowly in her mink towards her waiting car.

The night I saw her leaving the theater she was pale and drawn with fatigue. Why was I there? I must have eaten in the neighborhood and was passing back along the sidewalk on my way to the subway. But even fatigued, she smiled that rich, warm smile of hers and flashed those brilliant eyes and everyone went home satisfied.

Margot Fonteyn was born in Hong Kong, and there was something Oriental in her background. Perhaps Indian. Which probably explains the dazzle she had that was not typically English. She was like an undulating wave that glittered where its breaking edge reflected the sun. This is not English.

The moments I remember backstage include an evening when Svetlana Beriosova was dancing *Swan Lake*. She was the daughter of the regisseur—ballet master, you know—of the old Diaghilev company, Nicholas Beriosov. So she descended directly from the ballet of the czars. She had an incredible Russian profile and those curvy long legs and arms only the Russians seem to have. I passed behind her as she was preparing to go onstage from a downstage-right corner, just near the electrician's box, and I could see clearly how thick with powder her strong, square back was. All those muscles flexing and working under that smooth white surface. I realized how strong women could be, had to be, to dance a ballerina's role. Hour after hour of effort that is akin to throwing the javelin or doing the hundred-yard dash. This is no joke, I thought to myself, as this tigress prepared to pounce and devour the stage, her partner, and the entire audience.

And, too, passing very close to Rowena Jackson, about to go on in the pas de deux of *Les Patineurs*, Frederick Ashton's ice-skating ballet. Her pretty doll-like face under the rakishly tilted little toque hat, trimmed with fur, was impassive. Quite still under its layer of lipstick and thick mascara and heavy powder. I realized that the face of a dancer is just another part of the machine, like the feet and the hands, the thighs and the back. Everything is there to create the effect. The face is just part of it. If your body can't weave those sinuous effects, those whirlwinds of flashing limbs, those icepick flurries of racing across the stage on the points of your toes, then a pretty face cannot carry you through. Pretty faces know that and do not pride themselves on prettiness: one more of the healthy aspects of classic dance.

I always enjoyed being part of the dance world because it was a place of no faking. There was no escape. Every day of their lives, you could see them in class. In a glance you could tell where they ranked in the pecking order of pirouettes and piqué turns. Did their feet point correctly? Were their legs slender enough, and were they in good proportion to the rest of their body? Could they do multiple pirouettes? Double tours? Entrechats? More than four? Did they move with grace and beauty when that music played? It was all there before your eyes, to please you or disappoint you. No faking. So dancers seldom bragged. It was too easy to be caught out.

Georgina Parkinson certainly had the most beautiful face in the Royal Ballet—something like Tamara Toumanova or a dark Garbo. But there was no impresario to move her above the position to which she was entitled. One of the six princesses in the *Swan Lake* dance done with huge feather fans, that was enough for now. She would advance later as her technique allowed. It was so very fair, and I liked that.

I liked the huge and glamorous sets of the Royal Ballet, too: great sweeps of forests and palaces with pillars leading off forever. Everything was very grand. They did one ballet called *Birthday Offering* with six ballerinas and six cavaliers. All the firepower the company was capable of. I think Frederick Ashton choreographed it for the queen's birthday. The tutus were large and sumptuous. There were feather tiaras in the ballerinas' hair. The cavaliers wore curly wigs with locks of hair stuck down in front of their ears. Each ballerina had a color that suited her: blue for Rowena Jackson, red for Beriosova, white for Anya Linden, and so on. Then Fonteyn came out all in black and gold, and it was royal. It was a kind of sumptuousness that would have been entirely out of place in an American ballet company. But for the Royal Ballet, it was their thing. They reveled in it and so did I.

147

When I talked about it later to Illy he said little. But I think he envied me the experience. And he envied me, too, I think, the ability to have done those meager little walk-ons without damaging my ego. That he couldn't do.

Fire Island

When the season ended Illy asked me if I wanted to go to Fire Island with him. To Davis Park. I had never been there.

"We can run around naked on the beach," he said.

That sounded good to me. We were so citified. Always taking off our clothes in dressing rooms and practice studios and cheesy bedrooms but only naked for those few moments. Then back into our beat-up corduroys or jeans, tired sweatshirts or shabby sweaters, and old Navy peacoats and on our way. Illy had such a wonderful body, it would be a treat to see it running wild and free on the sand.

So we went. He had friends who were renting a house for the season and weren't going to go out until the middle of June. So we could rent it from them for a week. From a Friday to a Friday.

The other boys in the dressing room at the opera talked about going to Cherry Grove and Fire Island Pines, which were where all the homosexuals went. Nobody talked about Davis Park.

Off we went to Davis Park on a Friday afternoon. A train ride to Patchogue, changing at Jamaica. I've always had great fear of changing trains, personified for me by the Jacques Tati film, *Mr. Hulot's Holiday*. The scene where all the passengers rage from one platform to another trying to catch their train and finally miss it altogether encapsulates all of my most deep-seated mid-western fears. The Jamaica change was idiot-proof. You just walked across the platform and there it was. I, of course, had to ask three people to make doubly sure. Illy lounged along behind me with a look of amused tolerance. He had no idea where he was going, either, but he had a knack for shrugging off the responsibility onto the nearest nervous person. Yet, when he had to go somewhere on his own, he handled it well.

Our train pulled into Patchogue and we hurled ourselves into a taxi. A row of them was waiting for the train, like racehorses champing at the bit. All the other passengers seemed to know the drill, rushing at the cabs, throwing themselves and their luggage in pell-mell, and away they went. We followed suit and were in the cavalcade rushing for the waterfront. A boat was waiting at the pier and the passengers tossed money at their taxi drivers and rushed down the pier. There seemed to be some urgency in what they were doing, as though the boat had a very strict schedule and to miss it was unthinkable. We were to find out later that there were boats every few hours and water taxis were available at any time, so if you missed the boat you could hire a little water taxi. But these were New Yorkers. Transportation is serious stuff. You don't fuck around with fitting into a schedule. You make that plane, train, boat, bus and don't anybody get in your way.

Weirdly enough, once we hit the long wooden pier at Davis Park, the people rushed away, never to be seen again. Some of them were met by friends with wagons; and throwing the luggage in, they rumbled off across the boardwalks. You frequently heard the rumble of wagons on the wooden walks in Davis Park, but rarely saw people. It must have been like that in the French Revolution. You heard the tumbrels rolling, but you ignored the beheadings.

Davis Park wasn't like Cherry Grove. There were no screamers there. There didn't seem to be anyone at all, as a matter of fact.

Just a few lines of little cottages strewn through the dunes, low shrubs flung around them in a careless way, and boardwalks connecting them all in a checkerboard fashion. There was one little store down by the dock where the boat came in.

There was no electricity in Davis Park. There was a telephone booth down by the pier, but that was it. We had kerosene lamps. I knew how to light and take care of kerosene lamps, because we had always had one in Michigan for those stormy nights when the lines went down.

How much the light we live in changes the emotions we have! When people lit up the nights with candles, everything must have seemed so much more dramatic, all flickering shadows, faces carved into high cheekbones and deep eye sockets. Evil or danger lurking just beyond the circle of light from the fireplace and the candles. And no streetlights. It was dark out there.

Davis Park was like that. The kerosene lamps threw off a bit more light, but the corners of the rooms were dark. A naked body seemed so much richer in texture and form, lying across a rumpled quilt. When you stretched your body across the one lying under you on the bed, it was nothing like the movies. It had no relationship to things you had seen in photographs. It was there in its own right, recalling nothing. You slid your arms under it, your penis in between the warm thighs. A mouth opened in the shadows to pull in your tongue. Quite a different world. We forget—most of us don't even guess it was different. And how much more so when you went to bed when the light went and got up when the sun arrived. Those long winter nights must have been pretty great for the peasants. That's when you stored up all the energy to get through those hustling summers when the sun went down at ten-thirty at night and you were out there bringing in those sheaves as long as you could see something. Not to mention getting your ass out of bed at four-thirty A.M. when the sun came up. Whew. Must have been some workout. Now we get up at the same time, go to bed at the same time. Keep the lights

151

on when it gets dark. No wonder everyone's bored. Talk about no change in the routine.

I guess I thought the Atlantic Ocean was going to be like Lake Michigan: sedate beaches and only occasionally roiled waters. The shore at Davis Park was quite different. Vast beaches empty of people and waves crashing in from far-off shores. I said, "Where are we?" when we walked down there without even unpacking. Illy gestured. "That way is New York. Down there is the end of Fire Island." And pointing towards the ocean: "That way is Spain." Just when I was beginning to think he was a kind of sumptuous fucking machine he would surprise me.

In June, there was still a chilly little breeze blowing, sweeping the sand free of any footprints. As it turned out, Illy and I both loved the shore and could walk endlessly along the water's edge looking for shells. He was less of a swimmer than I was. (He *was* from Moorehead, Minnesota, originally. What do they say, eleven months of snow and one month of poor skating?) But he loved to sunbathe. I learned that from him. Illy had a very rich body, not what you would expect from someone whose family came from Norway. He was very sensual and had his clothes off as much as possible. He said a married woman with whom he had an affair in Minneapolis before coming to New York had called him "my little Percheron" because of the rounded force of his buttocks and thighs. I sometimes wanted to watch him fuck somebody else just to see them in action. I never did. I have my limits.

You get the idea. I couldn't keep my hands off his cock while we were there. He was sort of Percheron-like in that department, too. It was big, beautiful, and it was highly visible with our boy romping around naked as often as possible.

Every day we walked far along the beaches, usually in the direction of Water Island, towards civilization. Beyond Water Island was Fire Island Pines, then Cherry Grove. In the years that came to pass I went to some of the other towns closer to the city. The very upper-crust Point O'Woods, cheek by jowl with the much more collegiate Ocean Bay Park. They had a high fence between the two communities to avoid mingling. But they mingled on the beach anyway. When you need to get laid there's always a way.

Further along, where Fire Island almost collides with Jones Beach, are Saltaire and Fair Harbor. Beach towns that date back into the early 1930s, probably the '20s, when people first started coming out to Fire Island for weekends.

Water Island, where we went on our walks, must have been an early town also, probably for Patchogue families from the mainland. Just a handful of frame houses strewn about, with no street grid or plan. All bleached out into a beautiful gray. There never seemed to be anyone in Water Island, either. We would sit on the front porches, dangling our feet down toward the sand.

There was something restful about Illy. He could calm down. He read.

Illy and I never went to most of the towns. It would have meant taking one of the beach taxis that bounced back and forth along the edge of the water where the sand was hard, and these were expensive jaunts. And it would have meant leaving the isolation of Davis Park. We preferred our outings to Water Island, on foot, because it was even more deserted than where we were staying. Illy and I enjoyed being alone together a lot.

Not because we were so in love, because we weren't. Perhaps I was in lust and Illy didn't mind me worshiping at the shrine of his body. But Illy and I really relished the sea and the sun and the emptiness and didn't want to be distracted from it.

While we were walking along the beach, we were often passed by the beach taxis, the drivers waving and shouting in a friendly manner. In the night you could see them, too, burrowing through the darkness, headlights flashing across the foamy edges of the incoming comers. Whole caravans carrying loads of people back and forth, mostly to the Pines and Cherry Grove, where the nightclubs were. The poet Frank O'Hara was lost on one of those deep-night caravans along the edge of the ocean, headlights tailing headlights. He was standing on the beach at night beside a stalled beach taxi, perhaps a little drunk, and another beach taxi ran over him. He died the next day on the mainland after being taken off the island by boat in the night with the greatest difficulty. I can only imagine it. His battered body being carried in a blanket to the pier. Frantic phone calls trying to unearth a water taxi to come across the bay by night. An ambulance waiting as they churned into Sayville. The kind of nightmare the fun lovers of Fire Island weren't prepared for.

We took a beach taxi only once, to go to Cherry Grove to check out the nightlife. All the flightiest were in the bar there, cigarettes braced and bracelets jangling. This was before the appearance of the Butch Queen. There were no muscled men playing at stevedore hanging around the Ice Palace in Cherry Grove. Illy and I were quite a masculine pair in comparison, and many a languorous glance was cast in our direction. Curious, isn't it? Who were the prototypes for these men? Maria Montez? Constance Bennett? Rita Hayworth? Always the least talented actresses. Later, Quentin Crisp said, "Why is it homosexuals always copy the least attractive members of the opposite sex? Drag queens always look like whores. Butch dykes always look like garbage collectors. What could possess them?" Indeed. Illy said something similar. "Why act like a girl? There are plenty of real ones if anybody wants one. Men are looking for men, not girls." This would have been very revolutionary thinking in Cherry Grove, where slinky hips and the shaking back of long, imaginary hair and invisible long earrings were all the go.

Men were dancing together to songs like "Blue Moon," but the ambiance was something like a ten-cents-a-dance dance hall. All the girls were waiting for customers, but the johns were missing. Illy and I danced. He led. He didn't do a great two-step for a professional dancer, but I was pleased that he wanted to dance. And hold me close.

Sometimes my lust for Illy approached love. His touch never thrilled me. My heart didn't stop when I thought I saw him in a

154

crowd. But I never was with him that I didn't feel like sleeping with him, and in all the many times we went to bed together, that was always true. That says something, doesn't it? I think you can almost put that under the heading of love.

Did you ever read a J. D. Salinger story called "Uncle Wiggly in Connecticut"? It was always my favorite of his. Much more so than "A Nice Day for Banana Fish." That always seemed rather overdone. But in the Connecticut story, the central character is a woman who had once been in love with Seymour. (I assume you know Salinger well enough that you're aware he often writes about the brother of the narrator, Seymour.) This woman is now married to a stockbroker type and lives in Connecticut. A school friend who works in New York comes up for a visit and they get a little drunk, talking about the past. She says to her friend, "I was a nice girl then, Elouise, wasn't I?" And I knew the feeling. When I look back on the days with Illy I think I was really a nice person. I wanted to be in love, to be loyal, and stay with someone all my life. And I thought Illy might be the one. I was giving it everything I had. Now it seems so sad. Now I am loyal and with one person. And I'm not really a very nice person at all. Although I always act as though I am. I blame life. But I would, wouldn't I?

So, what is it about the sun that makes one so brainless? All I remember of that week with Illy was the sun, the cool June air, the empty beaches reaching away as we faced the glittering sea, the sea grass blowing in the dunes behind us. I don't remember it ever being night. I don't remember eating. We must have, but what? And the food was from where? I guess I brought it with us or bought some at the little store. And I must have cooked. Illy never cooked. I remember none of these things.

I remember shaving Illy's legs. He had decided he would have his body entirely hairless. His upper body had no hair except for his armpits. He left that.

Stripping down, he braced his butt on the edge of a stool and extended his legs in front of him. I had already agreed to do the shaving when we came in from the beach. I had hot water, but how I don't know. There must have been a gas tank somewhere to heat water. I used my own shaving brush and shaving soap in its wooden bowl and whipped up some good, firm lather. I worked from the bottom up. With my own razor I shaved one leg from the knee down. And then the other. I was careful and didn't nick him.

He sat naked above me, his arms folded, watching me. It was like some kind of sex ritual, but an unclear one. I don't think Illy imagined it would be. But I made it into one. He said to me once while we were having sex, "You should have been a whore. You're always dreaming up something new."

Then I lathered up his strong thighs. His penis swelled and sank back as I got nearer it, and then I would move the razor down his leg away from it. Perversely, I didn't put it in my mouth. The Puritan ethic, I guess. Start what you finish. One thing at a time.

I think it was more than that. It was the first time I ever felt truly perverse. I knew he wanted me to drop the razor and pull him down between my lips. And knowing that, I didn't. If he had gotten a real big boner, that would have been flattering and I probably would have. But Illy always needed to be aroused, massaged, played with, sucked on. He wasn't going to desire you more, or rather, before you desired him. So you learn to be a bitch, no matter how nice you are to start out with.

I don't remember how it ended. Certainly with Illy's powerful and shapely legs slick and smooth and monumental in their hairlessness.

These are the other fragments of that week on Fire Island I recall. I'm in the water naked. It's chilly. Our Illy with his big willy is hovering around at the edges of the blue, blue water. Dancing about like a three-year-old. Dipping in a toe and darting back. His body looked like an Ingres drawing. All sloping lines, one honey-tan color, honey-blond hair standing straight up, slanting Oriental eyes.

A beach taxi was coming. Being naked on the beach wasn't that common then, so I gestured for him to come into the water. To not shock the solid burghers who might be in the taxi on their way to Ocean Park. Illy didn't understand. The crashing waves covered the sound of the taxi's motor. And then it was whizzing behind him. He whirled around, giving them a real flash. Surprised, he threw himself into the ocean, sinking that beautiful body from their sight. I laughed. It was high delight in those chilly, blue waves, sparkling in the high sun, the dunes behind, long grass blowing, the taxi churning away down the beach, sexy, tan Illy stroking his way through the water towards me.

Perhaps it was on our walk back from that dip that we went up into the dunes. Illy wanted to sunbathe naked where it wasn't so windy. Somewhere more private, he said.

In the high, blowing grass he stretched out on a towel. He shut his eyes. I sat down beside him on another towel. I looked at him. He had a slight smile. His penis was saying hello. I touched it. It said hello very clearly, nodding and getting to its feet. Illy didn't open his eyes. He always surrendered himself to pleasure without a moment's hesitation. He spread his legs slightly and flexed his pelvis. "Martha Graham," I said.

I was sure that we were in plain sight of any passing beach taxi or shore walker, so I arranged myself to be seated casually leaning on one arm, watching the sea. The other hand was getting busy. A towel stood by to throw over Illy in an emergency.

I wet him up with my mouth a little, but he preferred a hand to be tugging on him. Phallic worship, there you had it, and something well worth worshiping. Illy could hang on a long while. He loved the to-ing and fro-ing, the little quick movements near the head, the long, long strokes pulling way down to the base. Any imaginative innovations were much appreciated.

157

At the end, he tightened his stomach muscles and pressed his hand down hard on his abdomen. His thighs and buttocks tightened, he erupted with a great "Gaaaah!!!" I looked around and mopped him up with the spare towel.

Illy got up and pulled on his black trunks. Whether I had an orgasm or not was of no concern. The phallus had been worshiped. It was time to move on. I always had the impression Illy enjoyed a hand job more than intercourse. Less personal.

Isn't this just the kind of stuff you always want to know about people? Particularly if they're famous? I'd love to know what Dwight Eisenhower's story was. I read recently he had to fight not to appear effeminate. Hmmmm. What a story Mamie could have told. Maybe that was why she was always under the weather on the top floor of the White House, enjoying a martini or two. I mean, after all, who cares hearing about where somebody went to college? If you could hear about their real sexual carryings-on . . . Richard Nixon. I wouldn't even want to get started.

Illy did have an amazing body. One afternoon during that endless week we were making love on a daybed in front of a window that gave onto the boardwalk in front of the house. I don't know why I tell you that except to give you an idea of how deserted Davis Park was. That someone might walk by and look in and see us was beyond the realm of possibility. Illy was kneeling and I had him in my mouth. He slowly let himself back down onto the bed backwards so he was lying flat out with his legs folded under him. His penis jetted upward from the low-lying triangle of his body, making my work easy. Something like a drinking fountain. Is that what you find memorable about a fuck? The sensations coupled with exotic and unusual images? Or am I just a very visual person? It's true, I can enjoy a well-made porn flick.

Another memory. Going alone down to the beach one morning I passed a young carpenter working on a house at the edge of the dunes. He shouted, "Hi, Stuck-up." I looked up and laughed and walked up the boardwalk that led to the house. He was dark, stocky, not bad-looking. Like a thousand guys. He was probably in his early twenties.

"You're the snooty one," he said, shifting from one foot to the other. He put his hands in his bib overalls. He didn't seem to be quite sure why he had wanted to get my attention and I wasn't, either. In Michigan "snooty" was one of the worst things one could be called.

"Gee, I didn't mean to be," I said. I didn't think it would do to tell him I didn't remember ever seeing him before.

"You're always walking past here with your friend and you never look around or say hi or anything," he said. I decided he was lonely working all by himself in deserted Davis Park.

"Hi," I said.

"Hi," he said back.

"You don't ever come down to the beach," I said.

"No. I have to work all day. I have a lunch break, but I never remember to bring a bathing suit."

"You could go in without one," I said.

"Aah." He laughed. That was obviously a very far-fetched idea for someone who must have hailed from across the bay in Patchogue.

"I'd like to go in *somewhere* without one," he said. He looked at me meaningfully. This was no high-school kid. Fire Island had spoiled him.

"Meaning?"

"You."

I was a little taken aback. In Michigan, carpenters don't chat you up and then want to get it on. Perhaps they do, but I never experienced it there.

"Oh, gee, I couldn't," I said. "I'm out here with somebody."

"He'd never know," he said.

"I'd know," I told him.

"You're just the kind of guy I'd really like to meet," he said.

"You are meeting me," I said. "My name is Harry. Harry Potter." I stepped closer and manfully shook his hand.

He didn't hang on to my hand very long, but his grip was firm. "Lloyd," he said, but didn't give me his last name. So I couldn't call his mother, I guess.

"If you want to come around and say hello, we're right down the boardwalk." I pointed. "It's called Bide-A-Wee."

"Oh, yeah. We call that place Bide-A-Wee-Wee. Maybe I will."

But he didn't. We said good-bye. I went down to the beach. I don't know why Illy wasn't with me. Perhaps he was reading and was tired of lying in the sun. He could be like that. When I came up from the beach, the carpenter wasn't there. And he was never there again. You have to believe in destiny. Otherwise you'd go crazy thinking that perhaps your fate was a carpenter named Lloyd who just slipped through your fingers one noon on Fire Island.

The last day it rained. I went down to the pier to check boat times and discovered one was to leave in half an hour. The next one was three hours later. I rushed back to the house. "Let's leave on the next boat," I said, throwing things into a suitcase. "We can make it."

Illy was not a quick turnaround. He started to pack, but it was too much for him. He dithered in the bathroom, couldn't fold his clothes neatly enough to suit him, forgot sandals under the couch, ran back and found them while I stood in front of the house in a rubber poncho with the wagon.

We hurried to the pier just in time to see the boat pull out. I was already enough of a New Yorker to be pissed off at missing a connection. Illy was furious. "You did that deliberately," he fumed. "You just wanted to upset me. You knew we couldn't make it." I turned with the wagon and started back on the rain-

slippery boardwalk towards Bide-A-Wee. Illy sulked along behind me. I had never seen him in this childish high-dudgeon
state. Where had my sex god gone? Into a pouty, handsome guy
shuffling along a wet boardwalk, shoulders slumped, hands in his
pockets, scuffling his feet as we returned, to read for three hours
until the next boat departed.

Another Summer Season

After our holiday on Fire Island, I went back to the Lambertville Music Tent for the summer. Illy was going to the Santa Fe Opera, because there was a chance he could choreograph something there for one of the operas. For very little money. I, on the other hand, was always ready to make money.

Sally Ann had urged me to come back. They were going to do *Finian's Rainbow, South Pacific, The Boy Friend,* and *Kiss Me, Kate.* She thought I could get the Harold Lang part in *Kiss Me, Kate.* I told her she should audition Rex Ames, from the opera company, who I thought would be better for the part. I knew Rex longed to become an actor and was studying singing and would like to do the role. We weren't really friends, but occasionally we chatted during rehearsals.

She did. He got the part. I wound up in the chorus. That started the ball rolling in the direction my life was to take.

Rex didn't join the company until the end of the summer. He didn't want to do chorus and had jobs floating around the summer-theater circuit. He was doing the lead dance role in *Brigadoon,* the one I had done the summer before. It was up in New York State somewhere. Then he was doing a lead in *The Boy Friend* in Kansas City, not in our production. He showed up in Lambertville in mid-August.

Of course, he was a hit in the company. Everybody wanted to fuck him, and the nice thing about Rex was that he wanted to fuck everybody. Regardless of race, creed, or place of national origin.

Rex really crept up on me. I knew him fairly well from the opera and knew his story, so none of this surprised me. And didn't embarrass me, even though I had recommended him. I don't think Sally Ann thought there was anything between us.

But Rex had a car, and I started going back and forth from the city with him. He didn't want to stay in Lambertville because he didn't like leaving his mother alone any more than he had to. That stopped me. Mother? He seemed the last person on earth to be concerned about his mother. But such was the case.

I wanted to take classes from Alfredo Corvino in the summer course he was giving in a studio over on Eighth Avenue. So I was going into the city to stay overnight in my awful little flat on Sixteenth Street. We usually got back at about one o'clock in the morning and I was up for Alfredo's at eleven o'clock. It was pushing it, but it was worth it. I wasn't about to start the second season at the opera with my technique falling apart.

My contract had been renewed, with a slight increase in salary, and I really didn't want to go anywhere else. The New York City Ballet had made vague gestures in my direction, but I didn't want to audition and fail. I thought one more year and I would pass their audition and then could decide if I wanted to go into that frigid, female-oriented company.

Riding back and forth, Rex and I started to get friendly. He confided in me. He didn't have a lover and he liked to sleep around. He started to pull me over and kiss me on the lips when I got out of the car on Sixteenth Street in the middle of the night. And Rex was a good kisser.

He also told me his real name was Rinaldo Ambrosino. He changed it so that he would have a real star's name when the moment came. And he was sure it would.

We didn't have any nights off at the tent, so I didn't get a chance to miss Illy. I called him in Santa Fe once a week. He was going to choreograph *Die Fledermaus*. I knew he had to be sleeping with people right and left but I didn't really care. It wasn't happening right under my nose.

One night Rex said, "Maybe I'll stay over one of these nights. If my mother goes to Baltimore." I said, "Mmmm." The mysterious mother. I wasn't even so sure there was such a person. It would certainly make a great excuse for getting out of anything you didn't want to do.

When he dropped me off, Rex and I were taking longer and longer to say good night. He loved to kiss and would be on top of me in the front seat, pressing his blue-jeaned groin into mine. Through his jeans I could feel his hard-on, which was pretty rampant, but he always pulled my hand away when I tried to unbutton those jeans.

One night when we were practicing our usual maneuvers he said, "Let's go upstairs."

I said, "What about your mother?"

He said, "She went to Baltimore today to visit my aunt Alice."

So we did go upstairs. We both got undressed pretty quickly, without much small talk. I got into bed first and turned off the lamp on the bedside table.

"You don't have to do that," Rex said.

"I want to," I said. I was very nervous and very excited.

He climbed in and immediately got on top of me, placing his penis between my legs. It felt very big. He kissed me and we pressed our crotches together as we had been doing in the car, but this time sans blue jeans.

He put his hands under my buttocks and said, "I'm going to have to go in you." And I came. All over the place. Just like the first time I slept with Illy. Really.

And you know how the last thing in the world you want to do is have more sex just after you've had an orgasm? Rex immediately pulled out from between my legs, rolled off, and turned on his side. He didn't seem particularly disappointed. I went into the kitchen and cleaned up, and when I came back he was sound asleep.

Rex jumped right up in the morning, looking at his watch. "We've got to get out of here," he said. "We've got early rehearsals for *Kiss Me, Kate.*"

There would have been time for a little action, but he was clearly not interested. Probably felt he'd already gone too far the night before.

So we did our two-week run of *Kiss Me, Kate.* Rex's mother was back from Baltimore after a very short visit. Her story was that she couldn't sleep until Rex was in the house. So his staying overnight must have been quite an event even if it was so abortive.

Rex was still kissing me when he brought me home from the show, but it was pretty clear he was putting our relationship on hold. A little heavy petting and that was going to be it.

I didn't really object. Summer stock ended. The opera season was in the offing and we were back in rehearsals. I was concentrating hard in my classes with Margaret Craske and Alfredo Corvino. It was one of those rare periods in life when sex was in perspective and not more important than anything else.

The ballet evening had never materialized the season before, but now Antony Tudor was ballet master, and the ballet evening was definitely on. There would be a *Così fan tutte*, and Callas would be back. It was going to be fun.

And somehow I was seeing both Illy Ilquist *and* Rex Ames. It was really Rex's fault. There was no reason to stop seeing Illy, because Rex didn't really want to sleep with me. He just wanted to neck furiously, sometimes fondle me, but never masturbate me. His own penis never came out of those blue jeans again. I was fascinated. And I didn't have any real relationship with Illy, did I? We met on Thursday nights, sometimes on weekends. But falling in love wasn't in his repertory.

165

So Rex Ames sort of snuck in the back door. I have no explanation except that I was really concentrating on my dancing and wasn't giving the situation my full attention. Would it have been any different if I had?

Illy in St. Vincent's

I stopped by to see Illy every day. As with most dying people, there was no way to know exactly when he was going to die. The dying can linger on for months and months, or they can suddenly be gone. So I tried not to miss seeing him.

His only other visitor was Anne Hatcher, who had been a dancer with us at the Met. She had been an all-business, no-nonsense dancer, and now she was an all-business, no-nonsense advertising executive. She and I had never been particularly friendly, but we had the bond of former dancers who have escaped into other worlds.

Somehow I realized that Illy and she had been lovers at some point as well as friends. I could only admire her loyalty, since no one else ever appeared.

Illy told me that both his parents were now dead and buried in far-off Moorehead, Minnesota. And that his beautiful, curly-haired younger brother had disappeared into the Pacific Ocean in northern California. He said he had been asked to come to California and identify the remains of a corpse found floating but that it had been impossible. I had met the beautiful brother, who had been my age, several times. He hadn't seemed to be the kind of person to be devoured by New York, but he was. I suppose he fled the city and headed west and when he reached the

Pacific Coast realized there was no farther to flee and he was still who he was.

I couldn't stay too long at Illy's bedside, but I would hold his hand and chat a few minutes while I was passing through on my rounds. He asked me one day if I ever saw any of the people we had known at the opera, any of the boys from the Sex Squad.

I told him that as far as I knew Antonio was still there, unbelievably enough. Alfred had gone to art school and was now teaching in Philadelphia. He sent me cards, though I rarely saw him. He was the only one to stay in touch after I went back to Michigan.

And I told him about Robby Schmidt. I told him that I had run into Robby on the corner of Bleecker and Carmine Streets shortly after I had seen him at the Metropolitan Museum. He really had become a street person; a wrinkled little creature with stray, gray hair, mad eyes, and a bad smell. He smiled, teeth loosely scattered in his mouth. "Hi, where are you going?" he asked.

"Mona's Candlelight," I said. Robby blinked. Mona's had been down at the other end of Carmine Street thirty years ago. An after-hours hangout when all the other clubs had closed. It was really called the Royal Roost, but had been Mona's Candlelight in an earlier incarnation. I guess no one got used to the new name. As I remember, Mona was on hand, tiny and ancient, and in something that looked like a Chinese robe. There was always a mix of homosexuals, lesbians, drag queens, and unrepentant celebrities. When you had scoured the town until four in the morning you could go sex shopping at Mona's among the dregs. A very similar crowd to the Five Oaks up on Grove Street. When the Five Oaks closed, they moved en masse to Mona's. Mona's had closed at least twenty years ago.

Robby's drug-crushed brain was trying to process the news that I was on my way to the now-nonexistent Mona's. He was thinking, What year is it? Is it 1958? Am I in fact still young and beautiful and this old wreck of a body is just a bad dream? Are we still at the Opera? Is Harry on his way to meet Rex Ames or Illy Ilquist at Mona's Candlelight?

Out of the chaos that was his brain he asked for twenty dollars, so I gave it to him. It was a bad idea. When I came home from the hospital the next night he was waiting on my doorstep. I don't know how he had found out where I lived. He still had some cunning in that drug-raddled little brain. He wanted another twenty dollars. Of course, I gave it to him. Then he proceeded to wait every night. This went on for a month. It was pretty depressing. Yet I knew it was for his night's lodging and if I didn't give it to him he'd wind up sleeping on the street.

It had to stop. It wasn't that I didn't have the money. It was the oppressiveness of knowing that at the end of every day Robby would be waiting. Crazy as he was, he realized he'd stumbled onto a good thing. Even when I worked late, he was always there. He would have waited all night for his twenty dollars. He had nothing better to do. One night I told him, "I'm going to rent you a hotel room, Robby. This is ridiculous. You're living from day to day and I'm being driven mad by your hanging about like this." Robby didn't seem to be particularly pleased. Being able to take care of yourself seems to depend on how far ahead you project your life. For Robby, it was one day. As long as he was all right until the next day, that was good enough for him. When the next day dawned and he had no money or lodging, no food, no bed, he became hysterical. Until he got some money. Twenty dollars would do. As soon as he was secure for the next twenty-four hours, his hysteria subsided and he lived in the moment.

Some people are okay as long as they know what's going on for the next two weeks, from paycheck to paycheck. Only when the paychecks stop do they unhinge and worry about their future.

169

I have a two-year span of projection. I look ahead and have some idea of what I'll be doing for the next two years and that's enough of a plan for the future. There are some people who need to project to the end of their lives. I'm not *that* uptight.

So I created a one-month plan for the future for Robby. After some hunting and inquiring, I found a cheap hotel near Times Square. Not a fleabag, but grim. They changed the sheets and towels weekly. A small but not too dismal corner room with its own bath. I paid for it one month in advance. Now Robby had a key in his hand and a roof over his head. A few times after he continued to show up at my home and I turned down his requests for money flat, he got the picture.

That was when I got an answering machine on the telephone at home, too. I thought it was pretentious. I didn't have the kind of life where a missed phone call mattered very much. But then Robby began to call nightly to complain about his hotel room. Could he be moved to a better hotel? The spoiled child he always was hadn't disappeared into the clouds of drugs he'd taken. When he was young and beautiful, he had demanded petulantly of older lovers any number of unreasonable things, and they'd always been delivered. Continuing to demand unreasonably still worked pretty well for him. People who pitied him delivered to his demands, but they soon disappeared and had to be replaced with other pitying people.

So when the phone rang, I stopped picking up until the machine told us who was on the line. It was rude, and I hated doing it, but it weaned Robby of calling. When he fell upon the answering machine time after time, he stopped calling. But I was never able to dispense with it, because he would randomly call from time to time, hoping I had let my defenses down.

I paid for that hotel room for a year, rarely seeing Robby. Then one day he was at the hospital. He had the reception desk page me. He had never done that before. When I went down to the reception area, he confronted me in an angry manner. "I want to go to California," he said. "I have friends there I can stay with, in Los Angeles. I hate the weather here. I want an airline ticket."

I knew what he would do with an airline ticket. "I'll get you a ticket, but it will be one-way and unchangeable and nonredeemable," I told him. "You pick the date and it will be done." He turned and rushed out.

The next day he was back. He paged me again, and when I came down he angrily said, "I want to go to L.A. by train." This was a ruse to get some kind of ticket that could be exchanged for money. "Same deal," I said to him. "I'll get it, but it will be for a specific day and you won't be able to change it or exchange it." As before, he turned and disappeared.

That was the last of him. The hotel said he had left when I went to pay at the end of the month. I didn't worry about him. His nuisance value was so high that his absence only created a great feeling of relief.

It had been almost a year since he fled in high dudgeon. I told Illy about my dealings with Robby and he laughed.

He said, "He'll be back, I can promise you that." Then he said, "I should have come back to you."

I said, "I don't know if that would have worked out, Illy."

He said, "You were *really* in love with Rex Ames, weren't you?"

I was feeling very uneasy carrying on this conversation within earshot of the passing nurses, but I didn't let go of his hand. I nodded.

"I've thought about you many times, Harry. You probably didn't know it, because you didn't sleep around that much, but you were a great little piece of ass. For my money, you had the best little make-believe pussy in New York."

I laughed and let go of his hand. He laughed, too. "Coming from you that's a real compliment," I said, and reached down and patted him on his lank, limp penis.

I didn't care if a nurse saw me or not. Illy had been a very

171

sexual being. It had been his life. I knew it made him feel good to still be considered that same sexy person.

I put my hand on his cheek and told him I'd be back before I left the hospital. When I dropped by at the end of the day, he was sleeping and I didn't disturb him.

Whatever Happened to
Belle-Mère and Levoy Ping?

I never was really out of touch with my mother and Levoy. I had gone over to see their apartment on Twenty-second Street that they shared with Afro Afrodisian. It was large and bare and I noticed that they each had their separate bedrooms. That is, Belle-Mère and Levoy each had their bedrooms, and Afro slept on a folding couch in the living room.

Belle-Mère and Levoy had started studying with a new teacher in the village, Robert Joffrey. They were crazy about him. They believed he was going to be very important in American dance.

Evidently Robert Joffrey also liked them. He was using Levoy in the little company he had pulled together to do concerts. It looked like a station-wagon tour was in the offing.

My mother was helping in the office and also with the children's classes. Because there wasn't any other ballet school in the Village, they were doing very well with children. In fact, it was supporting the school.

I went there to see her and she proudly introduced me to Robert Joffrey, a short, dark, and stocky man. He had danced with the Roland Petit company when it was on tour in the United States from France. Perhaps he was in the productions Belle-Mère and I had seen when Zizi Jeanmaire did *Carmen*. Belle-Mère introduced me proudly to her boss and told him I was in the

Metropolitan Opera Company and that the New York City Ballet had put out feelers in my direction.

"Feelers how?" he asked politely.

"Lincoln Kirstein sent me a note after he saw me dance in *Faust*," I told him.

"That could mean any number of things," he said. "But it's good. It's good. It means you're getting noticed. I'd like to see you in class here sometime." I told him someday I certainly would do that. But I never did.

At about the time my second season got underway at the Met, my mother surprised me. She called and wanted to have lunch, something we never did. Neither of us could think of a good place to meet, so we wound up eating at the Pam-Pam's on Sheridan Square in the Village.

As we sat down, she said, "I'm going back to Whitehall."

I stared at her and said nothing.

She went on. "This is ridiculous. I'm a nice person. I think you could even say I'm a lady. And I think living with a gay guy and a transvestite in Chelsea is a very educational experience. But if I go on with this much longer, I'll become a bohemian. I don't want to become a bohemian. I want to do some kind of real work and earn some kind of real money."

I was thunderstruck. Belle-Mère was growing up faster than I was, that was for sure.

I said, "But you *are* doing some kind of real work."

"Oh, come off it, Harry. I'm never going to dance professionally. I'll always be a hanger-on in the world of ballet. I think Levoy is going to do something with the Joffrey company, and Afro is actually making a good bit of money at the club where she works." She corrected herself, "Where *he* works. And the Jewel Box Revue has asked him to go out on tour with them, so I'm not leaving them in the lurch if I move out."

"You're going to hate being back in Whitehall," I said.

"Maybe yes, maybe no. I'm going to open a little ballet school and I think I can do fine. If I have to, I'll open one in Muskegon, where there are more kids. But I know where tights and toe shoes come from now. I know how to teach beginners' classes. I'm not going to ruin anybody's body. And I've been out in the big world and seen a lot of famous dancers. I can talk a really good game now."

I was impressed, even jealous. Knowing she was leaving New York made me feel lonely. I realized that just knowing she was in the same city had made me feel that I wasn't really all alone.

"I'll miss you," I said. "And I worry about you going back there and then thinking it was a big mistake."

She said, "I can always come back, but I think the fact that I really love ballet will fill my days. I *do* love it, Harry, and it will be a pleasure getting those little girls started on something that might really go somewhere for them. Being a dancer is a great career for a woman. It's one of the few where they get more respect than men. A girl can have a real career early, and if she becomes a star, she can go on and earn money and be important for a long time. If she doesn't, she can get married, have children, and keep working her own hours to earn money as a teacher. And keep her figure. I think I'm going to be fine."

We talked a little bit about the new ballets I was going to be doing. I didn't mention anything about Illy or Rex or my illicit and flamboyant sex life. I figured she didn't really want to know.

After she left I went to see a Joffrey concert at the YMHA on a Sunday afternoon. Levoy danced the Arthur Saint-Léon role in Robert Joffrey's re-creation of *Les Déesses*. He was good. His long-legged, slim figure had a real nineteenth-century quality to it, and he was dancing very cleanly. He had really gotten his tours en l'air down. In many ways he was doing better than I was, since he was doing truly classical ballet in a ballet company, small as it was.

I went backstage to congratulate him and he was glad to see me. He said he would like to see me sometime and I promised him we would get together. But we never did.

Sleeping with Rex Ames

It was weird. Rex and I saw quite a lot of each other. He came home with me at least once a week, on evenings after a performance, if it wasn't too late. Just to neck. It was bizarre. He always told me all about the other people he was sleeping with. About how he went to a party and the host said, "There's someone in the bedroom you need to take care of." When he was shown into the bedroom, there was a naked boy on the bed shouting, "Aren't there any men here? I need taking care of and four guys aren't enough!"

According to Rex, after he took care of the kid, he wasn't yelling for more.

He also told me that one night he just couldn't get enough. He called one friend to come over, who was staggering when he walked down the stairs. But Rex needed more, so he went out cruising and found someone else, fucked him, and still wasn't happy. It was late by now, about midnight, but he went out again and brought home a Puerto Rican boy. "He was the best. He just lay there and let me go at it," Rex said.

Is there a name for this? I thought.

We necked a lot and pressed our crotches together. I was more than ready and leaking very badly, but even though we'd been to bed together once, he wouldn't even let me take his cock out of

176

his pants. Kissing has always been my weakness, and Rex was a great kisser. He had a beautiful mouth and he really liked kissing. Not lots of tongue, but that hot, ripe, juicy mouth searching yours for some kind of answer got me all heated up. I was taller than Rex, so when he backed me against the kitchen counter and pressed that denim-covered crotch into my spread legs and kissed me for ten to fifteen minutes at a time, it definitely made me long to tear his clothes off. But no dice.

He was also having sex for money, I found out. Sixty dollars an evening. That was excellent money. His picture was carried in one of the photo albums the call-boy services provided. He said he was in the book at Mulroney and Weaver, the smart men's haberdasher on East Fifty-seventh Street. They called it "the Tie Catalog." Supposedly, when someone came in and asked to see the Tie Catalog, he was shown this looseleaf binder of young men in a variety of ties. When the client made his choice, he asked for a delivery, and the young man would arrive wearing the same tie. So the client could be sure that the right person had arrived. Particularly good if one was meeting in public, I guess.

"But you never wear ties," I said.

"I do when I'm working," Rex said.

I said, "Aren't you at the opera almost every evening?"

"There's Sunday. A lot of these guys come in from out of town. So Sunday isn't bad. I work during the day pretty often. Brunches and matinees. You know.

"And there are lots of nights we're not working. When they're doing *Butterfly* or *Cavalleria*. And we're out early lots of times, too.

"The last guy I was with asked me how I could do this kind of work when I had so much going for me. I told him it was my way of earning back something for all those fucks I gave away free to people who didn't care."

"I care," I said.

"That's why you aren't getting fucked," he said, pushing me down on the bed and piling on top of me. "I don't kiss anyone else," he said when he pulled his mouth off me for a moment.

"Oh, that's great," I said.

"Would you rather I didn't?" he said. I pulled him back down and ran my hands up under his T-shirt. He had very smooth skin and was hairless on his upper body except for a few hairs between his pectoral muscles.

He often wanted to take a bath at my place, and liked to lie in the tub and kiss me as I knelt beside it. I used to run the bar of soap up and down his spare body. He had more of a gymnast's build than a dancer's. He didn't have particularly heavy thighs, and his legs weren't long, either. A little short if anything. Although his hair and eyes were very dark, his skin had a faintly ivory color. Not like mine. I'm really white. Too white. You look at me and you know that I'm made out of meat. Rex, I know it's corny to say, had a kind of marble-ish quality to his body. You could understand why sculptors thought they had captured someone perfectly in marble. He actually looked like that.

Looking at our naked bodies, you could see that my ancestors had been hidden away in the fogs of Northern Europe and that Rex's forebears had obviously posed for those Greek kouroi. Very Mediterranean in the best sense. His nose wasn't very large, and I found out later he had had it redone. He had wonderful white teeth. And he could place his voice at a certain pitch on the telephone that always gave me an erection.

If beauty is the promise of happiness, Rex had a kind of cocky, taunting male presence that held the promise of sexual fulfillment. He eventually came through on that promise.

We had kind of gotten into a routine where I would put on a cotton bathrobe over my Jockey shorts when we came in, and we would tussle. One night he had to call someone and broke off our heavy necking to do so. Evidently the man on the other end of the line asked him who he was with, and he said, "I've got one here I haven't even tried yet," as he looked down at me. I guess that's what he thought of our first abortive run-through. I crawled over and sank my teeth into the bulge in his blue jeans, and he looked down and smiled and patted me on the head. He was an expert at withholding.

But later this night we were in a position that was the closest to sex we'd ever been in since that first fateful night. I had my legs up wrapped around his waist, and as he was kissing me, he was pressing into my upturned butt. He suddenly reached down and pulled my underpants off so my rear was exposed but my crotch was still caught in my Jockeys. I couldn't really spread my legs very well trapped in my underpants like that, and I was about to suggest he get up and let me take them off when I felt his hand struggling with his fly and he had his penis out and was pushing it in me. It hurt. No grease, no saliva, no nothing.

I said nothing. I knew if I made any suggestion, his penis was going to disappear right back behind those brass buttons, perhaps never to be seen again.

Rex was very vigorous and not quick to come. I clung to his neck and kept my legs around his waist so he wouldn't suddenly change his mind. I held him very tightly when he came. It was exciting. His breath got shorter and shorter. Those last moments just before a man comes, he loses all self-awareness, and it's one of those rare times when you know he's really there. No pretense, no preplanning, no searching for an effect. He's at the point of no return and there's no turning back. He's in the arms of the enemy and surrendering completely. Does that tell you something about me?

I was in shock. I didn't come, but it still felt like some kind of sound barrier had been passed. He didn't stay in me and didn't stay around very long. It was as though he had let himself down in some way. He never was really undressed. He said at the door as he kissed me good night, "Let's see each other again tomorrow night. We're not working. We can eat Chinese."

We saw each other at rehearsals the next morning. *La Gioconda*. The Dance of the Hours. The boys were doing double tours. Mine were passable. Many others' weren't.

Rex didn't pay any attention to me. He never did. I don't think anyone in the company tipped to the fact that there was something going on between us.

That night he showed up just after I was getting out of the tub. "Leave the water," he said. "And don't get dressed." I went into the bedroom and lay down on the bed to read *The New Yorker* while he finished his bath. I didn't even want to watch him getting out of his clothes. I had seen him naked at the theater many times in the dressing rooms. I knew his penis was uncircumcised and ran off a bit to the left. Not oversized when relaxed.

But this was different. A naked man in my little apartment was a bigger event. I didn't want to start things out by sucking his cock in the bathtub before we even hit the bed.

He was there, hardly dried off, his hair still very wet. He didn't have an erection. A true professional. I couldn't say the same thing.

He fell on me, and pulled off my bathrobe as he was kissing me.

I had Vaseline and a towel under my pillow. I reached for it as I rolled over on top of him and sat up, straddling him. I could feel his erection pressing up between my buttocks. I pulled the Vaseline out from under the pillow and greased him up thoroughly. He groaned as I did it. I greased myself, too, with a big gob of grease, so he could slip in without a struggle. He went in very deeply and groaned again, twisting his head on the pillow.

It was something like fucking a fantasy. He was so beautiful there on the bed under me. His head turned. That perfect nose, his eyes closed with their long Tyrone Power eyelashes, his curving upper lip pulled back off those white teeth.

His hands held my thighs and he raised his head off the pillow, his eyes still shut. His abdominal muscles and his pectorals were strained tight as he pushed up into me. He was driving upwards to get everything he could into me. Pulling in and out frantically. He came sooner than he had the night before. He groaned over and over again. I pushed down on him hard and leaned forward to kiss him. He hung on to me hard. I pulled my-self off in a few seconds on his stomach. I'd been almost there since we started.

I slipped myself off him and lay down on top of him, letting my full weight push him down into the mattress. I reached over and put out the light. He had a little smile on his mouth. I could see this in the shadows. Perhaps it was more beautiful than it would have been with the lights fully on. But no, in his slapdash biker way, he was perfectly beautiful, any way you looked at him.

I thought of Romola Nijinsky, who felt she was sleeping with a god when she was made love to by her husband. Rex was like that. Like a faun or a satyr who had slipped out of a thicket, leaped out of a mountain stream and into your bed.

When I came back from the toilet in the hall, the light from the kitchen was falling into the bedroom and Rex was lying across the foot of the bed. One arm was covering his eyes, and his chest was lifted, his stomach concaving down to where his thighs lifted up on either side of his penis, half hidden between his legs. Here was a little godlet, fallen across my pale blue blanket.

"Can I take another bath?" he said.

"Do you want Chinese?" I said.

"Yes, but I'm going to feel like something else a lot more, I think," he said.

"Well, let's get the Chinese first," I said. "You need your strength." He laughed and ran his hand across my buttocks as he headed for the tub.

When we're in love, how lucky we are to be fulfilled by the sight of someone. This was one of those brief periods of my life when nothing was missing.

Harry Thinks About Sex

Before I drop the subject, I want to talk some more about being "in lust" with Illy. Because it's important. Because Illy is here in the hospital. I can see the other end of that arching rainbow that began at the opera in the 1950s when he was so beautiful, he was known as the Handsomest Man in New York. I think they were right.

When we made love, Illy used to say, "It goes in like six and comes out like eight." Meaning me. It's so interesting how the pattern of the sex you have with people changes as you continue to sleep with them. You both change as people because of the sex you're having together.

I think it would be interesting to do an autobiography only in terms of your sex life. No details, no descriptions, and no identifications. Just what the other person was like and what you did together. They could be identified as A, B, and C. That would be best. I guess you'd have to include masturbation, too. Those fantasies are all part of the changing pattern.

With Illy, we started out with him always wanting to fuck me, but it wasn't always accomplishable because of his king-size equipment. Sometimes I just couldn't handle it, it hurt too much. So we usually settled for me sucking him and masturbating him to orgasm. Which was, in fact, more monumental that way than when he just climbed aboard. He certainly liked it. I had to take care of my own orgasm. Sometimes I masturbated us together, holding them both in one hand. That was good.

Then he wanted me, occasionally, to put it in him, without moving, while I masturbated him. And after we had been sleeping together for about six months, I regularly mounted him, face-to-face. He came to like that a lot. Although he never moved and we never kissed. Sometimes that passivity irritated me, and I would take his shoulders and shake him—hard—as I pounded in and out of him. He reacted only when he had his orgasm. Then those magnificent legs would open up and point to each side of the room, pushing himself up to me as hard as possible. He had a perfect turnout, Illy did, and he was big. So when those strong thighs and calves and the beautifully pointed feet reached out like a compass from the center of the bed, you had to make sure the sides of the bed were clear. If I didn't prepare, he was knocking over lamps and chairs, right and left. It was actually quite magnificent to see that muscled body pushing itself up to me, seeking the last little moments of pleasure from his orgasm. But it was always *his* orgasm. Never ours. When his body was drained of pleasure and drowsy he would sometimes want to put his arms around me and hold me, but I always felt there was something dutiful about it. Not dutiful, really, but a kind of shy effort to be loving, now the lovemaking was over. Curious, huh?

The reason I tell you all this is to explain how love and lust are quite different but can be equally satisfying. There was a feeling of completion and accomplishment in having sex with Illy that had nothing at all to do with love. It was more primitive than that. It was something like worshiping at a shrine of beauty—the eternal male beauty that is at the source of procreation. Is that too fanciful? I don't know. I do know that my feelings linked me in some way with the Greeks and the Romans. Pre-Christian. Did you ever see *Satyricon*? Fellini kind of got at that feeling there. There was no love in *Satyricon*, only fucking. Of course, in the films of that period there was no real fucking, but Fellini

183

came close. You really felt the excitement of beauty they must have experienced and the feeling that this excitement brought them closer to the gods. Only with no hangover the next day or feeling bad because the one god didn't really want them to do it. So strange, how Christianity has gotten such a stranglehold on the idea that sex is bad. Wonder where that came from? It isn't in the Bible. All those old coots of monks sitting on their pillars in the desert trying to avoid temptation, thinking it kept them from finding God. What was good for them was good for everyone else, that goes without saying.

Illy certainly was pagan. He was devoted to orgasms and that large penis of his. Sometimes when I was in the mood to have sex, he would say, "Oops, I just masturbated." He would suddenly masturbate while taking a pee in somebody's bathroom. He would have it out, it would look good, would stiffen, and he'd have it off. That's what is so weird about looking at him in his hospital gown, the nurse rearranging him, the still sizable but somehow blackened and desiccated-looking cock hanging below the gown's edge. Like an aged banana. Who would think of the splendor it had once been capable of? Large, violent, bursting with semen ready to jet forth. Illy was symbolic of sex. He was all that sex really is, and it was gratifying to share it with him. You didn't get tired of it. It never became a routine experience, largely because he valued it so much. There was never the quickie in a darkened room that one could roll off and fall asleep, hardly aware of where your penis had been. That was all to come later for me. With Illy, it was like a ritual visit to the shrine of Priapus. Something you did regularly and necessarily. There was no reason to search for another sex object to make it interesting. The sex object of Illy was more than enough for fulfilling the ritual.

With Rex it was a completely different experience. Rex didn't have that kind of godlike body. To tell you the truth, for all the times it was in my mouth and in my body, I never really got a really good look at Rex's penis. Once it was erect, he didn't like having it out of something. I remember seeing it in a mirror once, in candlelight, and noticing that it had a distinct swerve to the left aroused as well as limp.

Rex was all about domination. Our sex really never varied from the beginning to the end. It didn't shift, because our relationship never shifted. Rex kissed; he liked to kiss. I think the real Rex was only present from the time he started kissing you to the time he stopped fucking you. The rest was all facade, barriers, self-defense, and manipulation. Rex saw the world as a place to be used, like Genghis Khan storming across the steppes. But once he was on top of you kissing you, his marauder personality was focused on you and his defenses were down. Does that make any sense?

Rex was a man who took a long time to come, and somewhere in that self-centeredness was the feeling that his partner deserved a good fucking, so he shouldn't come too soon. When you got fucked by Rex Ames, you stayed fucked for a while. His concentration on getting to his orgasm was complete. He wore a gold cross on a chain around his neck, and frequently, while he surged on top of me, the cross would hit me repeatedly in the face and I would slip it over his head to get it out of the way.

Rex didn't have to have the lights on. He wasn't stimulated by what he was looking at, only by what he was feeling. Occasionally, he would get very casual and want to make love with my head hanging off the head of the bed while he watched the television. It was so modern, I couldn't really say anything. I didn't feel neglected. It was a kind of double jolt of pleasure for him.

Once, when we made love in daylight, he supported himself off my body at the full length of his arms so he could see his own penis going in and out of my body. He looked down at himself the length of both our bodies, while I put my arms behind my head so as to give him an unobstructed view. We were both very relaxed, lovers of much experience by that time, so his enjoying seeing his own body invading and dominating mine amused me. What Rex enjoyed looking at while making love was himself, not me. Yet he never masturbated, couldn't masturbate. He was brought up a Catholic—that strange contradiction Italian men have to deal with. On the one hand, all the sexual sins one is forbidden, and on the other hand, the ancient dictum, probably from Roman times, that you're less than a man if you don't fuck everything you possibly can. That includes other men. Italians don't like to talk about homosexuality because, *of course,* it isn't acceptable. But in the world of unspoken things, it's quite acceptable, because it feels good.

Rex was like that. He made love to women when it was available, but only readily available. He made love to men because it was readily available, he loved all the attention, the pursuit, and even the money. Orgasms were falling into his lap, so to speak, right and left. Some people were even willing to pay for it. A handsome little guy from Baltimore wasn't going to say no to that.

But *my* feelings for Rex were completely different from those I had for Illy. With Illy, I was visiting the shrine of the gods. With Rex, the gods were visiting me. There was a kind of all-consuming dedication to the act of sex on Rex's part that was thrilling. I honestly believe I had something to do with it. I wasn't just another body lying there under him. After intercourse with Illy my body felt fulfilled. After intercourse with Rex, my whole self felt as though I had accomplished something I was meant to do. Very different. It was because of those feelings for Rex that I decided to throw my lot in with him. Which was a silly decision. One shouldn't make decisions about sex. One should just let it happen and hope you don't get too seriously shipwrecked on the rocky shores you'll inevitably be flung against.

Getting Rid of Illy

I can really be a bitch. You know, I don't really blame myself. Minda Meryl said to me once, "Your problem is that you don't feel guilty enough." Perhaps that's true. But I do tell myself I was young.

More and more as I slept with Rex, I didn't feel like sleeping with Illy. It was carnal and fun, but as far as I was learning to define love, I was in love with Rex. I think, actually, I always knew what being in love was. It was when you not only *wanted* to sleep with someone, but when you *had* to sleep with someone. I had to sleep with Rex. Not that Rex *had* to sleep with me. I have no idea how many other people he was sleeping with regularly. I say "people" advisedly. He would often tell me he had slept with someone's secretary after he had been for an audition for a television soap opera, or something like that. Rex was determined to rise above being a dancer to being an actor. He also had a good singing voice and was taking singing lessons. I always thought he could make it. I'm not sure why he never did.

At any rate, Minda and I were talking about love one Sunday afternoon in her kitchen. Josh was watching a football game. Finishing the dishes, she turned and said, "It's so tiring always having to pretend you're not totally in love with someone so as to not lose their interest."

"What do you mean?" I said. I knew pretty well what she meant.

"I can't ever let Josh know that I'm absolutely nuts about him, or he'd start having that 'Well, that's done' feeling and start looking elsewhere. It's not deliberate. It's genetic in men. You know, scalps, notches in their belt. That kind of thing."

"I don't," I said.

"Maybe that's your female side," Minda said. We had advanced enough in our friendship that I had told her I was having a kind of romance with both Illy and Rex. She had said, after looking them over, "I see, the two best ones."

"Maybe," I said. "Maybe I've never had anyone tell me that they were very much in love with me and wanted to stay with me forever."

"Mark my word. When they do, you'll immediately feel that little slackening of interest. You have to be smart to realize that it's just automatic. Of course, if you think very well of yourself, you may just admire them more for their good taste. It's when you think poorly of yourself that you can't help but feel sorry for anyone so stupid and with such poor judgment that they would fall in love with you. Know what I mean?"

Minda had wiped her hands on a dish towel and was sitting down on the other side of the kitchen table. I would ordinarily have wiped the dishes, but she had put them in the dish drainer to dry.

"Which are you?" I said.

"Oh, definitely someone who admires anyone who falls in love with me. What good taste they have to love wonderful me!" She laughed, but she meant it. She was great that way.

"I love you," I said.

She said, "I know you do, and that's why I admire you. So smart. And so good-looking. If I was a boy I would want to look just like you."

"You do look like me a little," I said.

"When I bleach my hair blond I do," Minda said. "I guess that's why I spoke to you that day when we were both wearing white wigs. I guess I thought that I could look like you. In that role, I *should* look like you. You *are* sort of the perfect Octavian. If only you were a mezzo-soprano."

"I'd have to get fixed," I said.

"And that would be a pity. For Illy and Rex."

I let the subject drop. I was willing to discuss Illy and Rex with Minda, but not the details of my sex life with them. She, on the other hand, would have loved to discuss the details. She said she was hoping to get ideas for things she could do with Josh. I don't think anyone needed to give Minda ideas on what to do. I'm sure she was a great innovator when it came to doing the big thing. "Bumping uglies," she usually called it. She asked me once *exactly* what men did in bed together. I told her that they take all their clothes off and lie down and then improvise. She laughed a lot. I was not going to go into detail.

But that was the conversation that prompted me to think about what I should do about Illy and Rex. Illy usually spent Thursday nights with me, whether we had a show or not. Weekends he wasn't always available because of that roommate who was more than a roommate. Sundays were always completely out, so that told me something.

So whether we had a performance or not, Illy usually spent Thursday night at my apartment. I asked him if "the roommate" was suspicious that he was having an affair. It was obvious that he did not think that what we were doing constituted an "affair." He said, "We sort of have agreed that Thursday night is my night to myself. That's the night the store is open late, so he doesn't get home until late anyway."

And is too tired to fuck, I added in my mind.

"So he probably thinks you're just out catting around on Thursday nights. Hanging around at Mary's or the Cherry Lane."

"Probably." This was clearly a subject Illy didn't want to

pursue while the zipper on his fly was going down and my hand was pulling him out of his Jockey shorts, in the back of a cab. He loved that kind of stuff.

The next Thursday night I told Illy I loved him very much. He said, "Well, I want to thank you." We screwed our brains out.

The next day I wrote him a love letter. Something I had never done. He looked at me weirdly the following Tuesday at rehearsal. "I got your letter."

"Did you like it?" I said.

"Yeah. Sure. I'm not quite sure why you wrote, since we see each other every day, but yeah. Sure. It was nice."

So I wrote him another one that he would have Friday, after our usual Thursday-night bout. Not to say I wasn't enjoying those Thursday nights. But I was beginning to feel like you do when you pat your stomach with one hand and make a circle over your head with the other. I couldn't really concentrate on either one of these guys. Sleeping with both of them was getting to be a kind of juggling trick. Something had to be done, and I thought I knew what it was.

Illy didn't mention the second letter. That week, Wednesday night, he was working in *Salomé*. Zachary Solov had choreographed a kind of dance thing around Salomé where she threw torches and the dancers caught them. I wasn't in that, so I went up to the theater and waited for Illy after the show. He was surprised to see me when he came out. It was cold and I was kind of shuffling about, trying to look a little miserable. It wasn't too hard.

"What are you doing here?" he said.

"I wanted to see you. I thought maybe you could come down and stay tonight."

"Tomorrow night. I'm going to come down tomorrow night."

"Could we have a cup of coffee before you go home?"

He looked at his watch. "Stan will be expecting me," he said. "But okay. Let's go. Bickford's, right?" So we went to dreary Bickford's and I really had nothing to say. Nor did Illy. Fifteen minutes later, he was ready to go.

"It would be nice if we could be going home together," I said.

He just looked at me, tapped me on the ass, said, "See you tomorrow," and bolted across the street. Our subways went in opposite directions. I went down the stairs to mine. Seventh Avenue downtown to Eighteenth Street. I felt rather lighthearted.

Rex and I often made rendezvous on the weekends. He wasn't available in the evenings very often. I learned if we both had the evening off he would sometimes go to the theater with me if I got tickets. Never a dance concert. He really didn't have a very high opinion of dance. But theater he wanted to see, particularly if there was a famous actor he could watch.

We went to see *Tiger at the Gates*. It was still running from the season before. Diane Cilento as Helen of Troy was great. She played the role as Marilyn Monroe. She had one wonderful line. When Cassandra pleads with her and says, "Helen, have pity upon us," she replies, "Why have pity on you? I have no pity upon myself."

Rex had liked Julie Harris in *The Lark* better, the Joan of Arc story. I tend to not like anything that has to do with Jesus. But Rex liked it because it was a star turn and all very serious and haunting and desperate and all that.

Looking back, Illy had the better sense of humor. His crack about "maybe Christ was German" could never have come from Rex. Rex had been brought up a Catholic. They never make jokes about God. In case God doesn't like it.

Sometimes after the theater we would go back to Rex's if his mother wasn't there and let things fly. He had recently moved to a semi-basement on Twentieth Street. A strange kind of curving metal staircase went down to the door in front of a great panel of mullioned windows. It must have been a shop at one time. He had his bed in that room, back far enough that you couldn't see it easily from the street. One night after the theater, as soon as we descended the staircase and got in the door, I pulled him to the floor, tore his pants open, and gave him a blow job. Still in our overcoats. I just couldn't wait any longer.

"Whew, what was that all about?" he said as he staggered around trying to find a light switch and decide whether we should button our clothes up or take them off altogether. Both Illy and Rex were alike in that they rarely were in the mood to initiate sex; but once it was initiated, they were always interested. Probably because so many people wanted to initiate sex with them. They never had to make the first move.

My next step was to put a love note in Illy's shoe in the dressing room. I didn't sign it. But I knew some inquisitive shit would find it. Robby Schmidt, of course. After *La Gioconda*, he was running around the dressing room when we were getting ready to leave. He'd put the note back, of course, but then he was telling Clifford Fearing in a loud whisper that he'd found a love note in Illy's shoe, which he had started to put on by mistake. Naturally. You could count on Robby to do the wrong thing and then talk about it.

Clifford shouted across the dressing room just as Illy was pulling the note out of his shoe, "Hey, Ilquist, who you fucking here in the dressing room? It sure isn't me. Except once."

Illy was not quick on repartee. He didn't say anything, just shoved the note in his pocket. As we left the theater together he said under his breath going out the door, "Don't ever do that again!" He was really pissed off. He just walked away from me. It was Thursday night, and he was definitely going off to spend it with somebody else.

I was reading *Remembrance of Things Past* right then, so I went home and read some more of the volume *The Captive*. I was really into Albertine, and just figuring out that no Victorian girl was going to be sharing an apartment with an older man and that Albertine had to be a late-Victorian boy. Smart, huh? Just about forty years after everybody else had figured out the same thing.

Albertine was a kind of role model for me. Liberated, young, inexplicable. I guess I fancied myself a bit mysterious and liked the idea of doing things that confused people about my motivations. I was into the French writers then and had just read Gide's *Lafcadio's Adventures* and *The Counterfeiters*. Plus Camus. Existential. That was me, insofar as I had any philosophy. "Selfishial" might have been more like it.

I knew I had to make one more move, so I went over to Illy's the next Sunday. No rehearsals for a dance concert, and I told Minda I was busy. She knew I was up to something, but I'm not a confider. This business of having to confide everything to your best girlfriend, who then runs off with your boyfriend, seems very female to me. And very gay. Keep your own counsel is my motto. So when the shit hits the fan you only need to look like an ass to yourself.

So I showed up there about noon. I rang the bell downstairs and Stan answered the intercom. "This is Harry. Is Illy there? Can he come downstairs?" Intercom cuts off. Illy comes on. Disbelief.

"Harry?"

"Yes. I came over to see if you could have brunch." His voice squawked and garbled through the box the way voices on intercoms do.

"I'll be down. Don't come up."

I stood around in the little foyer. You know how dreary those buildings are. The floor with those little black-and-white tiles. Some of them missing, filled in with cement, not very neatly. Those crumbly brown walls, the color of a cardboard box, the white plaster underneath bubbling through here and there. No graffiti, but random marks where the edge of somebody's mattress has grazed the wall going in or out. The mailboxes looking like somebody has screwdrivered every one of them open at some point in their lives.

Illy opened the door. He was wearing a T-shirt and jeans. He was not planning to go out. I threw my arms around his neck and tried to kiss him. Illy hated kissing. Kissing in the lobby of his own building scared the shit out of him. It was 1958, you know.

"Stop it. Stop it. Stop it." Illy wasn't even registering that it was me. He pulled my arms away from his neck. "Harry, get out of here."

"I want to talk."

"What about?"

"About us."

"Harry, just get out of here. Leave me alone." And he pushed me out of the door, slammed it, and ran up the stairs. He didn't even take the elevator, grimy and battered, at the back of the hall.

I didn't ring the intercom again. I thought about it, but decided I'd done enough.

Of course, any gay guy reading this is going to be saying, "Is he crazy or something? He has *two* great lovers and he decides to get rid of one?" Of course, little did I know where all this was leading, but I still thought I was doing the right thing. I'm not going to go so far as to say I *did* the right thing.

In my own way, I wanted Illy to drop me so he wouldn't feel rejected. I didn't think he was going to suffer much guilt about rejecting me. In fact, *that* wasn't what he felt guilty about later.

I guess, knowing what I know now, Illy felt so guilty just about being alive, that feeling guilty about what he had done to someone else hardly figured in it.

He had a religious-maniac mother, a beautiful alcoholic younger brother, and an ineffective father—what else do you need? Didn't Philip Larkin write something about how they fuck you up, Mom and Dad and how they don't mean to, but they do. Bizarre, isn't it? All that fucking up being done, generation to generation. You wonder where it all started. Centuries back, probably. It takes a strong personality, or brains, or something, to break the pattern.

Now that I had the afternoon free, I went to the Thalia and saw *Les Enfants du Paradis,* with Arletty. I loved her line "I call myself Garance. It's the name of a flower." So glittering and mysterious in her spangled turban. The theater in Paris early in the nineteenth century. Mimes. I've come to hate them since, like everyone else, but that was the first wave. Before Marcel Marceau spawned that tribe of street inanities. Pointy-nosed Jean-Louis Barrault was really quite sexy. I read just recently that when Arletty was interrogated after the war for having had a German lover, the lawyer said, "How do you explain having a lover who was German during the Occupation?" and she said, "Je suis femme." Not even "I am *a* woman" but "I am woman." I squirmed in my seat. I knew what she meant. In a way. Rex could have been a triple ax murderer. I was ready for my fulfillment.

I was on my way, at least partially. On Monday, Illy didn't ignore or not speak to me. It was just that we had returned abruptly to our relationship before I had ever slept with him. I was one of the boys in the dressing room again.

When somebody remembered the note in the shoe from Thursday night, he said, "I think they got the wrong shoe. Sure couldn't have been me. They probably thought it was your shoe, Robby." Everybody laughed. Everyone had already slept with Robby. Not much chance that someone had a crush on him.

Actually, Robby had figured out who it was. We were going down in the elevator later that day, made up to the teeth wearing nineteenth-century tuxedos for the ball scene in *La Traviata*. Callas was singing. I said nothing. He said nothing.

Just before the elevator got to the stage level he said, "Innocent little Harry. If people only knew, they wouldn't be calling you the White Virgin." And we walked out toward the set where Callas was already waiting, wearing a pink satin ball gown with an enormous skirt.

195

The New Ballet

No one in the ballet company noticed that Illy and I weren't in any kind of contact, but they had never noticed when we were. Everyone laughed and made wisecracks and talked to each other in a group, so the fact that two of their group didn't make any remarks to each other directly would never have been noticed, and it wasn't.

What was noticed, with a great flurry of talk, was that Mr. Tudor was going to do a new ballet. There was going to be a ballet night after all, one night only. The company would do a Zachary Solov ballet that had been mounted the year before. We were going to learn Frederick Ashton's *Symphonic Variations,* which was for three couples only, and Mr. Tudor announced that, after many years of creating nothing, he was going to do a new ballet.

It was going to be called *Inquiétante.* I looked it up in my French dictionary (I was trying to learn French, too), and it meant "disquieting." Well, he certainly was a disquieting person, if I understood the word clearly, so maybe this was a good title. We'd see if it was a good ballet.

We rehearsed the ballet for *Faust* until the lunch break. It had been getting sloppy. Zachary wanted to add what he called a *ballabile.* I guess that meant a big frenzied ending. Well, it was big and it was frenzied, that was for sure. Actually, Zachary was very wise. So many of the company couldn't dance their way out of a paper bag, it was better to fill the stage with a lot of activity, where the audience couldn't see if there was any precision or not. The less precision demanded of the company, the better. The last movement we just held hands and did a giant ring-around-the-rosy. Simple but effective. Certainly not hard to learn.

After the lunch break, Antony Tudor showed up and said we would start to learn his ballet that afternoon. He said he wanted to use the ballet to show off the abilities of the company, so he was going to have two main leads and eight soloists, and everyone in the company would have some solo or duo movement. Perhaps brief, but they would have their moment in the spotlight.

Everyone was very excited. All ballet dancers believe that with the right break, stardom is just over the hill. Wealth and even fame are of no great moment; it is the chance to dance that they yearn for, to have those few instants of flying and darting about in the enchanted gaze of their audience. That is what they live for, and to deny them is like refusing water to someone crossing a desert. They are famished for those moments.

I was in back and only barely heard Tudor say, "The leads are going to be Asia Mercooleva and Harry Potter. I think they will look very good together. She is very dark and he is very fair." He then went on to announce the supporting eight dancers who would be the soloists. Everyone had pulled slightly away from me. I found I suddenly was standing in more space than I had been standing in before. I could see Asia across the room, and the same thing had happened to her. Tudor's choice could mean so many things, but basically it meant that he considered us the two best dancers in the company. I don't think that was true. My tours en l'air weren't perfect, and because I'm tall, I could never get off the ground enough to do a lot of beats with my feet. More likely he saw us as crowd pleasers. Asia was very beautiful and had a very elegant line. I was tall enough to partner her well

197

and was unknown in the ballet world. He probably saw us as making a splash.

On the other hand, maybe the company thought they had missed something important: that I was sleeping with someone powerful at the opera who made a deal. Tudor would choreograph a new ballet and I would get the lead. It had happened before.

I certainly didn't think it was because I was star material. But I was excited at the idea that I would be learning a ballet that had never been done before from one of the world's great choreographers.

The music was going to be Poulenc. Hard to dance to. Indefinite rhythms. Wandering music lines. Helen beat it out of the battered piano in a not-bad way. For all of her pounding out of Bizet, Verdi, and the rest, when called upon, she could play with a lot of emotion.

Mr. Tudor did not improvise on the dancers or seek inspiration from their movement. He arrived with a notebook and had planned the first two or three minutes of the music. It doesn't sound like much, but two or three minutes is a lot of dancing. The curtain was going to open with everyone onstage. We were all divided into couples. Each couple had separate movements, as though each was alone on the stage doing its own pas de deux.

The idea was that through the twelve minutes of the piece, dancers would slowly leave the stage. It would not be clear who were the soloists and who the principals until the ballet proceeded towards its close. Asia and I would have the last three minutes alone on the stage, and I would actually have the last thirty seconds to myself. I would be left alone when the curtain fell.

The Poulenc music was very moody and I got the picture immediately. It was about the impossibility of love and aging and being left alone. At least that was how I was going to interpret it. Tudor made a point of not wanting to discuss what anything *meant*. That I knew. He had a horror of people who danced with their faces. Although Nora Kaye, who was one of the best interpreters of his ballets, danced with her face all the time, she danced with her body, too. I don't want to be unfair to her. Not a beautiful body and not beautiful feet, but a great dancer.

I could see from the movement that Tudor clearly *did* choreograph on himself. The movement was the kind of movement he did well himself. It had the qualities of his own temperament. It was contained and tied up in knots, then suddenly breaking out in yearning, then pulling back in hesitation. He *was* a genius, too. You had to give him that. He gave each dancer the kind of movement that was suited to their body. He had obviously thought it out well, watched the company, and decided who was going to do what before he showed up in the studio.

We really didn't accomplish all that much that afternoon. He started setting Asia's and my opening pas de deux while the rest of the company watched. It was really nice. He had her twist her sinuous body all around me, and I helped her place her limbs here and there. We didn't move around the floor much. He explained that with all the couples, we didn't have much room. Also, we would be onstage the entire ballet, and he wanted to conserve our energy for when we would have to fill all the stage space. I was nervous. This was going to be a big deal. A far cry from the *ballabile* and running around in circles holding on to people's hands.

Rex partnered Maggie Black. A perfect choice: he, all sexy bad boy; she, all neat and cool precision. She really could dance. He'd have to work to keep up with her. They were among the soloists, so I knew Tudor would give them something good to do. He liked Maggie.

As we headed to the dressing rooms after the rehearsal, Rex pushed past me and said, "I'd like to see you tonight. Are you free?"

I said into the back of his neck as he pretended he hadn't spoken to me, "I'm always free."

We did our class and then we went to the dressing room to make up and dress for *Faust*. We were going to try the new *ballabile* ending. It was a mess, but a jolly mess. It was the kermesse scene, so the audience wasn't going to be critical. They rather enjoyed seeing some good-looking young people with waistlines having fun. Whether it was good dancing or not was impossible for them to judge, anyway. It was just a break from watching the tenor and soprano waddle around.

Afterwards, Rex and I had something to eat at Bickford's. I had bacon and scrambled eggs. I liked eating breakfast at all times of the day and night; it was a meal I was always interested in eating. Then we took the subway down to my place.

I haven't really told you all that much about Rex, have I? He lived with his mother. I've told you that. She went back to Baltimore occasionally to visit relatives, and while she was away, we could get it on at his apartment. But that was rare. (The night I dragged him to the floor fully clothed was one of those occasions.) Rex didn't have any feelings about being more comfortable in his own bed. He was comfortable fucking anywhere. My apartment was kind of a second home for him.

"Let's get comfortable and watch some television," he said as he came in the door, strewing his leather jacket, boots, and blue jeans across the kitchen and little sitting room as he made for the bedroom.

I knelt down and bit his cock through his Jockey shorts. It started swelling. He stood there while I soaked his shorts thoroughly with my saliva. It was really big now. I worked my way back and forth on it, kind of like playing the harmonica. I started to pull down the band of his shorts to slip it into my mouth, but he stopped my hand. "Hold off," he said. "We're going to really get into it tonight."

I stood up and started taking off my clothes. I always hang up my clothes and fold things neatly, put everything away so I know where things are. I didn't get that from my mother. She's pretty messy. I guess it's a gene thing. Some ancestor was a neat freak.

Rex found a striped cotton bathrobe on the back of the bedroom door. He usually wore that around my apartment. I put on my other bathrobe. The terry-cloth one. Rex turned on the television. I had an ancient set that one of my neighbors had given me. I would never have bought one on my own. I never have.

I don't know what we watched. Rex was learning to like cuddling from me, so we arranged the pillows, he put his arms around me, and I put my head on his shoulder. He could be very reassuring and sweet, and he had a warm, reassuring body. Except that it was only there when it was there.

I asked Rex if he had ever slept with Tudor. He looked at me as though I'd gone mad. "Not unless he paid me," he said, "and not even then. And he's not going to pay anyone, not as long as he's got those sappy ballet boys to prey upon. He doesn't figure anyway, Harry. He's just got that leftover life to kill. He can't do anything for anybody. He's lucky he's got that job at the Met. Who else would have him?"

"I would always like to be hopelessly unimportant," I said. "Then I'll never have to worry about being a has-been."

"You probably have nothing to worry about," Rex said, flipping his legs over my shoulders and pushing my face towards his crotch. "Get down there."

"Italian foreplay," I mumbled as best I could.

I was the girl in our relationship. I liked it that way. Rex was older by a few years, and I enjoyed having the male presence to revolve around. Since then, I've wondered if it was because I missed my father. I remember very little about my father when we were in Michigan. He was so uninterested in having a home life, I find it hard to imagine that he was interested in running off with another woman. But he did. Married her and had two more children. My half-siblings. I don't even know what sex they are. When Dad got out of there, he really got out of there. So maybe Rex was a kind of surrogate dad. He said to me once, "I'm really not a difficult kind of guy to get along with." And I said, "As long as everyone obeys, right?" His look said it all. He couldn't imagine why anyone wouldn't. He got very testy when they didn't. Rex Ames wasn't a good team player.

I bit him through his undershorts. He had kept them on. I was completely naked. Rex had these little twinges of modesty. This time he let me snake the front end of his penis over his waistband. His eyes were fixed on the television screen, but he was playing with my hair, so I knew I had his attention. Rex had the most complete command of his penis of any man I have ever known. If he decided he was not going to screw someone, they could have his penis in their mouth for half an hour and it just wouldn't get hard. He could be dry-humping you with an erection the size of a baby's arm stretching his jeans to their limits and look at his watch and say, "I've got to get out of here." And stand up, push at himself to get things to subside a little, and be out the door. Only to get it up a few minutes later for some john he was scheduled to see.

He had decided not to regulate his penis that evening. Soon it had pushed its way above that blue-and-white band all by itself. Foreplay was not Rex's long suit. It was that Italian blood. He told me that Italian foreplay was "You . . . there." He wasn't far off the mark.

He stood up on the bed and pulled off his underpants and threw off the robe. I knelt in front of him. I could see us in the big mirror on the wall by the window. (I had found it in the street—very nice mahogany frame.) We had the lamp on the dresser on, so his body was lit with yellow light from the lamp and blue light from the television. A marble faun. Not classic. Renaissance. Did you ever see *The Sleeping Faun* in Munich? Like that—not overly long legs; but the slope of the thighs in one direction and the whole triangle of the shoulders down across the flat pectorals and the even flatter abdomen, directed everything to the cock.

He moved it in and out slowly. He didn't shut his eyes the way Illy did. He looked at me, but in a very absent way. Dancers have strong stomach muscles and very flat. His were like some cabled bridge, holding up the weight of his outstanding penis as though it were very heavy and straining to drop. Occasionally, when he

202

took me from behind, I could feel his abdomen slapping my buttocks and it felt good, flat and hard and powerful.

He pushed me down on the bed and lay down beside me, his head in my crotch. He took me in his mouth while forcing himself in and out of mine and started probing my anus with his fingers. Hard. Like some animal trying to eat you and tear at you at the same time. Rex didn't usually let himself go like this. "Hey," I said gently, taking him out of my mouth. He stopped, pulled himself up to me, took me in his arms, and started kissing me, equally hard. He slipped his cock between my legs and we lay on our sides, him holding me in his arms, his mouth and his penis probing deep, deep, deeper. "I have to have it," he said, and turned me on my back. I pulled the pillow under my buttocks. He knelt between my legs, pulling at himself slowly, downward, as though making it as long as possible. He wasn't masturbating, more checking the wonder of it. I always kept Vaseline under the pillow. I rubbed a handful up between my buttocks and used that hand to join him in pulling down on the swinging curve between his legs. He lay down on me and slowly pushed in.

"Easy," I said.

Rex knew what he was doing. Not roughly but steadily he pushed his way in and began rhythmically pulling in and out. He could do this a very long time. Rex enjoyed the feelings of his penis in another body as much as, if not more than, his orgasm. He was never in a rush to get there. It wasn't your pleasure he was concerned with. Never. But his pleasure *was* my pleasure. The more he relished those deep plunges into my flesh, the more pleasure I had. Not so much the thrill of the feeling of him in me, but the pleasure of giving him pleasure.

I heard a famous painter say, once, "I think homosexuality is envy," and maybe it is. Maybe I was loving his doing this leisurely penetration because he was my surrogate. He was having the pleasure for me. Surely I have never had an equal pleasure in penetration. It's okay. The orgasm is good. But I never felt the luxuriant writhing about, the seeking to get that cock in as deeply as possible so every little millimeter could have the pleasure of being immersed in warm interior flesh. He loved it, and his rich pleasure was something I could share. Since I *was* the rich pleasure, how completely ego-satisfying.

I had gotten pretty good at holding off my own orgasm until Rex came. I had to put my hand over my penis sometimes to keep the regular thrusting of his hard stomach from forcing an orgasm out of me. As he approached orgasm, he lost control of himself completely and the thrusting became frantic. You could tell that he held himself back from the edge as long as he could, and when he irrevocably slipped over that edge, he crashed down that slide to orgasm totally abandoned. It was pretty exciting. I took my hand off my penis and let his body push me over my own edge.

"Hold me," I told him. "Hold me very tight."

It felt so dangerous to be slipping into that oblivion. I didn't want to be there all alone. His arms clamped about me very tightly. His lips forced my mouth open and his tongue was deep inside me also. His buttocks worked furiously and then his mouth came off mine, his head went back and he groaned very loudly. He held his pelvis very tightly against mine. He was pulsing hard inside me without any movement. I was aware of this at the same time that I was out somewhere in the midnight sky, falling and falling and falling. His strong arms kept me from falling into many small pieces, difficult to pick up again.

He collapsed on me. I put my arms around his back. He was soaked in perspiration. Slowly he eased his way out, almost automatically.

"Let's get cleaned up," he said.

He pulled away from my body and, crawling to the edge of the bed, he put on my terry-cloth robe and went into the kitchen. I couldn't move. It was all right that his arms weren't around me, but I couldn't move my arms and legs and lift my head and be Harry. Not yet.

Rex came back with a warm washcloth and wiped my body off.

Then pulled the covers over me. He returned in a moment and, slipping off the robe, got into bed and pulled me to him. He kissed me with some tenderness on my forehead.

"I'm going to stay here tonight," he said.

"What about your mother?" I said.

"She's with my aunt in Baltimore."

He pulled away and turned on his side, putting one arm back to pull me up against his back. We went to sleep.

In the morning Rex said, "We're going to have four days over a weekend coming up when we don't have to work."

Yes? I thought.

"My agent wants me to go out to Hollywood and interview with some people. I think I can be free a whole week with those extra days. They're thinking about doing *My Fair Lady* as a movie and he thinks I might be right for something in it."

"That would be great," I said. I was a master at keeping my voice neutral.

"I wondered if I could borrow some money from you to make the trip. Mom's been real depressed lately, so I've been taking her out as much as I can and I don't have any money."

"How much do you need?" I said.

"Two thousand dollars."

That was just about what I had in the bank.

"Of course," I said. "Just let me know when you need it and I'll get it for you."

Easter

The time when Christ arose was upon us: Easter. The opera was doing *Butterfly* and *Cavalleria* for school children and a number of *Parsifal*'s. No boys. Just girls in the garden scene. It was traditional at the opera that the boys could have this week off—without pay. It wouldn't be fair to the girls if they had a week off and got paid too. So all the boys had plans to go somewhere and do something, except me.

Tudor had asked Asia and me to stay and take special rehearsals for his ballet *Inquiétante*. He thought we were doing very well, but he wanted the special performance to be more than the usual evening where the critics thought it was "good for an opera ballet company." He felt we were close enough that it would be considered impressive by the standards of any major ballet company. He said. He didn't say that this would make a big difference in the careers of Asia and myself, as we would be seen by the directors of all the major companies and would undoubtedly have contract offers for the next season. This said itself.

I was actually improving a lot, reaching to achieve things that we were never asked to do in the opera ballets. Tudor was a genius—an evil genius.

I think Tudor was stretching himself, too. His choreography

wasn't all the usual twirling in upon yourself with an upright spine, whirling this way and that. There was much more open movement. Long arabesques, which were my specialty. In my solo, I was doing double tours en l'air whirling around twice in the air like a top and coming down into a very drawn-out first arabesque—one arm in front, one leg in back. They were hard, because Tudor wanted them done with no preparation. No popping up on your toes and then coming down hard to give you the thrust to get into the air. Turning was not my best thing, but it was his, and his coaching was helping me a lot. With that spine and not-too-long legs, he could pirouette and do tours en l'air very easily.

"It's not in the legs, it's in the shoulders," he would say. "Don't flail around with your arms so much. It throws your shoulders out of line. Feel those shoulder blades. Place them. Hold them. Now go!" He was right. I was getting it down. Three of those in a line coming down at an angle across the stage. It was going to be a showstopper.

I was able to concentrate on the rehearsals completely, as my private life was on hold for the week. Rex had taken my money and gone to Los Angeles, for his interviews with the people who were planning the *My Fair Lady* movie and to see about television commercials.

Monday, Asia and I rehearsed our pas de deux. We would rehearse it again on Thursday. Tuesday, I was doing my solo for Tudor. Wednesday, Asia would rehearse hers. Then Friday we would run through the whole thing.

After the rehearsal Tuesday, which went very well, Tudor said to me very smoothly, "What are you doing for dinner? I thought we might go somewhere and just discuss some of the fine points."

So the time had come. I think I had lulled myself into some kind of false security, thinking if he hadn't made his pass by now he wasn't going to. Cunning of him: waiting until I had fallen in love with my solo and the lure of the critics seeing me in it. I didn't miss a beat.

"Of course. Where'll it be?"

At least he didn't say "my place." "Café des Artistes. About eight? You know where it is?" I did, actually. I wasn't intimidated. One good aspect of being brought up by Belle-Mère was that she hated cooking and eating in, so I had spent a lot of time in restaurants, many of them quite good.

I did have a good jacket, shirt, and tie, so I wore them. I might be the little beggar boy asking for crumbs, but I didn't have to look it.

Tudor was already at the table when I arrived. He was wearing his navy blue suit, the one with the double-breasted vest. He was trying to look his best and in his vulturish way he could be quite good-looking.

"You're very handsome, Harry," he said as I shook his hand. My thoughts about him coming right back in my face. I smiled. He asked me a little about my background. I told him very little. I had a glass of wine. At least I was enjoying the restaurant. That big splashy 1930s mural, the low lights. The food wasn't great, but for New York the ambiance was nice. Not loud, not bogus Frenchy. I had sole, always a favorite of mine. I was thinking of cervelle with capers, which I also like. When I told him I was considering it, Tudor said, "Brains is a very unusual choice for an American. They usually only like steak." I told him my mother had always loved France and French things. Funny, I hadn't thought of or spoken of Belle-Mère in a long time. We wrote every few weeks, so I knew she was all right.

Mr. Tudor was very amusing. I told him that, and that I was a little surprised. He said, "Do you think sexual beasts can't be witty?"

As we ordered dessert Tudor put his hand on my thigh. We were seated side by side on a banquette. "Pardon me," I said. "Am I in your way?" and slid over so his hand fell onto the seat between us. He said nothing.

At coffee he said, "Of course I want to sleep with you, Harry. You are so beautiful. Unusually beautiful. And talented."

"You don't want to sleep with me. I'm terrible," I told him. "Ask anybody. I hardly move."

He didn't take it as a joke.

"I don't believe you're terrible at all. You couldn't be. As for asking anybody, I couldn't do that, I'm sure. But I could ask Siegfried Ilquist or Rex Ames, I suppose."

That stopped me. How did he know? Or was I just kidding myself? Did everybody know? Did Illy know I was sleeping with Rex? And Rex know I was sleeping with Illy? And the whole dressing room know I was sleeping with both of them? As did Miss Craske, Alfredo Corvino, Mattlyn Gavers, Antony Tudor, and everyone else who might give a shit as to what the ballet boys were doing?

I felt like such a slut. I had been sort of priding myself that I was a cut above the rest of them. Not prowling the streets picking up tricks, doing quick blow jobs in the subway toilets, hanging around in the Ramble in Central Park. Even if there was a difference, to the casual observer there was none. Just another pretty boy screwing guys right and left.

I felt insulted and a little angry. "You really are determined to get me into bed, aren't you?" I said, turning and looking straight into his hard little agate eyes.

He didn't flinch.

"I'm afraid it's a must, Harry."

"Well, *I'm* afraid it's a must that you're going to have to get along without."

Later I thought there would have been other things to say. I could have said that I was so much in love with someone else I just couldn't, even though I found him very attractive. The usual. Or that I would, but I would have to work my way up to it, postponing the whole thing until after the performance and having the showdown then. But it would have been of no use. He would have insisted under any circumstances, and right then. Tudor was a man of no sentiment. Like a giant cobra, he wanted to gorge on the prey. Then. What the prey felt was of no consequence.

"It's too bad. You would have been wonderful in the lead of the new ballet," he said. Quite calmly. His card was down on the table.

I put mine down. "This means it's off, then?"

"That's how it is."

I stood up. "That's the way it's going to have to be, then," I said, and left him and his little bald head gleaming on the banquette in the low and glowing lights of the Café des Artistes. I took my raincoat and headed out into the cold spring night. It was raining. The Seventh Avenue subway entrance was very near, almost at the corner, and I ran down into it.

My mind was blank. I didn't even feel devastated. I couldn't feel much of anything. My big moment in dance had come and gone, and there was nothing I could do about it. Who could I complain to? I could talk about it, but who would care? It was a common enough story in ballet. Except a dancer turning down a chance at a role was rare, if not unheard of.

I went right past my Eighteenth Street local stop—I wasn't in any mood to go home. I got off in Sheridan Square and I walked around aimlessly. Bareheaded in the rain. (Dancers never wear hats.) My hair must have been plastered down over my eyes when I ran into Robby Schmidt on the corner of Bleecker and Carmine. I was vaguely thinking of going down the street to Mona's Candlelight and maybe picking someone up. I was really quite beside myself.

"What are you doing here?" Robby said, all bright eyes and impenitence in the rain. Obviously out shopping for some large cock. "Why aren't you with Rex?"

Obviously Tudor had not been prescient when he mentioned Illy and Rex. Everyone knew.

I didn't feign surprise. I said, "He's in Hollywood for some interviews. About a film or something."

"He changed his plans? I was just feeling so envious, thinking of him in St. Thomas."

"St. Thomas?" I said.

210

"Oh, I know I'm terrible, but I saw the tickets in his dance bag while he was in the shower Friday night, so I slipped them out and took a quick peek. He was going to St. Thomas on Saturday. That must have been a quick change of plans." Robby was swift of lip, but he wasn't so quick to jump to conclusions. For the moment he was believing there had been a change of plans.

I fell into my role of the concubine. "Yes, his agent caught him in the nick of time, late Friday night. He went out Sunday. I'm here because I'm rehearsing the solos for the new ballet."

"How's that going?" Robby said. For all his silliness he was a serious dancer.

"Really well. I think it's going to be great," I said. Let him find out for himself that I'm out of the lead when they start company rehearsals again next Monday.

I walked back to Sixteenth Street. I threw myself down on my bed and didn't sleep that night. The future gaped like a big black hole. The ballet had disappeared, and so had Rex, to St. Thomas with my money and possibly with his mother. He was always talking about how she needed a vacation. From him, that shithead.

I had nothing to do the next morning and was still sleeping when the phone rang shortly after ten. It was Mattlyn, the ballet mistress. She was always normal and nice and I guess had dealt with these kinds of things many times in her years at the opera. "Bad news, Harry. Tudor has decided to give the lead role to Richard Zelens. He told me this morning and asked me to tell you. It was my decision to call you. I didn't want you to come in and be told in front of everyone."

"I knew," I said. "Am I back in the corps?"

"Not even," she said. "You're out of the ballet."

Silence.

"You did the right thing, Harry. It wouldn't have been worth it. He would have been quite capable of giving it to Richard anyway. He likes the way Richard turns."

"Thanks, Mattlyn. Thanks a lot. I'll see you Monday. We're rehearsing Dance of the Hours, aren't we?"

"It's been changed. We're doing the *ballabile* from *Faust*. Poor you." There was real sympathy in her voice.

"Poor us," I said, and hung up.

I threw myself into action. It was only Wednesday. I had four days before Monday. I felt as though some giant hand had swept down and clutched me. I was in the grip of something, that was for sure.

I pulled on my clothes. No shaving. I went up Eighth Avenue to a travel bureau I had seen up near Twenty-first Street and went in.

"Can you book flights to St. Thomas?"

The girl was a pretty Hispanic. This was a very Puerto Rican neighborhood, and they booked lots of flights back and forth to Puerto Rico and further south.

"I'd have to see what I could get you," she said. "It's Easter. The hard thing would be getting you back. When do you want to come back?"

"I'm not sure," I told her. "Actually, I'm trying to find my brother, who is on vacation there. My mother is very sick and I'm not sure what hotel he's at. I think I should go down and tell him. Just calling him could be a shock." The lies just flew off my tongue. They even sounded real to me. They certainly sounded real to her. In the Spanish-speaking world, "Mother" is the big word. "We can probably find him," she said. "There aren't all that many resorts there. Here's a St. Thomas travel brochure. It probably has all the hotels listed. Why don't you go home and make some calls. I'll see if I can't get you down there this afternoon if you can find him. We can always cancel if you don't."

I rushed home. It wasn't even all that hard. I called the big ones first. Bluebeard's Castle and others. No dice. Then I started the second rank, and after about four calls, there he was. The Shibui. Japanese on St. Thomas. Mr. Ames was registered. Did I want to speak to him? He was still in his room, cottage four actually. No, thanks, I'd call back later.

I rushed back to the travel agent. She had gotten me out on

a four o'clock flight that afternoon. I wrote her a check. It was taking every cent I had left, but I had no idea of not going. I had to be with Rex, had to see Rex. Losing the ballet had shaken me. He was my only stability. I could handle losing the ballet if I had him.

The only ticket she could get me back on was in the morning the next day.

"If you are just going down to break the news to him, that should be all right, shouldn't it?" the agent said in a nurse's tone.

She was really concerned. I felt sort of shitty lying to her.

"You can try to change it when you get down there." She added, "It's always easier on the other end."

I threw things into a bag. No bathing suit. I was not planning on doing any swimming. By four-fifteen, I was over Long Island on my way to St. Thomas. It was the first time I'd ever been on a plane. We had taken buses from Michigan to Chicago and Chicago to New York. I didn't feel especially thrilled. I was too hysterical for that.

St. Thomas

Even when you're in a state of hysteria, landing in the tropics after a short flight from cold, concrete-bound New York has something of the miraculous about it. Can it be that there are palm trees blowing in air heavy with the smell of rotting vegetation? A sun so hot and high there are hardly any shadows? How can this be coexisting with the gray streets of New York, slick under the dirty spring rain?

I was no seasoned traveler, even if my mother had dragged me from Michigan to Chicago to New York. But I had the sense and the money to jump into a taxi when I saw the line waiting for the passengers as we emerged a few at a time from the terminal. I was among the first.

I told the driver I was going to the Shibui, which prompted no inquiry as to where it might be.

We drove through Charlotte-Amalie, charming and Danish-looking, with flat little mini-baroque facades painted rose, white, and dark red, submerged in bougainvillea and hibiscus. "Sensual" was the word. There was something in the air that made you feel like fucking.

Outside the town, we climbed a hill. I could see that St. Thomas was largely low mountains. The Shibui was on the flank of one, overlooking the town, and beyond it the far, far reach of the ocean, glittering in the sun. Which was thinking about setting soon. Was this all the same day that I had decided to find Rex on St. Thomas?

It was. Unfolding so quickly I could hardly keep up.

The driver dumped me beside the curved entrance drive in front of a low-lying Japanese-style building. More buildings in the same style with curvy tiled roofs spread down the hill behind it. There was a smallish swimming pool at one side beside the reception building. Someone who was neither Oriental nor black, as my taxi driver had been, was behind the desk—young, male, overweight, with a tie. I asked him where I might find Mr. Ames. He told me and asked if I was planning to stay. "I don't know yet," I said. He didn't seem very surprised or very interested in my dropping in unexpectedly. He came out in front of the building with me and indicated where the cottage stood that Rex was renting. Down the hill and off to the left, the fourth one over there. I'd see a number by the door.

There was a number by the door. I hesitated. Did one knock on a door at a winter resort? Or call out? Or just walk in? I knocked.

Rex opened the door. He was wearing a kind of blue-and-white flowered cotton kimono. Probably came with the room, I thought. He did not act surprised.

"Oh, hi," he said, and opened the door wider. There was a large room with what they called a cathedral ceiling. The rafters supporting the room were exposed, with no ceiling.

"Tudor kicked me out of the ballet," I said. "All I could think of was to come find you."

"You're not surprised, are you?" Rex said. He stood in place halfway across the room. I stood by the door. "Obviously you weren't going to get that part without putting out. Everybody thought you already had. And were regularly."

"Why didn't you say something?" I asked him.

"Who you sleep with is none of my business," Rex said.

I didn't say anything. I thought it *was* his business. Shows how dumb you can be.

215

"It's okay. Forget it. He made a pass. You leaped up like a nervous Nelly and ran away and came here. What's the big deal? Having his cock in your ass isn't anything more than having your foot in the door."

Rex was skipping over the fact that I had found him at the Shibui when I should have been looking for him on the West Coast. History was rewriting itself under my feet as I approached him.

I put my arms around him, dropping my bag at our feet. He immediately held me close. I could feel how warm his body was under the cotton robe. Suntan. The bulge of his crotch pushed itself against my leg as he kissed me. It was so stupid. Like the song about when he takes me in his arms the world is quite all right.

I pulled away. "Where's your mother?" I said.

"My mother? In New York, as far as I know. Unless she went down to Baltimore to visit relatives."

I went over to the open door and looked in the bedroom door. Illy was sitting on the side of the unmade bed. His head was slightly down, his hands placed between his thighs, as was his large penis. He had obviously heard us. He looked up at me and said nothing. Clearly they had just made love. And Illy was taking it up the bum from Rex. A lot of messages flashed back and forth in the few seconds Illy and I looked at each other.

The messages were:

> Me: "You were the macho guy who's now got his legs spread for my boyfriend."
>
> Illy: "You thought I didn't know you were putting out for Rex and me at the same time."
>
> Me: "You must have thought I was crazy, acting like I was in love with you when you knew I was sleeping with Rex. Maybe you thought I'd decided in your favor."

216

Illy: "You think I betrayed you when there's nothing to betray. It's all just about fucking. You felt like fucking with me. I felt like fucking with you. Now I feel like fucking with Rex."

Me: "What a complete jerk I am. I'm in love with someone who borrowed all the money I have. Lied to me about what he was going to do with it and spent it to go to the tropics and fuck the only other man I was interested in. They were both planning to come back and lie to me some more."

I snapped. I ran out of the house and stood for a moment on the porch that ran around the building under the overhanging eaves. Illy had never spoken. Rex came out and stood by the door.

He said, "I want you to come back in. I want you to calm down. Change clothes. Go for a swim. We'll go down into town later and have a nice dinner. You're letting this thing get out of hand." This thing was getting out of *his* hands, was what it was. He was using a tone of voice that calms down excited horses and dogs. Rex was used to throwing his sexuality across any situation, like a blanket over a fire. His voice was like a hand on my neck.

"If you don't come back inside now and just enjoy the rest of this vacation with Illy and me, it's all over with us. I won't be wanting to see you again." This was serious. I walked back in calmly, so he would think I'd agreed. Bent over and picked up my little carry-on bag with my money and my ticket in it and ran out the door, up the path. Going where? I heard Rex say, "Get back here, you little bitch!"

But he couldn't follow me. Not in his silly geisha robe. I ran past the pool, past the reception building, down the curving drive, and out onto the road. There were no taxis, of course, nothing.

I turned and ran down the road. Tarry, sand on the sides. I ran. I really ran. I somehow thought they were going to rapidly pull on shorts and T-shirts and run after me. They could have caught me. I'm not a great runner. What was more likely, I'm sure, was that Rex went back in, threw off his robe, and fucked Illy again. Just to make sure he'd have someone to have sex with for the remainder of his stay.

A truck came down the hill behind me. I was quite out of character by this time. No one in Michigan would have done this. No one in Michigan would have tracked down a male lover in St. Thomas and then run off half-crazed down a mountain road. The truck stopped, so I went to the open window. "Can I have a lift down into town?" I asked.

The very black driver reached over and opened the door. I jumped in. I must have looked like a maniac.

"You okay?" he said, looking straight ahead.

"Yeah. Sure. I'm okay." My ability to lie easily had fled. "I just have to get back into town as quick as I can."

How old could he have been? I don't know. Middle-aged by my standards then, fortyish. There was something reassuring and paternal about him. I had a feeling everything would be all right as long as I was with him.

I noticed things going down the mountain I hadn't noticed going up. The little wooden houses on stilts, painted bright blue, bright green, yellow, and red. Without windows, just wooden shutters to close out the night. Starved dogs wandered along the roadside. Chickens stepped high, picking here and there in the dirt under the houses. This is what it's really like here, I thought. Not the Shibui. It's really all flowers and dirt and cheap paint and no money.

"Where you want me to drop you?" the man said. His voice was polite, but I don't think my being white made any difference. He sensed I was distressed and wanted to be helpful. A good man. They are hard to find, as you well know.

"Where are you going?" I asked him.

"I can drop you where you want to go," he said.

"Oh, anywhere. In the middle of town."

"By the hotel?" he asked.

"That would be fine."

He dropped me in front of the big, dark-red stucco hotel. Very Danish, with white trim, white porches, lots of flowers in pots and boxes. As I got out, I turned and shook his hand. It was warm and solid and callused.

"Thanks a lot," I said.

Under the forepiece of his cap, his eyes were so black they were each like one large pupil. The same blackness as his face.

"Take care of yourself," he said.

He probably would have been a good person to know. He's probably there right now. Driving a different truck, certainly. With all the money that has poured into St. Thomas since then, he probably owns the hotel. I can only hope so.

It was so stupid. I was hysterical and at the same time I felt like I was someone in a spy movie. Where to hide? Assuming they were going to look for me. I *was* on an island.

In the hotel was a small tourist bureau. I calmed myself as much as I could and asked the young woman at the desk when the next flight left for New York. To give her credit, she made an effort, but it was hopeless. "It's the height of the season," she said. "The only thing you can do is go to the airport and try for standby." I figured I was a sitting duck at the airport. I was just going to have to hang around Charlotte-Amalie until my flight the next morning.

I'm not sure why I was so determined not to see Rex and Illy again. I guess the feel of that bulge under his robe pressed against my thigh was telling me something. I might just let my emotions do the talking and wind up staying with them and doing a threesome, which is what I'm sure Rex had in mind.

Who was it that said, "Men like to give a nickname to their penis because they don't like to take orders from a total stranger"? Somewhere in my subconscious I was trying to avoid taking orders.

I went into the first café next to the hotel and sat in the back.

It was dark and shadowy there, and I could see everyone passing by in the fading sunlight beyond the door. I ordered an iced tea. The sunlight was almost over; the sun set fast here in the tropics. That I knew. I just had to hope that there would be enough light in the streets that I could see if Rex and Illy passed by.

I wasn't hungry, even though I hadn't eaten since the awful little tray on the airplane.

I looked up. Rex and Illy were coming in the door. They wouldn't be able to see, coming in from the sunlight, so I moved quickly towards the toilets in the back. I'd noticed they were moving in the direction of the kitchen. I pushed open the door marked Men. No lock. Kind of a swinging door with a shutter in it. I went into the toilet booth and squatted on the seat, locking the door. I held my bag on my knees. And sat. And sat and sat and sat. Someone came in and took a pee. That was all. Were they sitting out there having a drink? Maybe they weren't looking for me at all. I came out of my squat, hardly able to walk.

I looked into the café. It was empty. I thought of going out through the kitchen but didn't quite have the nerve. I found a waiter and paid for my iced tea. They probably thought I'd skipped out on it. As I came out of the café, I saw why it was empty. Everyone was on the terrace outside under the hanging lamps. It was murky. And just as murky out on the street. I stood a good chance of going unnoticed. I walked the streets of Charlotte-Amalie, not really knowing what I planned to do. Trying to stay in the shadows. I probably looked like a ragamuffin, dusty and rumpled, dragging my carry-on bag with me. Just another boy looking for some place to stay for the night.

I must have walked for hours. Stopping to sit on a city bench where there was one deep in shadow. Looking into little restaurants. I was beginning to get hungry but didn't want to risk being seated at a table, not being able to escape if Rex and Illy were suddenly to stumble upon on me.

A little Spanish-type place had a window on the street where I saw men buying tiny cups of coffee and sandwiches. I bought one of each. A ham sandwich on long French bread, except the bread was very light and almost nonexistent once it hit your mouth. The coffee revved me way up.

After a while the restaurants and cafés were closing. If Rex and Illy were looking for me, we weren't on the same circuits. One place, the Heavenly Blue, was full of people, and it was fairly obvious they were all men. The gay bar. I never went to gay bars alone in New York but decided to go in. Either I was going to run smack into Illy and Rex or they would never think of looking for me in here.

The Heavenly Blue was full of older men in open-necked shirts and blazers and younger men, many of them black. I went to the bar and asked for a Coke and went deep through the crowd to a back wall. What I always hated in gay bars was the aimless pickup conversation. But tonight I welcomed it. I told everyone who came over to chat that I was waiting for friends. Yes, I had just arrived that day. Yes, I thought St. Thomas was great. No, I couldn't go to another bar or to their apartment or house with them, because I'd miss my friends. I had promised to meet them there. Yes, I had a room, in a rooming house over in that direction. Indicating with my head. Sometimes in one direction, sometimes in another. It was hell and it was endless, but I could see through the crowd pretty well. I was near the toilet, and if Rex and Illy were suddenly to show up, I could pull my hideaway trick again. Or try to. The bag between my feet was of course noticed by everybody, who figured I was really looking for someone to go home with but hadn't found anyone I liked yet.

A young black guy standing against the wall near me struck up a conversation.

"Boring, isn't it."

"It's certainly always the same, wherever you go," I told him.

"My name's Cedric," he said, holding out his hand. He had a kind of English accent. I must have looked startled, curious. "I'm from Jamaica. I'm here working at Bluebeard's Castle."

"As a waiter?"

221

"Nothing that fancy. I help take care of the grounds."

We talked a little bit about this and that, which kept other men away from us. He offered to buy me another Coke. I agreed only if he took my money to pay for it, which he did. When he handed it to me, he said, "You're not here to pick up somebody, are you?"

I said, "Actually I'm here just waiting until I take a plane out of here tomorrow morning."

"You couldn't find a hotel room?"

"I didn't want to."

"Broke?"

"No. Not at all. I just don't want to be any one place."

"Police looking for you?"

"Not the police. Some people I don't want to see."

"This must be a romantic emergency," Cedric said.

"You could call it that, I guess. I'm sorry. My name's Harry. Harry Potter. It was rude of me not to give you my name before. It really is Harry Potter. I'm not a fugitive from justice."

"You're a fugitive from love," Cedric said, and laughed. Hard.

I was beginning to feel better. "Look," he said. "I have a really terrible little room at the hotel, but you're welcome to come back there until it's time to go to the airport. Your pursuer isn't going to look for you there."

I looked doubtful.

"You don't have to put out," he said, and laughed again. "I would like to do the putting out, if you're interested. But somehow I don't get the impression you are."

"I'm sorry. You've got it right. Could we go there now? I'm really exhausted."

"Of course. This place is dull at its best and it isn't even that tonight. You're the only handsome new face in the entire bar."

"How do we get there?" I asked.

"I usually walk, if I'm going straight back. But we could take a cab."

"I'd like to take a cab if you'll let me pay."

222

"It would be my pleasure," Cedric said.

Outside there were plenty of taxis roaming the streets, and we hailed one. In the brighter lights outside I could see that Cedric was quite handsome, about my height, wavy dark hair, and prominent nose. Something like a very dark Stewart Granger. I could have gotten very interested in Cedric, somewhere else, some other time.

Pulling around a corner, I saw Rex and Illy heading down the street in the direction of the Heavenly Blue. My luck was holding. Now all I had to do was get to the airplane and get the hell out of St. Thomas. Or the hell off of St. Thomas. However you want to put it.

Cedric did have a small room, in a frame building down the hill from the hotel. A long hall gave onto many small rooms, all their doors closed. Two-thirds of the way down was Cedric's door. The hall was dimly lit and looked none too clean. Bandbox-neat Cedric in his sharply pressed gabardine slacks and white shirt looked more out of place here than I did.

The room had one single bed, very narrow, a bureau, a chair, and a closet with no door. Cedric had obviously placed the small mirror on the bureau top, and the few clothes in the closet were neatly hung, with one pair of shoes on the floor beneath them.

"This is home," Cedric said in a low tone of voice. The walls were obviously thin. "There's a bathroom down the hall. You can take a shower in the morning if you want to. It's okay that you're here. The hotel doesn't encourage it, but many of the men have family stay over when they're here. You take the bed."

"I couldn't," I said.

"You're the exhausted one," he said. "I'll take the blanket and lie on the floor. I've done that before when my father was here."

I accepted. I went down the hall to the bathroom and then lay down on the bed, taking off only my shoes. Cedric neatly hung up his trousers and shirt. He had only Jockey shorts on underneath. A very beautiful body. He saw me looking at him.

"I played a lot of sports back home. Football—not your kind

of football, what you call soccer. And I am a really good cricket player. Wouldn't you know? The one sport that they don't play anywhere except England and its colonies, so I'll probably never play again."

"You're not going back to Jamaica?" I said.

So we talked most of the night. Me lying on the bed looking up at the ceiling in the dark; Cedric propped up on one elbow, telling me how he hoped to get to the United States. Hoped to find some kind of work, be some kind of professional. Get his family to follow him.

They were, of course, desperately poor in Jamaica, as they were on all the islands. He had a high-school-level education but wanted more. Cedric was older than I was, about twenty-two at that time, I'd guess.

In the morning, Cedric had to go on yard duty, or whatever they called it. He explained where I could find a taxi after I took a shower and where to hide the key after I left the room. Dear Cedric. He's in the United States now. In Detroit. We keep in touch.

I took the taxi to the airport, and of course, when I went to check in, Rex and Illy were there. They were wearing different clothes than they had on last night, so obviously they had been back to the Shibui before they showed up here. I wondered if they had time to squeeze in a fuck.

Rex was in a threatening mood. "You're not leaving," he said.

Illy said nothing. I had a feeling he would be very pleased to see me leave, only because the whole thing was so embarrassing.

"I have to," I said.

"We could keep you here by force," Rex said.

"But you don't want to," I told him.

"No, you've already ruined our vacation."

I said in a very loud voice that surprised even me, and certainly the people standing in line behind me, tickets in hand, "Goddammit, do you think I care! It wasn't your vacation in the first place. It was mine. I paid for it!"

224

Illy looked at Rex. Rex didn't flinch. He just raised his eyebrows in surprise, as though he had suddenly encountered an irrational person who was being insulting to poised and faultless him.

I said, "You've been inside hundreds of people but you don't know anyone."

Rex turned and walked away; Illy followed him. He didn't look at me. Illy hated any kind of emotional display, and most especially in public.

I went aboard the plane. I cried a lot during the flight. The fat man next to me wasn't nonplussed. He just pretended it wasn't happening. The stewardesses were very sympathetic. I'm sure they've seen a lot of crying aboard planes. They asked if I wanted lunch, and I nodded yes. I kept right on crying into my pasta with tomato sauce and soggy broccoli.

From that point on, I guess you could say I went back to Michigan, went to school, and went straight. Certainly I left the Harry Potter I was then in the airport on St. Thomas. In many ways, I've felt like I was leading somebody else's life ever since.

The Afterword

Funny, I haven't thought about these things for so long. When I returned to New York, I never went back to ballet class. I never went back to the opera.

I lie. I did return once. I did not show up for rehearsals or performances at the opera, and finally this came to the attention of the General Manager's office. Mr. Bing's secretary, Florence, called me as I was packing to go back to Michigan and asked me to come see Mr. Bing Wednesday at two-thirty. I remember that.

I did, dressing very neatly, wearing a jacket and tie. Haircut. Mr. Bing was cautious. "Why aren't you reporting to work?" he asked politely with his faint Viennese accent from behind his desk, his polished pate nodding towards me. He had those kind eyes, brown—the great difference physically between Antony Tudor and him. He didn't call me by name.

I lied slightly, or distorted my real reasons for avoiding the opera. "Mr. Tudor demanded that I sleep with him in exchange for dancing the lead role in his new ballet. It was a shock to me."

Mr. Bing blinked. Clearly he was struggling with a new idea. I'm sure he had never heard that a ballet boy was shocked that someone wanted to sleep with him. "And you didn't want to do that?"

"It was a shock," I repeated. Later, when I saw Harold Pinter's

226

plays, I was reminded of this interview. The calm emptiness of our dialogue didn't match well with the subject being discussed.

"A shock, yes. You're sure that was what he wanted?" Mr. Bing asked.

"Quite sure. Positive. There was no doubt," I said. It did sound like a drawing-room play of some kind.

"What did he say?" Mr. Bing wanted to know. There was a gleam in his eye, the voyeur's gleam. Mr. Bing may have been a gentleman, but he was not an innocent gentleman. Perhaps not even a very nice gentleman.

"I don't think you want to hear that, Mr. Bing," I said.

"I will have to ask him about this," Mr. Bing said. "It seem so unlikely."

Yes, I thought. About as unlikely as the Pope's being Catholic. I felt myself being pivoted into the wrong. Even then, young and stupid as I was, I knew the one thing that threw people off when they were trying to manipulate you into a position was to *not* act as they expected you to. Clearly Mr. Bing expected me to get angry and sputter and protest. I didn't. Or wise off. I said nothing. Only sat and looked at Mr. Bing.

He went on, "What if Antony . . . Mr. Tudor . . . denies it?"

"He would, wouldn't he?" I said. In a businesslike voice. I felt I was gaining the upper hand by remaining calm. Perhaps I *was* lying. It didn't matter. What mattered was how one played the hand. Somehow, I was playing it correctly.

"You're not trying to leave the opera before the end of the season to go to another company, are you?" Mr. Bing's matter-of-fact voice was beginning to sound a little sinister. As though more brutal interrogation might be in store if I didn't answer fully. He wasn't German for nothing. I know, I know, he was Austrian. For some of us it's the same thing.

"No, I'm not going to dance anymore. Anywhere. I'm going back to Michigan. I'm going to college next fall."

"Oh, where?" It seemed the conversation about Antony Tudor was over. And my Met contract. And all the rest of it.

"I'm not sure. The University of Michigan, if I can get in."

Mr. Bing stood up. "Well, I certainly wish you all the luck in the world." Still no name. Perhaps he wasn't sure what my name was. "Of course, you won't be paid after this date, you know that."

"Of course," I said, smiled, and walked out. I didn't shake his hand. His young secretary said good-bye. A nice girl. Florence was probably a society girl. Maybe even with some money. She had no idea where she was working.

Minda Meryl called as soon as I was back in my cold-water flat. It was really bare-looking now. I was letting Alfred take it over and was leaving the Salvation Army furniture for him. What he wanted of it. But all the little personal things, pictures and ornaments, were packed up, or I had given them away.

"How'd it go?" Minda asked.

"He questioned whether I was telling the truth. But he didn't make any effort to keep me," I said.

"The old trout." That's all she said. "Come on over about eight. We'll go out for a splendid dinner tonight before you leave."

Minda had been a "brick through the whole ugly mess," as she put it. I had cried my way back from St. Thomas. Cried all over my apartment and all over her apartment. Cried on the phone to my mother. For Belle-Mère, the Tudor story was sufficient. Minda had to be told the Rex-Illy story, even the part about my driving Illy out of my life by pretending I was in love with him. I wasn't very proud of that.

Minda had dealt with things head-on when we first talked about it. "There are times in this business where you either become a slut or get out, Harry. I think you should get out. I knew you'd never sleep with the sleazy people like Antony Tudor to get ahead, but you *could* drift into a three-way and very casual sex hanging around men like Rex Ames. Sex pushes us into strange highways and byways."

228

I said nothing. Stopping dancing was like coming off oxygen for me. It was going to be a struggle trying to breathe in the normal world.

Giving up Rex was something else. That was beyond breathing. That was amputation, self-amputation. Like a wolf chewing off its own leg to escape from a trap.

"I know, I know, I know," Minda said in one of our long conversations. "It's like some kind of horrible tropical infection. You think you've gotten rid of it but it just keeps cropping up. Hopefully, it doesn't linger on in your bowels forever. My first husband was like that. He was a lion tamer—tiger tamer, in fact. It took forever to get over him. I really married Josh as a kind of antidote. I knew I couldn't be in love with two men at the same time. He was everything Josh isn't. His name was Roman. Can you imagine?"

"He was like what?" I said.

"Arrogant, self-centered, domineering, childish, violent," Minda said.

"Don't hold back. It's no good repressing everything," I said, laughing.

"Unfaithful, crazy, handsome, and that's the good part," she added.

"Why did you marry him, for God's sake?" I asked.

"I don't know. I never liked him. He insisted on it. Of course, he may have been a fucking maniac, but he was a maniac fucking. Insane people can be great in bed. I'm here to testify to it."

"He sounds great. You're sure it wasn't Rex?"

"In an earlier manifestation, or half-life. No, he's still alive, Roman. Torturing some millionairess in New Jersey. They keep tigers right there on the farm. They eat a cow a day or something like that."

"Not alive, I hope," I said.

"I think not." We both laughed. "I can laugh, but you never get over being one of the walking wounded, Harry. You're younger than I was. I was twenty-four when I met him, twenty-six when I left him. I used singing as a kind of drug to keep him at bay in my heart and my crotch. Poor Harry."

She looked at me and she really had a sad expression on her face, sitting there at her kitchen table. "You're not even going to have dancing to tide you over. I know it all seems very hopeless now, and I don't want to sound like some smiley-face Pollyanna, but I can promise you that someday you'll be interested in things you can't even imagine now. Even though it seems as if everything and everyone you've ever been interested in is swept from your life.

"And one thing more. It's all right to have an all-consuming love. In fact, it's a must. But once you've had it, Harry, you don't need another one."

It was good advice. It was true, I was to come to find out. But it took a long time.

When I came out of Minda's building to go back alone to my dingy apartment, the sun fell on a little tree standing alone against a red brick wall at the end of the block. One little tree with its new, bright green leaves trembling in the spring wind. Alone in a square of bright sun against that glowing wall, everything in shadow around it. I thought, *You* don't have to have a reason to live. You live because you are alive. Like that little tree, I am alive and I will keep on living. Because my heart is beating and I'm breathing. I'll never have to have a reason to live again. Not a person, not a thing. I live because I am alive. That's enough.

My mother said, "Come on home, honey."

Minda said, "Go home, Harry."

So I went home. I sat around my hometown for a month or two. I didn't even take my dance clothes with me. I just left them in that empty front room, hanging over the barre.

All Alfred said when he came to get the key was, "Perhaps it's best that the only people who stay in New York are people who were born in New York." I knew Alfred felt New York was too crowded because so many people moved there from out of town.

230

I was doing my part to return New York to normal. I was moving back home.

I didn't stay there long. I stared out the window as the crocuses were followed by forsythias, the hyacinths by tulips. Dandelions were infesting the front lawn when I wrote the registrar's office at the University of Michigan for an application. Belle-Mère kept her counsel, made meals, taught her kiddie classes, and didn't discuss ballet. She did ask if I wouldn't like to teach a class or two. Then said, "I guess not." I refused to look at her.

The rest is history. It all seems very brief and inevitable actually. I started in the literary college, studying English literature. Then changed to pre-med. I did my medical school there and met my wife there. I found the job at St. Vincent's after graduating. We had the girls. Antonia has moved around a little from one clinic to another, but now she's established at that place down on St. Mark's Place. That place on the Place.

We've moved a couple of times. Now we have a really nice house on Greenwich Street in the Village. With three bedrooms, so the girls can have their own rooms and share a bathroom. All quite lavish compared to Sixteenth Street. When Belle-Mère visits, one of the girls goes to her sister's room. They take turns.

Do I fool around? With guys? That's the big question, isn't it?

I think of it. Who wouldn't? But I'd have to fall in love first, and I don't want to fall in love. It would have to creep up on me. There is no place in my life for falling in love. It's all occupied. I'm quite aware that I've done this deliberately. I'm sure my wife is aware of it, too. I'm barricaded behind my hospital schedule, the girls, school plays, the PTA meetings, holidays in Europe, going to the theater. When would anyone ever see enough of me that I could fall in love with them? It's impossible, and it's an impossibility I created myself. So be it.

My happiness will never come from fulfilling my duties to others. That's like brushing your teeth. Of course you do it.

I had my happiness. I overdosed on it. I've been on automatic ever since. And I'm fine, I assure you. I'm perfectly fine.

231

Harry Thinks About Love

Marilyn Monroe recorded a song called "After You Get What You Want You Don't Want It." She sang it in her little baby-doll voice and at the very end interpolated "I know you" in her speaking voice. Marilyn, you were so right. So right. All the time I was balancing back and forth between Illy and Rex, they were interested. Because the ball wasn't really in their court. I don't know what I was thinking, but I wasn't thinking that I wanted to spend the rest of my life with either one of them. So the pressure was off. As soon as I concentrated on Rex it fell apart.

Love is such a weird thing. It seems to be all about need. Either we need to be loved, or we need to love. Needing to be loved is probably the most usual and the most normal. Selfish, selfish human beings. I often meet women nowadays who want so much to be married, have a lover, something. So I ask them, What would you be willing to accept in a lover? What faults could he have? Could he be missing a limb? Or an eye? Could he have a low income with no prospects for a better one? Or no income? Could he be a widower or a divorced man with children? And one of the children has a major health problem? Cerebral palsy? The answers are always no, no, no, no, no, no. To anything except a good-looking, single lover with a good income and no children. Okay, maybe children, but no health problems, please.

Conclusion: We want to be loved, but the love can't come with any baggage. How realistic is that? After a certain age, everyone comes with baggage.

Love doesn't come without problems. I think people have it all wrong. Being loved is one of the least interesting situations you can find yourself in. Being loved gives you all the power in the situation. But in a funny way, you're not getting anything out of it. Your own emotions are just lying there, doing nothing. There is nothing worse than sleeping with someone when you don't feel like it. Nothing. For men, of course, it's usually just out of the question if you can't get it up. But women can just lie there. Maybe that's what many women do all their lives and don't have any idea that it would be quite different if you loved that person lying on top of you pumping away.

And of course, there's loving someone and being in love with someone. People say there's a difference. I don't really get it. I think being in love is loving. It's quite clearly different from being sexually attracted. The difference revolves around kissing, I think. If you really love kissing someone, that indicates to me that you're in love with them. If you don't feel like kissing them but you like fucking them, that's sexual attraction. In some ways, kissing is more personal than fucking. Rex always said to me, "You're the only one I kiss." Which, at the time, I thought was pretty ridiculous. I was supposed to not mind all the middle-aged johns from out of town he was screwing, because he wasn't kissing them. Now I have a better view of the whole thing. Rex was sort of like an electric stove: you turned on the burner and he heated up. He was Italian; maybe that's the way Italian men work. But kissing someone indicated for him that he was actually aware of the person he was fucking. It wasn't just a warm place to put his penis. I guess I should have been flattered.

Anyway, there is that difference. I see it as three entirely different categories.

Sexual attraction. Obviously only good for as long as you're attracted. Some people know how to spin that out for a long time by limiting the amount of sexual contact distributed to others. I guess this is pretty much a female thing. Men who are sexually attracted to another man aren't going to hang around very long if there is sexual rationing going on. Unless it's a much older man and his little tootsie. Diaghilev and Lifar. That kind of thing.

Then there's being in love. Which has to do with some sort of necessary life experience. I really think when you lie down to die, you really don't feel good about the whole thing because you were president of a big company. Or a famous painter. Or gave millions to help the poor. I think you feel you lived because you felt a lot. You really felt those tidal waves of emotion sweep over you, caused by the fact that someone else exists. That's what I think we want. We want to feel that thing. There are people who back away from it because it makes them feel too much and they're afraid of those feelings. They go to their graves feeling they missed the boat, and they did.

If you believe in reincarnation, they'll only have to come back again and see if they can screw up enough courage to fall in love and be swept off their feet into unmanageable situations. Love isn't for control freaks. Earning millions of dollars and running the lives of others is for control freaks.

It's funny. You see these guys coming into the hospital who have control-freaked their way to the top, and now they have everything under control. Surprise! They have controlled themselves right out of contact with any other human being. It's a very big punishment, success. You don't dare ever be alone.

Then there's love. The kind of love you feel for children, your family, your friends, and your pets. It's a strong feeling, but it doesn't come out of genetic programming. So it isn't powerful. Except for a mother's love for her child, and not all mothers have that. I don't think mine did. I don't think my wife has it. Antonia should have it in spades—she's Italian. But there's some-

234

thing cold about how she handles her responsibilities as a mother. She'll go to school and discuss problems with the teacher. And she'll reassure the girls when they start worrying about God. Or if they're pretty enough. That kind of stuff. But I don't get the feeling there's any kind of blood rush about it. She isn't like a mother lion defending her cubs. It's more that she knows what a mother's responsibilities are, and she will never fail to discharge them well. She's very upper-class. I, on the other hand, am not.

So do I love my wife? I have to say that I was never in love with her. I was in admire with her. Our marriage was like a train that pulls into the station and it is obvious you are supposed to climb aboard and travel away on it. Staying behind in the empty station has no point to it. If Antonia hadn't come over from Italy to finish her training, if we hadn't met in my last year of med school, and, probably most important, if she hadn't decided she wanted to marry me, most likely I'd still be single. I certainly haven't ever felt I needed to get married to be a convincing subject for advancement at the hospital. I don't really care if I advance or not. I like taking care of people. And I get the chance to. Dancing was my career. That's over. This is my work. Whether I'm an *important* doctor or not couldn't interest me less. It interests Antonia. She really wants to be head of that children's clinic, and I'm sure she will be. In many ways she's the man in the couple we make. She even looks like a Roman senator now that she's gone gray and cut her hair short. I wouldn't want to overstate that. She was beautiful when we met and still is.

What about the sex? Sex with Antonia is definitely in the sexual-attraction section of human relationships. My body responds to her body and we get it on. We don't kiss much. Never did. Our life together is a real life based on doing real things. It has nothing to do with fulfilling deep-seated emotional goals. At least for me, it doesn't. That was all over once I left Illy and Rex behind. I think I learned what there was to learn and that I won't do that again. At least I hope I won't have to. Whether Antonia has a need to fulfill herself emotionally beyond me, I don't know. We have never discussed it. We probably will never discuss it.

Let's face it, if we didn't have our demanding jobs, the two girls, and the house to deal with, I'm not sure what we would be doing with each other. But that's a very abstract question. We *do* have our responsibilities and they are all-consuming. At the moment, I have to believe many people's lives are like this. I notice that I say "I have to believe" quite often. I guess I do.

Back to being "in love." Finally, I guess I'd have to say that I was "in love" with Rex Ames and "in lust" with Illy Ilquist. And that's where it stands. The kind of "in lust" I had with Illy had its monumental side. I never got tired of sleeping with him. There was something about his physical presence that always made me feel sexual. And his penis, if we're going to be really up-front. He was a kind of penis with a person attached. His life revolved around it for the most part. And I did too, when we were involved with each other.

What did I know about love? Nothing. But it was clear to me that something was going on with Rex Ames that wasn't happening with Illy. I made my decision on that basis, to throw in my lot with Rex. Which, as it turned out, was of little or no interest to Rex at all. So much for love and being in love.

Illy's Death

Illy died. I wasn't there. "Who is Harry?" the nurse said the next day. "He was calling for Harry over and over." I said nothing. I'm Dr. Potter to her. If she looked up my first name in the files it would say Harold. Some of the other doctors at the hospital call me Harry, but most doctors aren't known by their first names or called by their first names.

I wasn't surprised by that information. I don't know how I feel about not being there. I wish I'd been there only because Illy had called for me. But for myself, I can't say my life is more empty with his passing. It has been empty with his absence for almost thirty years.

I never saw Illy after he died. The body had been taken away when I reported in to the hospital. A woman friend had claimed the body. It must have been Anne. The nurse said she had been told that the body was to be cremated. I wonder if Anne planned to return his ashes to Minnesota. That I didn't care about. The dead body is like a sort of old overcoat, a suit of worn-out clothes, once the wearer has flown. Often, when I pass a cemetery, I think how ridiculous those rows and rows of stone look, holding down all those empty black suits and worn-out black dresses. There is no one there. There never was. Only expensive boxes holding ill-assorted fragments of neutrons and protons,

237

trying to leap apart and re-form into other elements. The spirit that once made those scraps of bone, muscle, and flesh beautiful and lovable has gone.

I never told Illy about the letter I'd gotten from Robby Schmidt after he had gotten to California. I'm not paranoid, but perhaps I should have been a little bit. As some people are destined to play positive roles in your life, evidently there are others who are there to have a malignant influence. Mine was Robby. His letter went:

You silly bitch,

I grew tired of your attempts at controlling my life in such an obvious and contemptible way. The price I had to pay in emotional subservience was not worth the petty physical comforts you provided.

Now I am in California far from your harmful grasp. You always were a pathetic cunt, even at the Opera. You conned everyone into thinking you were such a sweet, virginal young thing, but I saw through you. I knew better and always could perceive the deceit and manipulation. I figured out that you were sleeping with both Ilquist and Ames, our two best dancers, so you could control them and gain ascendance over them. I told Tudor that. You never knew I lined up boys for him, did you? There was a lot you didn't know, you idiotic faggot. He was one of the few that saw through you and your ridiculous conceit as I did.

I told Ilquist and Ames, too. While you were doing all those rehearsals with Tudor for that ballet, and rehearsed spinning around on his cock, too, I'm sure. I should have had that lead role, but you made sure that I was relegated to the least important role. I told your lovers, "Why don't you guys just go somewhere and fuck." They did. Ha, ha, ha. Anything to escape from you, you evil twat.

I'm telling you all this just in case you think I'm un-grateful. No one needs to be grateful to the sheer evil that is you.

Wishing you all the worst,
  Robert

Well. I read the letter very quickly. I could hardly bear to keep my eyes on the pages. I didn't reread it, just crumpled it up and threw it in the wastebasket. I guess you could categorize it as the worst letter I ever received in my life, on quite a few levels. It was all pretty clear. I had been playing in a league that was way over my head. A major league of ambition and deception I hardly per-ceived, even when I was up to my neck in it. I had been chewed up and spat out. Robby made that very clear. But then indeed, who wasn't? Certainly there were no winners among Robby, Illy, Rex, Tudor, and me. Rex maybe. An unknown quantity, but he has never surfaced on Broadway or in Hollywood to my knowl-edge. He had done a lead in an off-Broadway musical based on a Shakespearean play in which he had colored his hair blond; that I knew. I had seen the ads in the *New York Times* Sunday edi-tion, which we got in Michigan. But nothing more after that. Did he borrow that money from me just to even the score? Somehow I don't think he even cared that much. He just wanted to go to St. Thomas with Illy and figured out a way to do it.

After-Afterword

Now it is a month later. Illy died at St. Vincent's and my life has gone on as though nothing had happened. My wife just became the director of the clinic where she has worked for so long. This was always her goal, and she is content in having achieved it. Like many psychologists, she is not very aware of the emotions that surge within the people she sees daily.

One daughter has abandoned her plans for a career as a geophysicist and now plans to live on the Main Line in Philadelphia with a doctor husband and two children. Good luck to her.

The other daughter, the younger, is very involved with computers. In what way, I can't exactly tell you. I know I can't hope she'll outgrow it.

Two weeks ago, while I was crossing Seventh Avenue near the hospital, my evil genius, Robby, emerged in my life again. He wasn't in California very long. I wondered whom he had conned for the return fare.

"Oh, hi," he said, smiling brightly, or as brightly as he could with the two or three teeth left to him. I didn't mention his letter. He probably wouldn't have remembered it. That was another channel, another life. "Where ya going?" he wanted to know. I didn't tell him Illy had just died. I said, "To class." He looked to see if I was carrying a dance bag.

Then he said, "I saw Rex Ames last week." Now it was my turn to wonder what year it was. "He asked about you. I told him you were a famous doctor now."

"Where did you see him?" I asked cautiously. With Robby, he might have met him in a hallucination.

"On Eighth Street. He was just up here for the day seeing some old trick of his, I guess. He lives in Baltimore now. He's a waiter. You should call him. He'd like it."

"I'm never in Baltimore," I said.

Robby was playing the role of the old pal. When we had never been old pals. "We should get together. We have a lot of old times to talk about," he said.

"Too many," I said. And left him standing like a grizzled garden gnome on Bleecker Street.

I have come to believe in destiny. That all things must unfold in their own time. Our path, no matter how we may want to leave it, is our path to tread alone. There is no hurrying down it to get to a better part, or lingering upon it to enjoy the present moment more. We move along it inexorably.

The next day there was a letter on my desk inviting me to a doctors' convention in Baltimore the following month. At the Peabody Hotel. I asked my secretary to accept it. I could have turned it down, but decided to cooperate with destiny.

I called information for Rex Ames's telephone number in Baltimore. I called and an answering machine came on. As I started to leave a message, Rex came on the line. His voice was still sonorous, with a thick edge that gave me the beginning of an erection.

I told him I was coming to Baltimore and suggested we meet. He didn't ask how I happened to know he was in Baltimore. He said he was working most evenings as a waiter but the Sunday I was arriving he would be free. I told him I would arrive in the late afternoon. I suggested eating at the hotel. He agreed.

"You were quite a little fuck bunny," Rex said.

"You were the love of my life," I said.

241

"I know. Kismet. It is written in the stars. I loved you as much as I ever loved anybody, Harry. You were the only one I ever kissed."

"You wouldn't want to sleep with me now?"

"No. You know I never slept with anyone on the spur of the moment." He laughed and took a sip of his double martini.

I felt relieved.

There were moments when Rex was still handsome in the shadows of the restaurant dining room. In the turn of his head, the flash of his still-excellent teeth, the Rex I knew was there. He seemed shorter—or was I taller? His torso bulged under the thick sweater he wore. His taut body was gone. His face wasn't wrinkled but drawn and pale like parchment, making his large dark eyes even larger. He was nervous, and his smile flashed on and off with no connection to our conversation.

At no time did Rex ask why I was in Baltimore, what my profession was, anything about my marriage or my children. Although he must have known something of all this from Robby. It had always been important to Rex not to appear interested in other people, and much of his lack of interest wasn't feigned. I don't think he ever was very interested in other people.

"I brought these pictures," Rex said, and pushed a small cardboard album across the table. "Remember these?"

I opened the small book. In the front were black-and-white Polaroid photographs of a woman who must have been his mother. "Polaroids," Rex said. "They didn't even have color Polaroid then. Only black-and-white." His mother, posing stiffly, smiled timidly in a black dress against plaster walls and venetian blinds. In some, her head posed in profile or turned upwards in an attempt at an "artistic" pose. Suggested by photographer Rex, I'm sure.

Then there were pictures of me. "I don't remember these," I said. "You must have seen them," Rex said, tipping the top of the little album down with one hand to check what I was looking at while lifting some salad to his mouth with the other. I was being careful to keep the album out of my bean-and-broccoli soup.

"No, never. I'm sure I've never seen these." There were Polaroids of me seated on a bed in a white shirt and a sweater. A tan cardigan, it was. My best sweater. There was one photograph of me standing at a door, my profile reflected in a wall mirror. I looked good. I looked handsome, lively, animated, even beautiful. My profile looked not bad in the mirror. I hate my profile. Not enough chin.

"My hair looks nice," I said.

"You always had beautiful hair," Rex said.

It did look good, my hair. Glossy, silky, falling over one eye in some shots. My hair was honey-colored then. Not blond-blond. I seemed relaxed, smiling, turning to look at the camera as I sprawled on the bed. Nothing at all as I remember myself. Tormented with desire. Exhausted with ballet classes. I had never thought of myself as alluring or fuckable. It wasn't that I had thought of myself as not being fuckable, I'd just never thought I was. A clear-skinned, shiny-eyed, gleaming-haired young man looked back at me. In only one, where I clasped Rex's dog in my arms on a couch, did I look like myself, as I remember it. Tremulous, a little sad. That poor dog. Poor me.

"Let me keep these photographs to make some copies, Rex," I said. He had no objection. I put them in my pocket.

On my way to Baltimore, I had thought that after dinner perhaps Rex and I would go to my room and make love in that savage, senseless way we used to. Few preliminaries. Just a long, pounding mounting of my body by Rex.

I had no desire to do this with today's Rex, and he clearly didn't, either. We talked about opera for the most part during dinner. He now had a great passion for it. I didn't remember him being so passionate about opera when we were dancers. Now he said how thrilled he was to find a CD of Bizet's *The Pearl Fishers* at his local record store.

He leaned over and squeezed my shoulder as we ate our shrimp creole (me) and lamb cutlets (him). "Your shoulders are tense," he said. It wasn't a come-on for a later massage. "I think

I'm just strong," I said. He demonstrated simple exercises of bending the head backwards and forwards and from side to side to relieve tension and stretch the muscles. "Keep your chin in," he said, as he demonstrated them for me. "That's not hard," I said. "There's nothing wrong with your chin. There never was," he said. Almost paternally. Certainly with affection.

Rex talked about his job as a waiter with all the enthusiasm he had once talked about dancing a lead for a Valerie Bettis recital. He was well respected at the restaurant, one of Baltimore's best, he assured me. He had the best tables and he didn't have to bus. It didn't make me feel sad. But distant, distant, distant. The other Rex was far, far away.

It was something like Lina Wertmüller's film *Swept Away*. We had been two lovers alone on a desert island so long ago. We didn't love each other anymore. But I think we both loved the memory of that love. At least I did. I don't know about Rex. I don't know what he thought. It was important to him, as I've said, that no one did.

We finished dessert, we went to the lobby, we hugged good-bye. "Your body feels good," he said.

"I exercise every day," I told him.

"That's good," he said. And walked away. With that cocky, feet-out walk short men often have. Shoulders back, head up. Another dancer would be able to tell immediately that Rex himself had once been a dancer.

In my room, I undressed slowly. The conference started tomorrow. I didn't look forward to it. Rex and I hadn't made any plan to see each other again while I was in Baltimore. He was only free in the daytime, and I was going to be tied up with the conference every day. I am forty-eight. Rex must be fifty or over. I saw a funny gay card in a bookstore just last week. On it was a 1940s-type illustration of a gray-haired professional type smoking a pipe. In the balloon from his head it said, "God, he was handsome. He had big muscles and a big car. I'll bet he's still thinking about me." In a lower corner there's another 1940s-style drawing of an older man looking upwards. This man's balloon reads, "Get a grip on yourself. That was in high school."

At the top the card reads, "How Long Is Too Long?" Exactly.

I snapped on the radio. It was playing Rachmaninoff. That terribly sad one that wraps up all there is to say or feel about love and longing. I started to dance in my sleeveless undershirt and Jockey shorts. My legs are still good, I still have buttocks, and my stomach is flat, and I have pectorals.

Other people in the privacy of their rooms may drink. Or masturbate. I dance when I'm alone, and that is rarely. When there is classical music on the radio.

I danced. Slow-revolving pirouettes, deep first arabesque, *piqué* to second. I can still do all that stuff. My body has never changed. Only I have. It's a tough thing, this life. It can break your heart if you let it.